Highland Harry

by

Gail MacMillan

This is a work of fiction. Names, characters, places, and incidents are either the product of the author's imagination or are used fictitiously, and any resemblance to actual persons living or dead, business establishments, events, or locales, is entirely coincidental.

Highland Harry

COPYRIGHT © 2015 by Gail MacMillan

Cover Art by *Debbie Taylor*

The Wild Rose Press, Inc.
PO Box 708
Adams Basin, NY 14410-0708
Visit us at www.thewildrosepress.com

Publishing History
First Tea Rose Edition, 2014
Print ISBN 978-1-62830-622-4
Digital ISBN 978-1-62830-623-1

Published in the United States of America

He sat savoring another wee dram. God knew he needed it. He'd just been proposed to by the stepmother of seven children with mills, a farm, and an apparently dangerous enemy threatening her and her family. The widow of a fellow Highlander, a woman—together with her children—he was duty bound to help and protect.

In the flickering firelight he walked to the door of her bedroom and peered in through the space she'd left open to allow heat from the hearth to enter. In the wide bed, her shining chestnut hair adorning the pillow, Maggie slept, long eyelashes spread out over creamy cheeks. In her arms she cradled the golden-haired cherub named Eppie. On a rug on the floor beside them, Pig woke, looked up at him with strangely knowing eyes, grunted, then lowered her head and went back to sleep. What was a man to do with such a rare and unexpected family?

He wandered back to the hearth, put a hand on the shelf above it, and stood staring down into the flames. Wind shrieked around the corners and snow buffeted the windows, but inside the log house, protected from the storm, he let a warm, secure feeling settle over him, a warm and secure feeling he hadn't experienced at night since he'd been a lad in his father's croft cottage during a blizzard much like this one. The ambience was seductive but perhaps false. After all, the family had a dangerous enemy.

He banked the fire for the night, then glanced back toward the bedroom where Maggie slept. Beautiful, unassuming Maggie. What would the future hold for her and the children if he decided not to stay?

Praise for Gail MacMillan

"Be prepared to be hooked on the first word of the first page and go on to the next with anticipation. Her stories will live in your heart long after the last page is read."

~*Rebecca Melvin, Publisher, Double Edge Press*

~*~

"Gail MacMillan's stories delight the senses and brighten the dark days of winter like a candle glowing on a windowsill. Best enjoyed while curled up in your favorite chair...with some hot cocoa and a faithful canine companion."

~*Sue Owens Wright, author, newspaper columnist, and two-time Maxwell Medal recipient*

~*~

"Gail MacMillan's stories place you in a well-worn comforting chair. She writes of deep-rooted rural customs and traditions, of her love of dogs and horses. She shows glimpses of truth in revelatory detail."

~*Heather White, Editor, Saltscapes Magazine*

~*~

Other books by Gail MacMillan
Available from The Wild Rose Press, Inc.

Lady and the Beast
Caledonian Privateer
Ghost of Winters Past
Holding Off for a Hero
Shadows of Love
Rogue's Revenge
Counterfeit Cowboy
Heather for a Highlander
How My Heart Finds Christmas

Dedication

To my equine adviser Jessi and her Eric,
wishing them many happy and continuing
adventurous years together

Chapter One

Sleet blinding him, he charged through the night. Trusting to his mare's surefootedness, he let her have her head, but when the hollow sound from beneath her hooves told him they were on a bridge, he swung her sharply to the left and down the embankment. He muttered a curse as the frigid water of the stream splashed up his legs.

He halted his mount to leap from the saddle and pull her head against his chest. His heart hammered at his ribs, nausea welling in his gut. They'd got Brodie. They wouldn't stop until they had him as well. Bloody hell, he should have known it was a trap. Damn Lady Annabelle Spencer to hell!

Hoofbeats. A thunder of them. A regiment? Part of a regiment? Did it matter? Like hounds hot for blood, they were hell bent on running Highland Harry to ground. The hot breath of his mare wheezed against his frozen coat. He rubbed her nose. She'd given her best this night. If he were caught, it would be through no fault of hers.

Closer. They were coming closer. Then they were on the bridge, the sound of hooves like the beat of a hundred crazed drummers over his head. His mare shied and muttered. He covered her nostrils with his hand and whispered words of reassurance into her ear. And then, as quickly as they'd come, they were gone off into the night. He could breathe easy again.

But he didn't want to. Not now, not ever. Brodie was dead, captured by that marauding hoard. Brodie, his brother in all but blood. He leaned his head against his horse's arched neck and submitted to the trembling that he'd managed to hold at bay. By now his best friend would be swinging from a rope. They'd waste no time on trials or courts with Brazen Brodie, that miserable rabble pulled from the slums and prisons of England to pass for an army, their officers worthless bastards who'd had their commissions purchased.

Only vaguely aware of the icy water soaking through his boots, he realized the truth. It was time to quit, to give up this madness that had no chance of success. Over a half century earlier, Culloden Moor had sounded the death knell for the cause. He and Brodie and the others should have been wise enough to recognize it these many years later.

He mounted the mare and headed her back onto the road. Hunched against the driving sleet, he turned her toward the coast where, in a collection of caves, he and his fellows had gathered supplies in readiness for the day when they had to escape across the sea. That day had come for him. It was time to head for British North America and a place named Riverhaven, in the province of New Brunswick.

****

Maggie Fowler paused inside the door of Riverhaven's mercantile. The only other customers, three women, turned to face her. Lillian Gardiner, Hazel Green, and Hazel's daughter Morag. A tight, hard knot formed in Maggie's gut as the trio stared at the young woman in boy's jacket, trousers, and boots, hair shoved up under a black knitted cap. Lillian's long, narrow countenance retracted into a prune-like shrivel. Hazel pursed thin, colorless lips into a tight pucker. Morag lowered her gaze to the floor.

They won't cow me, miserable witches who think themselves the souls of respectability!

Maggie pulled herself up to her full five-foot-six-inch height. Mustering her courage, she advanced across the room to where a big, potbellied man behind the counter leaned on it with beefy, hirsute hands.

"Good afternoon, Angus," she said. "I'm in need of supplies."

"And just what might those be, Mrs. Fowler?" He glanced furtively at the other women.

"Tea, salt, molasses, sugar, and a few other items we've run short of over the winter," she said.

"Mrs. Fowler, indeed!" With a disgruntled sniff, Lillian Gardiner grasped her companion by the arm. "We'll be back to do our shopping later, Mr. Harper," she addressed the storekeeper. "When you're serving decent clientele."

Drawing her companion along with her, the woman marched past Maggie. Hazel Green ducked her head to avoid Maggie's unflinching stare, while her daughter followed the pair, her gaze downcast as they exited the building.

"Sorry about that, Maggie." Angus Harper's flushed countenance gave credence to his words. "They're a bunch of self-righteous hens. Now as to the order, I'm afraid I have to ask if you have coin to cover it."

"At this time of year? Hardly. But our pond is full of logs, ready to be cut. Within a month, two at the most, I'll have squared deal and sawn planks ready to ship. As you well know, since the war closed the Baltic ports, the British are looking to this colony to fulfill their need for forest products. Processed timber will fetch top prices. 1813 is going to be an excellent year to make a profit for saw mill operators like my family. Angus, you granted my husband credit. He told me you did. Surely you won't go denying the same to his widow…just for a short period."

"Maggie, if it was up to me, I'd give you whatever you need and you'd be welcome to it." Looking down at his hands, he rubbed thick fingers over the scarred counter. "But, the truth is, I've had a spot of trouble lately. I got into a game of chance with one of Joe Carmody's men last week." He looked up at her, his jaw working in a nervous tick. "I'd had a few too many ales and didn't realize he was baiting me into a trap, that he was using Joe's money to lure me on. Bottom line is, I don't own this store anymore."

"Oh, Angus, I'm so sorry." She'd known Angus Harper had a weakness for gambling, but she'd never thought he'd go so far as risking his means of livelihood.

"That's not the worst of it, Maggie." He stared at her, blinking fast. "I got so desperate to win the store back, I put my house on the line."

"And lost it, too." She exhaled, letting her shoulders droop. "What about your wife and children? Where will they live? What is it you have now, five?"

"And number six on the way. Joe will allow me and my family to live on in the house, and I can run this business, just as long as I do his bidding. Maggie, I'm living on the grace of an almighty dictator who will tell me what I can and can't do, probably for the rest of my life."

"Damn Joseph Carmody." The tone of utter defeat in the big man's words and expression wrenched at her heart. "He's out to control everyone and everything in this valley. And he's well on the way to doing just that. This store is the life blood of the region. What will people do if they're denied credit at the only place to buy supplies?" Angry frustration snapped from her words.

"You have to understand the fix I'm in, Maggie. Your William was a great friend, a truly good man, and now I'm forced to deny his widow credit, or else..."

"Or else he'll take away your home and means of making a living." She heaved a deep sigh. "I understand. I also understand the attitude of those so-called ladies who just left. In their eyes I'm still a tavern girl who married a man for his holdings barely a month after his wife had passed. A conniving trollop."

"Maggie, you know none of us who are genuinely acquainted with you believe such nonsense."

"You may not, Angus, but I wonder about your good wife's opinion. Ladies do not take kindly to women who've made their living pouring drinks for men. Never mind." She heaved a deep breath and started toward the door. "We'll manage. Our cows are milking, our hens are laying, there's moose meat in the ice house, maple syrup in jars on the shelves, and we've enough vegetables in the root cellar to see us through. I'll just have to learn to get by without my morning tea."

"Sorry, Maggie. If there was anything I could do..."

A bolt of pink cloth near the entrance caught her eye. She stopped to touch it, to feel its softness between her work-roughened fingers. Three-year-old Eppie would look sweet in a dress made from it. A swift, hot wave of outrage and frustration welled through her body.

"You know Joseph Carmody had my husband murdered, don't you, Angus?" The accusation she'd never previously voiced burst out, loud and clear in the silent room. "Well, you can tell the old blighter for me, the next time you see him, that Margaret Fowler isn't about to be driven from her land by the likes of him! William Fowler struggled for years to build up his holdings, and I'm not about to let some greedy bastard steal them."

"Maggie, Maggie, be careful what you say!" Angus Harper glanced around the empty store and wet his lips.

"Why should I? Joe Carmody is out to ruin me, and nothing I can say or do will make his efforts any more heinous than they already are!"

Head held high, she threw back her shoulders and strode out of the store into the blustery overcast of an April afternoon as bleak and cold as the feelings in her heart. Pausing to regain her regular breathing, she looked around the settlement, at the log and plank houses and buildings. With the current desperate need for timber products in England and this region ready to supply them, someday soon the community would become a bustling township. She planned to see to it her family held a position of respect in the opinion of its citizens.

Glancing downriver, she saw the skeletons of three ships in various stages of construction. Joseph Carmody had begun a shipbuilding industry the previous year. Now he was going ahead as fast he could, the need for vessels to carry forest products across the ocean as vital a necessity as the trees and men who brought planks, squared deal, and white pine spars for masts to his wharves.

She drew a deep breath. She'd been foolish. Yelling unsubstantiated accusations in the mercantile had been a rash thing to do. She had no proof William had been murdered, let alone on orders from Joseph Carmody, yet she felt as certain of it as if she'd been present at the event. Fortunately, Angus Harper had been the only witness to her outburst. In spite of his changed circumstances, she believed he would remain her discreet friend.

But enough of such thoughts. She had more immediate problems to solve. Pulling up the collar of her shabby woolen jacket against the biting east wind and forcing her emotions into control, she headed back to where she'd left her team of Clydesdales tied to a hitching post. Widowed less than a month, she'd been forced to learn to harness the big animals and do a myriad of other tasks of which she'd previously had no knowledge. But she'd managed, and she'd handle this latest setback as well.

A commotion in front of the tavern where she'd formerly worked drew her attention. Curious, she left the team tied and went to stand outside the circle of men gathered around a man she recognized as Nate Bendel, a local fisherman.

"I tell you, Captain Duffy was right flabbergasted," he expounded to the group. "He thought the fella was a dandy, someone what had never dirtied his hands or wielded a sword in his life. But when those American privateers boarded the *Avon Queen*, the captain said his passenger was worth a half dozen of his own men. This fella come up on deck, his fancy coat and silk cravat thrown off, a sword in one hand, a pistol stuck in his belt, and waded right into the fray. He shot one fella in the leg, threw another overboard, and chased their captain back aboard his own vessel at the point of his sword. Charlie said they wouldn't have won the battle without him."

"Oh, right." One of the men Maggie recognized as Joseph Carmody's right-hand man Michael Kelly scoffed. "And where would you be hearing such tidings, Nate Bendel? Captain Charlie Duffy's ship is just now coming up the river."

"I was fishing salmon out in the bay. When I saw the *Queen* riding at anchor, waiting for the tide, I decided to drop aboard and say hello to Charlie and his crew. That's when I got the story."

"And did you see this great fighting man with your own eyes?" another jeered.

"Aye. He was standing at the bulwarks, ignoring Charlie and his account of the fight, like he wanted no one to speak of what he'd done."

"A soldier, perhaps?" someone in the small crowd suggested. "A soldier given a grant of land in this country for his service? He wouldn't be the first to be so rewarded."

"Nooo…" Nate Bendel dragged out the word thoughtfully. "He hadn't the stance of a military man."

"But where else could a man learn to fight as you've described, unless…"

"Unless he's a highwayman," came another

possibility. "Aye, that's probably it. A highwayman fleeing justice in the Old Country."

"Well, it little matters, does it?" Nate Bendel barked. "Most of us have things in our past we'd rather not have raked up. If this man saved Charlie and his crew, I say he deserves a hearty cheer when he arrives."

"Go and tell Mr. Carmody." Michael Kelly ordered a man at his side. "He's always ready to recruit a good fighting man. He may be interested in this one. Come on, lads." He turned to the rest of the group. "Let's go down to the dock and get a look at this mighty warrior for ourselves."

An idea forming in her mind, an idea so bold it made her innards flutter, Maggie eased away from the edge of the crowd and went back to her team. She climbed aboard the wagon seat and swung the horses around so she could see the river and the ship moving toward the village wharf. She recognized the *Avon Queen*, the ship reputed to be carrying that amazing fighting man. Wetting her lips, she squared her shoulders, mentally going over her plan and struggling to convince herself it was prudent.

She waited until the ship had bumped against the pier and the men on shore were hustling to secure the vessel to the wharf with lines hurled out by the crew. Then she clucked to her team and headed for the waterfront.

Their hooves thumped a hollow sound as she guided them onto the dock. Startled, the mare threw up her head and began to prance, jolting her great hind quarters and the wagon to one side.

"Whoa!" Maggie jerked on the reins.

The gelding that was the mare's teammate ground

to a halt, dragging the other animal into snorting submission. As he brought the situation back into his mistress's control, Maggie breathed a silent prayer.

"Good boy, Prince," she praised the big Clyde.

"Havin' a bit of a battle, are you, Maggie?" Maggie recognized Michael Kelly leering up at her. "Need a man?"

He reached to take the mare's bridle, but she jerked the animal's head away.

"I'm just fine, Mr. Kelly," she said, her words calm with an effort. "Now if you'll kindly step aside…"

"To be sure and certain, my lady." He swept her a mocking bow and let her walk her team and wagon past him.

She halted her horses halfway out on the wharf and watched from the high seat of her farm wagon as workmen moored the *Avon Queen* to the dock. The ship had been fortunate to have made the voyage across the Atlantic. The British North American colonies were engaged in a war involving frequent naval battles with their neighbors to the south. French vessels also roamed the seas, supporting the revolutionaries. American privateers sailed up and down the east coast of the British colonies, a bane to ships from the Old Country entering their harbors. Battles such as the one Nate Bendel had described aboard the *Avon Queen* were common occurrences.

But it wasn't thoughts of war or even the bitter April wind tunneling up the river that sent a shiver coursing through Maggie Fowler's slender body. Her heart pounded at her ribs and her head felt feather light at the temerity of what she was about to do.

She saw a man come to the bulwarks. Broad of

shoulder, with dark curls ruffling in the harsh wind, he had a face as handsome as any she'd ever seen. He wore an elegant black coat. His white shirt, devoid of cravat, had blown open at the throat. His bold stance suggested a spirit not easily cowed or diminished. He had to be the fighting gentleman passenger Nate had described.

Her heartbeat upped to a violent tattoo. She hadn't imagined he'd look as he did. How could she possibly summon the courage to approach such a man with her proposition?

You worked in this village's tavern for nearly two years before your marriage, Margaret Fowler. You faced down more ruffians than you care to count. Surely you're not about to be deterred by a man whose appearance bespeaks of his being a far cry better than such riffraff.

She nosed the team up against a stack of sawn lumber near the wharf, tied the reins to the whipstand with fingers so cold they could barely accomplish the task, and climbed to the ground. She adjusted the cap over her hair and attempted to brush some of the sawdust from her clothing.

Off you go, my girl. No time to back down now.

"Good morning, sir." She strode forward to greet the stranger as he came down the gangplank.

"Good morning." The stranger looked down at her with eyes so intensely blue that, for a moment, they froze words in her throat. *Get on with it, just get on with it.* Behind her she heard a group of men gathering, probably eager to see the amazing fighting man Nate Bendel had described. She swallowed hard and forced herself to speak.

"I'm wondering if you have a position, a job?" She asked the question from a dry throat out over parched lips. *Good God, but he was handsome.*

"Not as yet." The corner of his mouth quirked in what might have been the beginnings of amusement. "I've only just set foot on your fair soil. Have you one to offer?" His words carried the inflection of a cultured Englishman.

"Perhaps, but this is not the place to discuss it. Are you willing to take a drive with me?" Acutely aware of her own shabby appearance, she indicated the waiting team, their bellies and legs, like the wagon, splattered with mud. A man of this ilk wasn't likely to be interested in such a woman or any offer she might make to him.

"Why not." He surprised her with his answer and a shrug. "I'll collect my trunks and horse later," he called back to the sailors already bringing cargo up onto the deck. "This won't take long, I assume?" He glanced down at her.

"Not long at all." She turned to precede him back to her wagon, but a group of burly workmen, headed by Michael Kelly, blocked their way.

"Trying to get yourself another man, are ye, Maggie?" he sneered. "Ye are a brazen little hussy, taking a stranger off the first ship that hits the wharf this spring. But you'd no need to wait. Meself or any of the lads here would have been glad to satisfy your cravings."

Glancing up at the stranger, Maggie saw one of his dark eyebrows raise.

"Get out of my way, Michael Kelly." She stood her ground and glared up at the brute.

"Ah, now, Maggie, be a nice girl." He reached to grab her arm, but the stranger's fist was quicker. It came down with a wallop on the other man's wrist that sent him staggering backwards with a yelp of pain, clutching the point of impact.

"Bastard!" he yelled.

"The lady asked you to move aside." The newcomer's words held the stark cold of winter ice.

For a moment no one moved. Then, with a sneer and a mocking touch of his forelock, Michael Kelly stepped aside. The group around him parted to allow the couple access to the wagon. At its side, the man from the ship caught her about the waist with both hands and hoisted her as easily to the seat as if she'd been a sack of feathers. With a lithe movement, he vaulted up beside her, unwound the reins, backed the team away from the lumber, and halted them while he asked, "Which way?"

Astonished to muteness, she pointed down the road that led through the middle of the small settlement and into the trees at the rear.

"Hang on." He shot her a quick glance. "Hah!" he shouted to the team, cracked the reins over their backs, and sent them forward at a thundering gallop of great hooves. His urging drove them from the wharf to churn up mud from melting snow in the rutted road and send it splattering. Maggie lurched backward in a jerk that would have unseated her if he hadn't given her warning.

What manner of man is this? A second thought flew across her mind. *Will he prove more than I can handle?*

Once they were out of sight of the village along the

tree-lined trail, patches of lingering snow spotting its edge, he slowed the team to a walk and turned to her. "Now, what is this proposition you're about to put to me?"

"I need someone who can help guard my farm and mills." Afraid of losing her nerve, she blurted out the requirement. "Someone"—she wet her lips—"who is not afraid of conflict and is willing to fight for what is right and just."

"A tall order." His mouth quirked at her gush of words. "What makes you think I might be this remarkable creature?"

"I don't know that you are." Relaxed by the hint of humor in his reply, she gathered courage. "I only know that you are new to this valley, that you have not yet been tainted by Joseph Carmody and his heartless greed, that you have the bearing of a gentleman, and…" Her words trailed off.

"Go on." This time the corners of his mouth elevated into what might well be the beginnings of a grin.

"And I have it on good authority that you're not afraid of a fight and can acquit yourself tolerably well in one." She turned up the collar of her jacket in a pretense of warding off the cold, but afraid of seeing refusal mirrored in his expression.

"And exactly who is this good authority?" Humor drained from his tone as he asked the question.

"A fisherman encountered your ship at the mouth of the bay." *Why did it matter? Why had her words brought such an instant change in his demeanor?* "He told me there was a stalwart gentleman aboard, a gentleman who'd acquitted himself well in the skirmish that had occurred between the crew of the *Avon Queen* and that of an American vessel. As to why I accosted you so quickly on the wharf, I needed to get to you before Joseph Carmody claimed you…as he's determined to claim everything in this valley."

"It sounds as if you and this Joseph Carmody are in some kind of nasty dispute."

"More than a dispute." Her hands holding her collar high about the lower portion of her face knotted into fists. "My family's holdings include a farm, and a saw and grist mill. The grist mill is the only one in the county. He's determined to gain control of all of it and will stop at nothing to achieve his goal. I'm just as determined he will not."

"I doubt, given the vehemence in your tone, that this man has a snowball's chance in hell of succeeding."

She glanced over at him and saw he was grinning, good humor apparently restored. Allowing herself to relax for the first time since she'd driven the team onto the wharf, she flashed him a bit of a smile in return.

"At least not without a damned good scrap," she replied. "Once you see my holdings, I'm hoping you'll be willing to join in…on my side."

"And perhaps after you've introduced yourself?"

"Oh, I am sorry. Maggie Fowler. And you would be?"

"Harry…Harry Wallace."

"Mr. Wallace." She offered her right hand, and he, after a slight hesitation, gathered the reins into his left and accepted it.

They fell silent, Harry Wallace seemingly concentrating on driving the team and Maggie wondering how this handsome warrior stranger would react when they reached her farm and he discovered its realities. She'd been careful to refer to "her farm," "her holdings," all in the singular. What would he do when he met the children?

Chapter Two

What manner of woman was this? Harry cast a furtive glance in her direction as the wagon jolted over a root. No more than in her early twenties, she was fair of face, from what he could see of it. A few chestnut curls peeping out from beneath that ugly cap suggested lovely hair beneath, and even though she was bundled in male clothing he got an impression of a nicely shaped body. But she'd offered her hand in introduction as no lady would, talked of fighting, physically fighting, this Joseph Carmody. Bloody hell, the lass barely came to his shoulder.

About to urge the team to a brisker trot, he felt her lurch against his shoulder. As she bolted upright and struggled to regain her dignity, he guessed she'd dozed.

Poor wee lassie. Bone weary I'll venture a guess.

A crack that sounded like musket fire exploded to their left. The team snorted, half rearing. Tossing their heads, they jerked the wagon sideways as a massive pine tree crashed across the trail in front of them.

"Whoa!" Harry, no stranger to horses but unaccustomed to handling a wagon and team, battled to bring the pair under control. He caught a glimpse of two figures leaping astride horses and galloping off into the bush. Beside him, Maggie Fowler clung to the seat.

Don't let her get tossed. The words sprang across his mind like a silent prayer. *Bloody hell, these beasts are powerful. And the lass was driving them all on her own.*

Once he got the animals under control, he turned to her. "Are you all right?"

"Yes." She nodded, but her face was pale. "Damn Joseph Carmody! He's trying to scare you off! Or"— her eyes narrowed and her voice took on a bitterness that startled him—"kill you, like he killed William."

"William?" He frowned over at her.

"My husband. He was killed near this same place, accidentally shot by an unknown, careless hunter, so I've been told." Her words carried contemptuous disbelief.

"But you're not convinced?" *Sweet Jesus, what have I stumbled into? Murder and mayhem...again?*

"Not for a minute." Color returned to her face, red spots of anger brightening both cheeks. In her green eyes, he saw the outrage of a cat aroused to fury. "I have plenty of suspicions, but no proof. Therefore nothing has been done about it."

"Didn't you appeal to the magistrate? You should have insisted he conduct a further investigation."

"Do you know who the local magistrate is?"

"A man of integrity, I'd hope."

"Your hopes would be dashed. His name is Joseph Carmody." She jumped down from the wagon seat. "I'll lead Bonnie and Prince around this mess. They'll be skittish about going off a bit into the trees to get past it. Keep a firm hand on the reins in case they nevertheless decide to bolt."

She caught up the bridle of the gelding. "Come along, Prince. There's nothing to be afraid of, you great baby." Leading the team, she headed around the top of the tree blocking the trail and into the brush beside it.

Frightened by the swish of branches, they pranced, snorting and churning up the muddy earth with their large hooves.

"Whoa!" Pulling back on the reins, Harry fought to control the plunging pair as they seemed about to trample the slim young woman leading them.

"Let them have a bit more head," she called, dancing clear of the plunging hooves. "Don't be concerned about me. I know what I'm doing."

Nevertheless, Harry was relieved once the Clydes had been established back on the trail at the far side of the blockage and under his control, even if still blowing and pawing nervously.

Bloody cowards, that pair I saw in the bush! Attacking a woman. If someone had been with my mother and sister when such bastards came, they might have had a chance, they might have…

"Can you turn them about?" His thoughts broke off as she ran back to the wagon and climbed aboard. "Now that you've witnessed the kind of trouble you'd be walking into if you decided to come with me, I've no doubt you'll be wanting to get back to the dock to start looking for another position. I'm sure Joseph Carmody will be more than happy to add you to his ranks." The last came out with ill-disguised sarcasm.

He pulled on the reins, yelled a few commands, and managed to get the team turned back toward the village. Beside him on the seat, he sensed her body drooping.

"We're heading back to Riverhaven only to get my horse and trunk," he said. "I'm going to give your position a try." He flapped the reins over the backs of the team, sending them into a rhythmic canter. "Hang on to your hat, mistress. You're in for a wild ride."

"Thank you." The words bumped out as the wagon bounced over a root.

Satisfied, he returned his full attention to the team. The most he could urge out of them was a shambling gallop. Within a quarter mile, Harry gave in and let them settle to a comfortable trot.

These poor beasts must be exhausted from the stress of the day. They're farm animals, not war horses like Scotia. I can't expect them to take violence in their stride and then run like the wind.

"How far is your farm?"

"A good eight miles beyond where we were shot at," she replied, settling beside him. "But don't be concerned. Even with this return to Riverhaven, Bonnie and Prince have more than enough stamina to get us there."

"Very well." He adjusted the reins and slanted her a glance. "Suppose we pass the journey back to the village with your telling me about this position you want me to fill."

"That's only fair." She avoided his eyes and began her tale. "My parents and I came out from England three years ago. There was sickness on the ship. The stench and filth in the bowels of that miserable vessel defied description. My mother fell ill and died. My father, similarly afflicted, died shortly after we docked in Riverhaven."

She paused. A sideways glance caught her swallowing hard. He remained silent. He understood her grief.

"I was left alone." She cleared her throat and

continued, finally. "When I went to claim my parents' belongings, the captain said he'd be keeping them, that my father hadn't paid full passage. All he allowed me was my own trunk."

"Bastard!" Harry let the word fly out naturally, then muttered, "Sorry. Continue."

"The local innkeeper offered me work tending his bar and cooking meals for his guests. I accompanied him to his establishment, saw his clientele, and refused. A night spent alone on the dock with nowhere to sleep, terrified by drunken men and half-eaten alive by mosquitoes, changed my mind. At least at that tavern the landlord had promised I'd have a room of my own, a room with a good sturdily barred door to keep out intruders. I accepted his offer."

She drew a deep breath and stared ahead into the tunnel of pine trees.

"But you later married." He brought her back to her story when she seemed lost in thought.

"Yes. Two months ago."

"Two months! Woman, in the old country, you'd still be in widow's weeds."

"William Fowler, the man I married, had lost his wife Jane in February. She died suddenly of a fever. He came to Riverhaven in the days following. We'd met briefly at the mercantile the previous autumn and chatted for a bit. He remembered me, remembered my saying I was working at the tavern only until I found a better way of life. He said he believed me to be a strong woman, the only woman he knew who could deal with the situation at his holdings if anything happened to him. He proposed marriage. I accepted."

"Did you know the full extent of his troubles with

this Carmody fellow at the time? Did you fully realize what you were marrying into?"

"Yes." She rotated her shoulders. *Bone weary, no doubt.* "But saving the holdings of such a man as William Fowler, a hard-working, honest man who'd fought and struggled to make himself a home in this land, was something much more worthwhile than dishing out stew and liquor to noisy, disrespectful rabble."

"Aha. So you married William."

"Yes. Two weeks later he was killed, murdered by Joseph Carmody's men."

"Murdered is a strong word. Do you have proof?"

"Would it matter if I did? With Joseph Carmody representing the law, such an accusation would be laughed at." She broke off the subject. "Don't keep urging the team. They've had a long haul to Riverhaven, a bad fright, and we've still got miles to go. They're not racing stock, you know."

"You're right." He slowed the team to a walk as they came out of the forest and into the village proper. On a hill back from the wharves and rude structures of the village, a large, three-story white house with a wide front veranda overlooked the small settlement. He hadn't noticed it on their hasty exit earlier. It reminded Harry of a castle lording it over its vassals. Quite possibly the home of the infamous Joseph Carmody?

At the dock he saw sailors and shore workers busy unloading the *Avon Queen*. He turned the horses toward the area of activity. A trunk he recognized as his own had been shoved aside against a pile of deal, his saddle, its cloth, and a bridle thrown on its top. Tied to its side was a mare, a remarkable mare with a silver mane and tail, charcoal body gleaming from Harry's constant grooming during the voyage. She stood pawing the planks of the wharf and shaking her head, weeks of pent-up energy waiting to be released.

"All my earthly belongings." He quirked up one corner of his mouth, jerking a thumb toward the trunk and the restless animal.

"That mare is the most beautiful animal I've ever seen." Beside him, he heard her suck in her breath. A warmth flooded through him at her appreciation.

"She is a pretty lady." He turned the team toward the trunk and horse and stopped beside them. "And a clever one."

The animal, catching sight of him, whinnied, pranced, and tossed her silver mane.

"She appears glad to see you." Maggie smiled.

"Yes, well, we've shared more than a few adventures." He wound the reins around the whipstand. "Would you mind if I saddled her and rode beside the wagon back to your farm? She's been cooped up in that ship for weeks and needs exercise."

"Not at all." She smiled at him, and the thought coursed through his head that it had been a long time since he'd seen such a pretty face, cheeks pink from the bite of the wind, green eyes bright and expressive.

"Then I will." He swung to the ground and went to quiet the eager mare. "Easy, girl. You'll have a good run directly."

As he reached for the saddle cloth, he glimpsed, out of the corner of his eye, a group of men watching him from the wharf beside the *Avon Queen*. Heading the bunch he recognized the previous troublemaker, a man Maggie Fowler had addressed as Michael Kelly.

He threw the cloth over the mare's back, then the saddle, and began to fasten the girth, all the time keeping the men within his peripheral vision. When her bridle was in place, he tied her reins to the side of the wagon and went to retrieve his trunk.

"Let me help." She jumped down from the seat and grasped one of the end handles.

"It's heavy," he warned.

"Never fear," she emitted with a grunt as together they hefted it into the back of the wagon. "I'm accustomed to hard work."

"Hey there, dandy man." Harry turned slowly to see the men advancing toward them, Kelly in the lead. "Decided to throw your lot in with this doxy, have you?" He picked up a yard-long piece of two-by-four with one hand and smacked it into the palm of the other.

Ignoring him, Harry assisted Maggie back onto the wagon seat. His nerves taut and ready, he gathered up his mare's reins. He gave the woman a slight nod he hoped she'd interpret. Relief flooded through him as she returned the gesture, her hands easing toward the whipstand.

"Man for hire, I'm speaking to you!" Michael Kelly put a hand on Harry's shoulder.

Harry whirled. His booted kick sent the stick flying from the man's hand. A second later his fist connected with his assailant's jaw in a dull crack that sent the man sprawling onto the planks of the wharf.

"Drive!" he yelled to the woman who'd already gathered the team's lines and turned the pair toward the trail out of the village. As she sent the Clydesdales galloping with a yell, he vaulted into the saddle and shouted a command to the mare. She plunged into the group, rearing and kicking.

Whooping and crying out, some were toppled to the ground. Others managed to flee the flaying hooves. They staggered away from the attack, faces contorted with shock and fear. Satisfied, Harry swung his warhorse about and sent her bounding in pursuit of the wagon.

****

A half mile down the road, Maggie reined in the team. Riding beside the wagon, he also stopped. Her Clydesdales dripped sweat, but beneath him Scotia pranced and cavorted, little of her stored energy spent.

"I'd say they won't be following us…at least not for the present." He leaned forward to pat the mare's neck and grin at the woman in the wagon.

"And I'd say this wasn't your first battle." She eased up on the reins and leaned against the boards that formed the back of the seat. She surprised him with a small grin. "We make a good pair."

Tough, not about to let a bunch of roughnecks frighten her. Reminds me of Iona. But that nasty bit of refuse named Michael called her a doxy…

"Yes, well, we'll see." He wasn't about to commit himself, not yet. First he had to view her property and get a lay of the land. "Right now, we'd best be getting on. Scotia is fine, but your team wasn't made for racing. I doubt they've got much left in them."

"Scotia. A pretty name for a pretty mare."

"She's a pleasure, that's a fact, and clever enough to learn anything I choose to teach her." He patted her arched neck, letting her prance a bit, proud of her form and energy.

"What was it you had her do amongst that rabble?" She looked at him. "I caught only a glimpse as I was turning the team from the wharf, but what I saw was amazing. I've never known a horse to perform such defensive maneuvers."

"A little something I taught her after reading about similar tricks," he replied. "The moves originated with the ancient warhorses of Rome, where equines were trained to fight along with their riders. Kicking and rearing, they often brought down more of the enemy than their masters. It's come in handy on more than one occasion."

"You can read?" Her eyes widened in what he thought he recognized as delighted surprise.

"Yes. Can you?"

"No." She lowered her head and fingered the reins.

"Ah, well, no great problem. If I decide to take the position you have to offer, I'll teach you. I don't imagine the job of warrior will take up all my time. Now let's be off." He let Scotia have her head, and she loped off down the trail. He heard the wagon following.

****

She reined the team to a halt on the top of a rise and swept out a hand to indicate the valley below. "The Fowler farm and mills, sir."

He stopped his mare and looked down to where a boisterous stream had been dammed to form a large pond presently glutted with fresh cut logs. Beyond it stood a two-story building built into a rise with another long, level one jutting out from it. Sawdust and lumber piled around the latter branded it a sawmill, while he recognized the taller as one of the grist type. On the hill opposite the one on which they'd paused, in a wide clearing, stood a rambling, two-story log house and, several yards to its left, a large barn of similar material. Under a canopy of stark white clouds, the little settlement appeared a safe haven from both the biting wind and the dangers of the world.

But is it? This woman says her first husband was killed, murdered, and now she's expecting me to protect her and her holdings from a man she's already described as ruthless in his greed. Do I want to be drawn into a fight again?

"I'm impressed," he said aloud as he nudged Scotia closer to the wagon. "This is a much larger venture than I'd anticipated, a small community, in fact. But the sawmill appears idle even though there is no shortage of raw materials." He indicated the logs.

"William and the boys cut those last winter." She heaved a deep breath. "James and Geordie and Robert wanted to continue cutting while I went to Riverhaven, but I forbade it. If something happened while I was away…"

"James? Geordie? Robert? You have other hired hands?"

"No. Come along. It's easier to show you than explain." She flapped the reins, and the weary team set off at a spritely trot now that home was in sight.

As he rode down into the valley, across the bridge above the dam, and up the hill toward the log house, he glanced back at the pair of mills. *A promising-looking operation. The lass's deceased husband has set things up well.*

"Whoa." She brought the horses to a halt before the veranda that ran across the front of the house. The door at its back opened as an assortment of children flooded out. Harry's breath hiccupped. *Bloody hell, how many of them are there? Four, five, six... And the smallest one, a wee lassie...is that a piglet she's clinging to? What in hell...?*

"Seven." Maggie Fowler stopped his mental counting and faced him with proud defiance. "I have seven children."

"Seven? Ye never said anything aboot seven bairns..." Dumbfounded, he let his accent slip as he stared at the group and allowed Scotia to prance.

She jumped down from the wagon and advanced up the steps toward the silent, staring group.

"This is James." She introduced the tallest, a handsome lad well into manhood, with broad shoulders, light brown hair, and a strong build. "He turned eighteen last week. Next comes George. We call him Geordie. He's sixteen. Then there's Robert, who's fourteen. Over here"—she moved down the veranda to put her arm around another lad—"is Samuel. He's thirteen. Next comes Isabella—Bella—at twelve, and Elizabeth—Lizzie—ten last February. And this"—she moved to the smallest child standing on the bottom step, her arm about the pig, thumb stuck in her mouth—"is Elspeth—Eppie. She's three. Her friend we call Pig."

None of the children acknowledged her introduction but all continued to stare at the newcomer, the older boys with sullen, suspicious expressions, the two older girls with shy, downcast eyes.

"Children, this is Harry Wallace. He'll be helping us with the work about the place." She sat down on the step and drew the youngest, identified as Elspeth, into her arms. "Pig is Eppie's pet," she continued, looking up at Harry. "My husband found her abandoned in the woods, probably because she'd ceased to grow, a dwarf." She kissed the child, and Harry felt a lurch in his chest.

He remembered his mother, far from being the dour Scot his father had been, as a demonstrative woman who loved her children and made no attempt to hide it. *But, God in heaven, seven children...even if they were a handsome, healthy-looking bunch with their tangled golden-brown curls and bright blue eyes.*

"Now, boys..." She turned to James, Geordie, and Robert. "I'd be obliged if you'll put the team away and show Mr. Wallace where to stable his mare while I start supper heating. Bella and Lizzie, fetch that pot of stew I made this morning, from the ice house. Samuel, build up the fire on the hearth."

The eldest, James, after a slight hesitation, scowled, narrowed blue eyes, and came down the steps to take Prince's bridle. Geordie and Robert waited only a moment longer, then followed their brother's lead toward the log barn a few hundred yards away, with Harry, still mounted on his mare, bringing up the rear.

What is this lassie attemptin' to play at? These bairns cannot be her own flesh and blood. She told me she'd only married months ago. And she's aye no more than in her early twenties herself. Step children, aye, that must be it. Step children, bairns of her dead husband.

At the barn, the procession halted, and Harry dismounted. James backed the wagon into a shelter at one end and began to work at freeing the team from the traces. Geordie moved to help him.

"A fine-looking place," Harry commented, casting

a gaze around the large shelter, hoping to bring an end to the silence and shake himself out of the shock the introduction to Maggie's family had thrown over him. "You must have a fair bit of stock to warrant such a facility."

"Six cows and two dozen hens," Robert began proudly, but James shot him a look. The younger brother lowered his head and said no more, busying himself around the wagon.

The oldest lad thinks I'm taking inventory, sizing up the place, suspicious. Can't say that I blame him.

Glad to get out of the cutting wind, he led Scotia into the wagon shed beside the team and began to remove her saddle. As he threw his riding equipment over a sawhorse in a corner and turned the cloth up to dry, he made an effort at breaking the silence.

"Any of you ride?"

"We only have the Clydes." It was Geordie—was that his name? He didn't have them all straightened out yet—who answered.

"Aha. Wonderful animals, Clydes, and not bad riding animals once they're trained to it."

"Our horses are workers." James's response reeked of annoyance. "They've no energy left at the end of a day to go gallivanting around the country with anyone on their back."

"Well, then, since my mare has only been broken to saddle and might prove unfit for the type of activity required on a farm or in the lumber business, perhaps one of you might like to take her out for a run one fine day. That is, if you think you're up to handling her. She's got spirit."

"Mister, there's no man or horse we're not up to

handling." His expression bellicose and challenging, James strode to stand close in front of him. Harry realized he was nearly as tall as he himself.

A fine figure of a young lad, but with a chip as big as one of those millpond logs on his shoulder.

"I'm sure." *Not the time to push things any further.* "Therefore, the offer most definitely stands. Now, if you'll show me where I can stable her, I'll leave you to your tasks."

"This way." James took the team by their bridles and headed outside to another door in the barn. Leading his mare, Harry followed the young man and the Clydes into an area where several stalls stood empty while, in those at the far end, a half dozen fine-looking milk cows placidly munched hay.

"Good-looking animals you've got." Harry again attempted conversation.

"Yes, sir." The lad he believed had been introduced as Robert replied with alacrity. "Father was right proud of his herd. He said…"

A dark look from his eldest brother stopped his words. Looking quelled, he retreated to the rear of the barn to rub the nose of the first cow.

Except for the sounds made by the horses, the remainder of the stabling was completed in silence. Chores finished, the three young men headed for the house, Harry walking at what he deemed a respectful distance behind them. Glancing up at the white sky, he pulled his coat closer to his throat in the bitter wind.

Cold enough to snow. If I were back home, we'd be expecting a lambing blizzard. Ah, well, Scotia and I will be well sheltered in that fine barn, if we're invited to stay. And we won't be tossed and pitched about as we have been for over a month now.

Outside the back door, they paused at a small, rough-hewn table that held a basin, a piece of soap, and a length of drying linen. Beneath it, a bucket steamed with hot water. In the dull, late-afternoon light, James pulled off his jacket and shirt, poured water from a bucket beneath it into the container, and, in spite of the biting wind, proceeded to wash himself from the waist up. Harry couldn't help but be impressed. The boy had a remarkable build. Hard work and good food, he reckoned. Back in the old country, there was lots of hard work but precious little decent food.

The others sank wearily onto a bench beside the washstand and waited. Harry remained standing. When James had finished, he threw away the water, put his shirt back on, and, carrying his jacket, went inside.

Geordie, a similarly strong specimen, refilled the basin from the bucket and repeated his brother's performance, but when it was Robert's turn, he discarded the used water, poured more from the bucket into the basin and turned to Harry. "After you, sir."

Aha! At least one of these lads is willing to give me a bit of rein.

"I thank you, young man, but I'll wager you've had a long, hard day of work. You go ahead."

While he waited for Robert to wash, he glanced around the dooryard and saw a large, well-constructed beehive oven several yards from the log house's rear door. Images of warm, golden-brown loaves slid across his mind. How long had it been since he'd had such a treat?

When Robert had finished washing and gone inside, Harry stripped off his coat and shirt. The wintery cold chafed his bare skin, and he hurried with his ablutions. As he pulled his clothing back on, he felt better but knew a full bath and clean clothes from the skin out would have been his idea of nirvana.

Stop bellyaching, Harry Wallace. Take what's offered and be grateful. You could be eating beans in a louse-infested tavern, with a bunch of drunken louts as companions…or rotting at the end of a rope.

Chapter Three

When he entered the log house, an encompassing warmth chased away the chill of the day as the aroma of cooking food enveloped him—a delicious stew, if he wasn't mistaken. The smell made his innards rumble with anticipation. After weeks of ship's fare, he was more than ready for a decent meal on a table that didn't dip and tilt.

A massive stone fireplace to his left, an old musket propped up against its side, drew his attention. He wondered if this weapon was the family's only means of defense.

A pot from which issued the enticing smells hung over the flames. In front of the hearth, two rocking chairs were turned toward its warmth. To one side of the fireplace, a plank door was closed on what he suspected was a bedroom, on the other a stairway led up to a second story. Across the room, a curtain was drawn back to reveal a small chamber with a built-in bed at its rear. Dressers to his right housed an array of dishes, cooking utensils, and a dry sink. He turned his attention to the inhabitants.

Wooden bowls full of steaming stew in front of them, tin mugs of milk at hand, the children sat on benches along both sides of a long, plank table in the centre of the room. Empty chairs stood at either end— the parents' positions, he guessed. The table was laid with plates of bread and butter. On a hand-hooked mat in front of the hearth, the pig lay basking in the warmth, an empty bowl in front of her offering evidence of her recent meal.

"Well, I must say, this looks most inviting." He drew a deep breath and smiled as seven pairs of suspicious eyes turned on him.

These bairns aren't about to welcome me into their midst, not by a long shot.

"Mr. Wallace, welcome to our home."

His breath caught as she spoke and he saw her, carrying the youngest on her hip, coming out of the bedroom to his left. She was wearing a dress, albeit a grey woolen creation with no pretension to fashion, held in at the waist by a worn leather belt, but now, suddenly, he saw her for the first time as a woman. Her chestnut hair, a tangle of shining waves and curls, was caught back into a queue with a bit of frayed ribbon, and her face—it had to be the face of an angel with its healthy glow and heart shape.

"You sit here, and I'll fetch your supper in a minute, Eppie darling." She placed the child in the chair at the foot of the table and moved to the hearth. As she reached for a bowl on a shelf beside it, he remained mesmerized by her altered appearance and didn't realize he was staring until James cleared his throat and shot him a narrow-eyed glare.

Verrae well, young lad. I get the message.

He gave him a nod of understanding. James replied with a sneer.

"Here you go, Mr. Wallace." She brought his attention back to her as she held out a bowl of steaming meat, gravy, and vegetables. "Please take the chair at the head of the table. I apologize for the bread. I fear it may be a bit stale. I've had no time to fire the outdoor oven these past few days."

"Thank you." He accepted the meal and headed to the seat assigned. "No excuses necessary. After weeks of hardtack, any bread will taste like manna from heaven."

"That's Father's chair!" Samuel, the thirteen-year-old, burst out. His expression combined shock and anger as Harry started to take the indicated seat. He straightened up, holding the bowl, and paused, glancing over at Maggie.

"It *was* your father's chair." Her words were even and firm. "Tonight we have a guest. We cannot ask him to share one of the benches already crowded with you lot. I'll be sitting at this end near the hearth to keep an eye on the food, so there is no other space. Now say, 'Good evening, Mr. Wallace,' and let us get on with the meal."

Silence. Finally Isabella the oldest girl raised bashful eyes to him. "Good evening, Mr. Wallace."

Slowly the others, with the exception of the two oldest boys, followed suit, shyly from the girls, grudgingly from the younger boys.

Determined not to trust me. Ah, well, I can understand. Harry sat down in the chair and turned his attention to the hearty meal in front of him. He had to concentrate on the food to keep his gaze from wandering to the alluring woman moving about at the far end of the table. She brought another bowl of stew to the table and lifted the little girl from the chair to place her on her knee as she sat down.

"Look, Eppie, stew," she used a spoonful to tempt

the youngster. "Your favorite."

Eppie didn't respond. Instead, she stared at Harry with wide, blue eyes.

"That's Mr. Wallace, darling." She spoke softly. "He'll be staying with us for a while. Now eat your supper. Look, Pig has already finished hers."

Slowly the child opened her mouth and accepted the food.

"You're spoiling her," James muttered. "She's old enough to feed herself."

"Perhaps, and probably she will soon. But until she does, we'll give her a bit of time to adjust to the changes around here. Eppie, take a drink of milk." She returned her attention to the little one and offered a mug to her lips.

Harry was impressed with Maggie's calm tone. Surely these children must be a trial, challenging her at many turns in their understandable bitterness at having lost both parents in such a short space of time.

When they had finished their stew, she stood and went to the hearth, where a teakettle hung over the fire.

"Tea, Mr. Wallace?" she asked glancing back at him as she reached for it.

"Aye, if you please."

"James, Geordie?" She cast questioning looks at the pair.

"None of that swill." James reached for his mug and drained it. "I'll stick to water." Geordie grunted agreement.

"As you wish." She poured steaming liquid into two cups and returned to the table to place one before Harry and take Eppie back on her knee as she reseated herself.

Harry saluted her with the mug and raised it to his mouth.

Sweet mother, what is this stuff? He barely managed to avoid more than a slight grimace as he tasted it.

"I must apologize." She looked down the table at him. "We ran out of tea, and now we're making do with such as we can manage from the bark of spruce trees. It really is vile, isn't it? And I'm afraid we've no sugar with which to sweeten it. We have maple syrup gathered this spring that might help."

"No, no, it's fine just as it is." He steeled his stomach and took another sip. *Good God, how did the woman drink this witch's brew?*

"We're low on a few supplies…tea, salt, and sugar among them." She kissed the top of Eppie's head and avoided his eyes.

"And that bastard Joseph Carmody won't grant us credit to get more, even though he knows we'll have lumber ready for market within a few weeks." James's words were a snarl.

"James, I remind you again about swearing in front of the children." Maggie placed her hands gently over Eppie's ears for a moment. "We'll manage. We must not distress Mr. Wallace with our troubles at the supper table."

"Whatever you say…I suppose. Come along, lads." James stepped back off the bench. "Barn work to do."

"I'll help." Harry was quick to join the group heading for the door.

"We can manage." This time it was Geordie who met his offer with narrowed eyes.

"I'm sure you can, but my mare will make extra

work."

As he followed the boys toward the door, Maggie's words halted him.

"You can help Mr. Wallace bring his trunk up to the house. He'll be sleeping in the small room. Tonight promises to be bitterly cold. The barn won't do."

"Thank you, Mrs. Fowler." He half turned in acknowledgement. "Most appreciated."

Snowflakes swirled about the yard as he and the boys stepped out of the house. *Just as I suspected, a lambing blizzard. Maybe things aren't so different here as I'd thought. Cold as an iceberg and storming like hell, even though it's supposed to be spring.*

He turned up the collar of his coat, ducked his head, and followed the young men across the yard through the howling wind. The idea of sleeping safe inside the log house on such a night held a soul-warming appeal. And Scotia would be stabled from the storm, fed and watered, not standing saddled and waiting in the snow, her head bowed against the gale, crusted in ice. She deserved such comfort.

The barn work was another silent affair. Harry made no effort to break it with talk. Tomorrow would be time enough to begin to settle things with these lads. After taking care of his mare, he headed into the wagon shed for his trunk. Figuring he'd have to drag it to the house, he was surprised to see Robert running, head bent against the driving snow, to join him.

"That thing must be fair to middlin' heavy," the young man muttered, grasping one of the handles.

"That it is." Harry hefted the other end, and together they headed for the house, snow blasting into their faces.

"Come a fair distance, have you?" Robert yelled above the howl of the wind.

"From the Old Country, five weeks aboard a ship."

"Huh."

They reached the house and struggled the trunk inside. Maggie, seated in one of the chairs by the hearth, rocked a nightgown-clad Eppie in her arms and was singing softly…a Gaelic lullaby. Its words startled him, froze him in place, tightened his chest as memories flooded back.

Sweet Jesus, the woman's singing a lullaby my own mother used to sing to my wee sister. And me.

A lump clogged his throat as a stinging struck behind his eyes. Mesmerized, he could only stare at the scenario, Maggie's voice washing all other realities from the moment. His own mother, the croft cottage in the Highlands, a peat fire keeping out the cold of a lambing blizzard… With an effort he forced himself out of the reverie.

Buggar that, lad. Buck up. Don't let this lot see me reduced to tears by an old song.

The girls were busy washing the last of the supper dishes and tidying the kitchen. He forced his attention to brushing snow from his trunk as James and Geordie came in. They removed their outerwear, shook it, then hung it on pegs by the door. Harry followed suit.

"You can put your belongings in the little room over there." Maggie broke off from her song and indicated the cubicle. "There's a bed, with a bathing tub shoved beneath it, and room for your trunk. We generally use the space as a washing room for taking baths in private, but it also serves as a place for overnight visitors. We'll expect you to vacate when any of us needs to use the tub."

"It'll be fine." Harry nodded as he and Robert, carrying the trunk between them, headed into the small space with a narrow bed built against the outside wall, a big wooden washing tub visible beneath it. The trunk fitted neatly in the space at the bottom of the bed.

"Thank you, Robert," he said as the pair returned to the main room.

The reply was a grunt but not an unpleasant or defiant sound. Harry sat down in his chair at the head of the table and wondered if he'd be able to earn the respect of any of Maggie Fowler's children, if he stayed.

Chapter Four

When Eppie finally slept, Maggie stood and carefully carried her into the room Harry had correctly assumed earlier was a sleeping chamber. Pig followed. After they'd gone, he leaned back in his chair and enjoyed the ambiance of the big, clean, food-scented room. Even the sound of the storm blustering about the log house soothed him. This was the perfect place to be on such a night.

The girls finished in the kitchen, and together with the three youngest boys they went up the stairs to their beds. They looked tired, too spent from hard work to indulge in childish chatter or playful repartee.

A hard life it must be without a man at the helm to ease the strain.

James remained. Getting up from where he'd been sitting on a bench at the table, he went to the woodbox, picked up a stout length of log, and added it to the fire. Curious to see what manner of weaponry the family possessed, Harry reached for the musket leaning against the stones.

"Don't touch that gun! It was my father's!" Bristling, the young man whirled to face him.

"A thousand pardons, sir." Harry withdrew his hand and sat down. "I only wished to examine it. I haven't seen such a weapon in many years. Is it the only one in the house?"

"It serves its purpose." James threw another log on the fire, this time sending up a shower of sparks. "Papa brought down enough game to feed us over the winters with it, and I will do the same."

"I'm sure you will." Harry nodded. "But even without close examination I can see it's showing signs of wear. You'd best be careful with it. Old weapons can be dangerous."

"Don't concern yourself." James towered above him as he turned from the fire. "We've managed without your advice for this long. I dare say we'll do so again."

"Of course you will." It had been a long, arduous day. He wasn't about to challenge this tall, broad-shouldered man over a trifle.

"I'll take care of my family." James glowered down at Harry, blue eyes hard as ice. "Don't try to take over just yet. You're here on *her* good graces alone. My brothers and I expect you to understand your place."

"James!" Maggie stepped out of the bedroom in time to hear his remarks. "You will apologize… immediately."

"I'll apologize when he proves himself worth the effort, and not before." He swung away and strode up the steps, shoulders up, back, and rigid.

"I'm sorry, Mr. Wallace." Maggie sighed and lifted her shoulders in a small, weary shrug. "I haven't yet had an opportunity to tell him how you fought our battle at the wharf, or how you helped with the team…"

"No need to try to ingratiate me to your sons." He let a sardonic grin quirk a corner of his mouth. "I'm pretty certain the only way I'll gain their respect and trust is to win it on my own. So let's just leave them for the time being."

"If that's what you want." She heaved a sigh. "Nevertheless, it goes against my principles to allow a child of mine to fling insults."

"I think mistrust is as good a reason as any. And given what has been happening to this family recently, mistrust has become a way of life, I'll wager."

"You're a perceptive man. I hope this family will soon begin to give you a better impression."

"Now, I think an explanation is in order." Harry watched her as she began once more to rock in the chair by the hearth.

"Explanation of what?" She stopped moving and stared at him.

"For the children, for this house, for everything." He swung a hand out to indicate the surroundings. "That lullaby in Gaelic."

"Very well. Come, take the other rocker here by the fire, and I'll try. I'd offer you tea, but as you've discovered, we've run out of leaves, and I gathered from your expression that our spruce substitute is not exactly to your taste."

"Right now I'd prefer a wee dram." He stood, crossed the room, and shoved aside the curtain that served as a door on his new sleeping quarters. Pulling a key on a chain from beneath his shirt, he bent and unlocked the trunk. A bit of shuffling inside produced a bottle.

"Will you be joining me, Mrs. Fowler?" He held the bottle up to her. "You've had a full day."

"Thank you, I will." She stood, crossed the room, and took two mugs from the sideboard and placed them on the table. "Just a very wee dram, if you please, Mr.

Wallace."

"Excellent." He poured, more into one than the other, slid the lesser cup toward her, and picked up the one better supplied. "*Slainte*." He raised his drink.

"*Slainte*?" She looked puzzled.

"It's an old Celtic toast, for when one is about to share a drink with a friend."

She hesitated, then with a small smile curling her lips, repeated it. "*Slainte*." She took a sip, flinched slightly, and continued, "Now to business."

"To business." He saluted her with his mug.

Once they were seated in the rocking chairs before the fire, she fondled her cup between her hands, her gaze cast down into its contents. "The children are my dead husband's," she began slowly, softly. "His wife died in February. He needed someone to care for them. He came into the village, to the tavern, where he knew I'd been working since my father's death. He asked me to marry him. I said yes. Two weeks later, he was killed."

"You're one brave woman, to marry a man you barely knew and take on such a family."

"I'm pragmatic," she said. "I do what must be done. William required a wife. I wanted to be free of the tavern. Most of all, the children needed a mother."

"Look here…" He bent toward her. "I'm not judging you. I may be new to this country, but I understand that marriage, where the care of children is involved, is generally a necessity, not a romance. You did a fine and courageous thing in marrying this man to care for his brood."

"Thank you." She looked over at him, the sincerity in her green eyes going straight to his heart.

"But what about that lullaby? I'd have judged you to be an Englishwoman. Where did you learn Gaelic? And a Highland tune, at that?"

"William was a Highlander, driven out by the Clearances. In the short time we were married, he taught it to me. He said his wife Jane sang it to all the children when they were babes, and that Eppie was especially partial to it...wouldn't sleep most nights unless she sang it to her. William tried, but it seemed it was a woman's voice on the words that Eppie needed."

Hell and damnation! The man had been one of his own breed...a victim of the Clearances. That changed everything. He took a hefty drink from his mug before he continued.

"So you learned." He struggled back to conversation. "Not an easy task. The Gaelic is a difficult language to master."

"I'm probably singing a number of words incorrectly." She shrugged. "But it soothes the child. That's all that matters."

"I noticed very few amiss. Now that mystery is solved, suppose you tell me exactly what it is you're expecting of me beyond fighting for you? Farm hand, millwright...what?"

She took a swallow from the mug, coughed, wet her lips, and continued. "All that and more." She hesitated, then plunged on. "A husband to me." She met his startled stare with unflinching determination.

"Husband?" She couldn't have shocked him more if she'd lashed out and punched him squarely in the jaw.

"It would be a marriage in name only." Her words tumbled out. "You'll continue to have the small room

46

over there." She indicated the curtained cubicle. "I will sleep in the big bedroom beyond the hearth." She motioned to the other, where three-year-old Eppie slept with her Pig. "I'll see that you get a fair share of the profits from the farm and mills...and, of course, your bed and board."

"Why bother with this marriage thing at all?" He paused to take a drink from his mug. Something in his chest had begun to pound. "Why not just ask me to be your hired hand?"

"Because"—she placed her mug on the floor, got to her feet, and walked to the sideboard, where she began rearranging dishes—"the children need a father, and I need a man who will act as my partner against Joseph Carmody. A man with a vested interest not only in our enterprises but also our family. A man who won't run out on us at the first signs of trouble."

"Aha! And you think I might just fill the bill. What if I turn out to be a lazy drunkard, a black bastard who abuses women and children?"

"Hush!" she admonished, glancing upwards toward the children's sleeping quarters, then swinging back to face him before continuing softly, "That does not worry me. James and Geordie are perfectly capable of shanghaiing you onto the next timber drougher that docks in Riverhaven if you prove unsuitable. The captains of such vessels are always looking for broad shoulders and a strong back. They're quite willing to forego questions about how that help is acquired."

"And if I don't agree to this marriage proposal of yours?" He stretched long legs out toward the fire. "Might I still not stay on as a hired hand?"

"No." She stood, back against the sideboard, hands

clutching its edge. "Men who work for pay can be lured away by Joseph Carmody. After seeing you fight today, I don't want you as an enemy." She sucked in a deep breath before continuing. "If you choose to marry me, it need only last until James is old enough to take full ownership of the place. His father's will specifies that is to take place when he turns twenty. Then you may desert us with your share of the profits and go on to seek your fortunes elsewhere. And furthermore…" She paused, staring down at her hands.

"Yes?"

"I will not have it said that I'm living in sin with any man." She looked up at him, and the vehemence in her statement was backed by the intensity of those green eyes. "Above all, I want this family to be respectable, and respected by the community."

"And marrying me will do that?"

"Not entirely, but it will inform people that although I once worked in a tavern, I'm no doxy, that a man must wed me if he wishes to share my hearth and home."

"I see." He paused before continuing, slowly, thoughtfully. "A Highlander also who's suffered the ugliness of the Clearances does no let another Highlander down." He crossed the room in long strides to seize her by the shoulders. "I'm honor bound to stay and do whit I can for you and the bairns."

Chapter Five

"You're a Highlander, as well?" She turned on him, those beautiful green eyes widening. "But up until now you spoke as an Englishman, an aristocratic Englishman."

"Aye, well, there's no need to go tellin' everyone and his dog. I had a spot of trouble back there, and…"

"No need to explain." She drew a deep breath. "Most from the Highlands have at least one black mark after their name for protesting the Clearances. There's a reason the village is called Riverhaven. It shelters a goodly number of your kind. Now…" She returned to the hearth, picked up her mug, drained it, choked slightly, and headed toward the bedroom. "Now, if you'll excuse me, I'm off to my rest. I trust you'll see to the fire before you retire. It promises to be a blustery night. Thank you for agreeing to help us. And"—she paused at the bedroom door and looked back over her shoulder—"I apologize for James's behavior. He's normally a respectful boy. The rudeness from his tongue tonight is not typical."

"He's becoming a man, and we can be strange creatures, behaving out of character, when we feel threatened by another male in our territory." A corner of Harry's mouth quirked. "This is the lad's family, and he won't take easily to anyone he sees as trying to usurp that position."

"I'm glad you understand. Good night and pleasant dreams, Mr. Wallace."

****

After she'd gone to bed with the child, in the room beyond the hearth, he sat savoring another wee dram. God knew he needed it. He'd just been proposed to by the stepmother of seven children with mills, a farm, and an apparently dangerous enemy threatening her and her family. The widow of a fellow Highlander, a woman—together with her children—he was duty bound to help and protect.

In the flickering firelight he walked to the door of her bedroom and peered in through the space she'd left open to allow heat from the hearth to enter. In the wide bed, her shining chestnut hair adorning the pillow, Maggie slept, long eyelashes spread out over creamy cheeks. In her arms she cradled the golden-haired cherub named Eppie. On a rug on the floor beside them, Pig woke, looked up at him with strangely knowing eyes, grunted, then lowered her head and went back to sleep. What was a man to do with such a rare and unexpected family?

He wandered back to the hearth, put a hand on the shelf above it, and stood staring down into the flames. Wind shrieked around the corners and snow buffeted the windows, but inside the log house, protected from the storm, he let a warm, secure feeling settle over him, a warm and secure feeling he hadn't experienced at night since he'd been a lad in his father's croft cottage during a blizzard much like this one. The ambience was seductive but perhaps false. After all, the family had a dangerous enemy.

He banked the fire for the night, then glanced back

toward the bedroom where Maggie slept. Beautiful, unassuming Maggie. What would the future hold for her and the children if he decided not to stay? Shaking his head in confusion, he turned toward the small cubicle she'd assigned him across the kitchen.

Inside, he drew the curtain that served as a door, pulled off his boots, and shucked his shirt and breeches. With a sigh, he fell back into the narrow bed, with its straw tick and feather pillow, and pulled the down-filled quilt of many patches over his body. As he settled beneath it and listened to the wind howling around the eaves, the comfort of the moment once more enveloped him.

It was good to be out of the storm, to be warm, in a dry bed, to know that Scotia was also safe from the elements, watered and well fed, and, like her master, able to rest, without body and muscles tense and ready to jump into action if the need arose. He moved to settle for sleep, making the straw mattress crackle. No feather beds here, but that was just as well. Lady Annabelle Spencer's feather bed had proven to be a trap well laid for him.

And now, in spite of the aura of warmth and peace that surrounded him, he realized he mustn't be seduced by it either. This man, this Joseph Carmody, had designs on this property and wasn't above using any means within his power to get it. The incident that afternoon on the drive from the village had been proof that Maggie Fowler had a dangerous enemy. The question as to whether the entrepreneur had had her husband murdered hung in the air, a black cloud of danger and suspicion. Did he, Harry Wallace, want to once more get involved in a fight? Hadn't he come to this country to get away from trouble?

And yet William Fowler had been a Highlander. Honor bound Harry to help the man's family.

Settling on his back, his fingers laced beneath his head, he experienced the all-too-familiar sickness of loss and regret as his thoughts returned to his life in the Old Country…and Brodie. Nausea roiled in his gut as he remembered his friend, who hadn't been as fortunate as he, who hadn't made it aboard an outbound ship, who'd probably swung at the end of a rope while he, Harry, made good his escape. The best he could hope for was that Brodie's end had been swift. He wouldn't allow himself to think that members of that bloodthirsty pack who'd shot his horse from beneath his friend that night had taken their bayonets to him on the spot.

God help you, my friend. The thought was his last as he drifted off to sleep in a bed that for the first time in over a month was not pitching and rolling.

****

He was awakened to a babble of voices, a stream of sunlight beaming though the window above his bed, and the smell of food preparation. *Good God, what time is it? And what's going on?*

As consciousness brought his memory back, he pulled his lips into a thin line of resolution and heaved himself out of bed. Accustomed to sleeping away most of his days and working at night, he wasn't an early riser. Rubbing his head, he squinted out the window above his bed into the sunshine of a bright spring morning as it glared off the blanket of fresh snow covering buildings and yard. It hurt his eyes, and he grunted.

The memory of Maggie Fowler's proposal and

revelations filtered back into focus, and he sat back down on the edge of the bed, rubbing his temples. Finally he sucked in a deep breath and stood.

Might as well get on with it. I'm honor bound to help...at least for a while.

He pulled on shirt, breeches, and boots. Stepping out into the kitchen, he found a fire crackling on the hearth. The pot bubbling over the flames probably held oatmeal. The children lined the benches at the big, scarred table, tucking into porridge in wooden bowls with wooden spoons.

All except Eppie. She stood behind Maggie, clinging to the woman's skirts with one hand, the thumb of her other stuck in her mouth, Pig by her side.

At his entrance, all talk ceased and seven pairs of eyes focused on him. Maggie Fowler turned from stirring the pot hanging over the fire and smiled. "Good morning, Mr. Wallace."

Her hair brushed and tied back with a bit of frayed ribbon, she was as fresh and lovely as any woman he'd ever met. Marrying her wouldn't be such a hardship. The thought dashed across his mind.

"Good morning, Mrs. Fowler." He turned to the group at the table. "Good morning, children."

Sullen silence greeted his words.

"We'll have no rudeness." Maggie took quick exception to their behavior. She faced them, hands on her hips. "Mr. Wallace is going to help us out. Therefore, we have every reason to treat him with courtesy and respect. Now I'm waiting for a proper response to his greeting."

The room remained quiet except for the ticking of a clock in the corner by the door. Finally, Isabella, the oldest girl, put a hand to her mouth and murmured behind it, "Good morning, Mr. Wallace."

"Good morning—Bella, isn't it?" He cast her what he hoped was one of his most appealing smiles. "You'll have to give me time to get all your names straight."

"Sit here, please, Mr. Wallace." Maggie indicated the place at the head of the table. "I hope you've no objection to oatmeal porridge."

"Look at his clothes!" James's face contorted with anger as Harry moved to accept her invitation. "He doesn't look much ready for a full day's work. I'll wager he knows nothing about running a saw mill or a grist mill, never mind a farm."

"You're right, James." Geordie supported his brother. "He's a dandy. Couldn't fork hay or manure if his life depended on it."

"Now there ye're only partly correct, laddies." Harry deliberately let his Highland accent color his words. "My family were sheep farmers in the Hi'lands, like your guid father, before they were run off by the English. I know how to till the soil and grow nips and tatties. Furthermore, I can spread manure with the best of them. As to the mills, I'd be looking to you and your superior knowledge to assist me in those areas."

The pair continued to glare at him until, finally, expressions sullen, both young men returned to their breakfasts.

Aye, the battle between them and me is just beginning. Well, young laddies, ye're in for a fight.

"Now, Mrs. Fowler," he turned to Maggie. "If there's enough porridge, I'd appreciate a bowl. A Highlander cannot be expected to start a day's work without a belly full."

The meal was a silent affair. Avoiding eye contact with Harry, the children ate with their attention on their food. He didn't interfere.

Give them time…time to get accustomed to this new person in their midst.

He ate the bland porridge and recalled Maggie saying they'd run short of salt, sugar, tea, and the like. Maybe he could do something about it. He'd have to. He couldn't drink any more of that swill made from a spruce tree.

****

"Come along, lads." James stood and went to fetch his jacket where it hung on a peg near the door with an assortment of other outerwear. "Logs to be cut. Bella, you'll have to make do with Lizzie to help you with the barn work. I need Sam in the mill."

"Ye're leavin' a pair o' lassies to do the farm work?" Harry got to his feet and faced the young man.

"They've done it before, and I need the boys in the mill." James turned a defiant face on him. "It's no concern of yours. You're *her* problem." He jerked his thumb in Maggie's direction.

"Now just one minute, laddie." In two long strides Harry was across the room and yanked James upward by both sides of his jacket collar so that the young man stood on the tips of his toes. "You may insult me as you please, but not this guid woman. She's taken on the job of carin' for all of ye when a hundred others wouldn't. Ye'll speak respectfully to her or ye'll be feelin' my fist in your face."

Silence except for the harsh breathing of the two men facing each other engulfed the room. The other occupants stared.

"Mr. Wallace…" Maggie began to protest but let the rest die away.

"All right, all right," James conceded. Harry let him drop back flatfooted onto the floor and stepped off.

"Verrae guid," he nodded, wetting his lips. "Now…" He turned to Maggie, English inflection returning. "If you can find clothes that might fit me and are designed for mill chores, I'll be heading off to work with these fine young lads. And," he continued, "there'll be no need for you to accompany us to the mill today. I believe your sons can turn me into a passable replacement worker."

She hesitated. He winked at her, and she replied with a slight inclination of her head. She understood. He needed time alone with the boys.

"Thank you, Mr. Wallace. There is cleaning and baking to do. I can put hours in the house to good use."

Fifteen minutes later, garbed in William Fowler's woolen pants, shirt, jacket, and work boots that oddly enough fitted him tolerably well, he followed the four younger men down the hill to the mill, plodding through six inches of freshly fallen snow.

****

Maggie watched them go, then heaved a sigh and turned to the sideboard. There was bread to be made, even without salt, and meat to be cooked.

"He's very handsome, isn't he?" Bella came into the house carrying a pail of milk. She placed it on the floor, pulled the kerchief from her golden brown hair, and joined Maggie in watching the men head down over the hill.

"Yes, he is." She smiled down at the girl in the shabby woolen coat and realized she was growing into a pretty young woman. "But that's not the reason I asked him to come and work with us. Is Lizzie still in the barn?"

"Yes, there's a lot to do." Bella sighed and turned to go back to her sister. "I'll start churning as soon as we're finished. We used the last of the butter at breakfast."

"Bella." Struck by the hard work this girl, barely more than a child, had to do, Maggie slipped an arm about her shoulders and stopped her. "I know all this is difficult for you to understand, but I am grateful that you're trying." She looked down into the clear, honest blue eyes gazing up at her and made a decision. "I've asked Mr. Wallace to consider marrying me."

Silence. The old clock ticked. The fire crackled. Finally the girl replied.

"You want to keep him here. You don't want Joseph Carmody to lure him away, maybe even use him to betray us. That's right, isn't it?"

Her insight startled Maggie. And encouraged her.

"You're a clever lady, Isabella Fowler." She held her by the shoulders, at arm's length. "Yes, that's it exactly. He's a strong man, a man who knows how to fight. We need him here, loyal to us now."

"I understand." Her gaze never faltered as she faced her stepmother. "You're pretty. I think he'll stay."

Maggie looked down at this child only just entering her teens but with the serious eyes of a woman, and she saw an ally, the first in the family since William had been killed. She drew the girl into her arms, and Bella embraced her in return.

"Oh, Bella, you don't know what your approval

means to me," she breathed against the child's tangled hair. "The boys don't seem to understand we must form a united front if we're to win this battle against Joseph Carmody."

"But I do." Bella pulled out a bit and looked up into her face. "I'll help you convince the boys that Mr. Wallace must stay, that we need such a man if we're to keep our parents' holdings."

"Wonderful." Maggie smiled down at her, a lump thickening in her throat. "With two strong women in charge, how can we lose?"

"Now I'd best get back to the barn." Bella headed toward the door, then paused and turned back. "Perhaps you might wash your hair and at supper wear the blue dress that belonged to Mama. Gentlemen like ladies to look nice."

"Oh, darlin', I hardly think wearing your mother's clothes would endear me to your brothers." She smiled. "But I will try to do up my hair. And Bella?" She stopped the child as she once more started to leave. "Did your mother talk to you and Lizzie about...boys?" Maggie felt a small blush creeping up her cheeks.

"Not to worry." Bella grinned. "We're farm girls. We know all about where babies come from and such."

"Oh, well, then, good." Maggie felt a wave of relief wash over her.

"But she never got a chance to talk about courting and that kind of thing...like letting boys hold our hands and kiss us."

"Well, then, someday soon we'll talk about just that...you and Lizzie and I, shall we?"

"I'd like that." Bella nodded. "Lizzie and I should know a bit about such things in case we meet someone who is as handsome as Mr. Wallace." Her eyes twinkled mischievously over the last words.

"Go!"

Giggling for the first time since her father's death, Bella danced out of the house.

Maggie let a smile curl the corners of her lips. Harry Wallace's coming was already having good effects. Without it, she and Bella would not have had that woman-to-woman chat just now. And even though she didn't believe in violence, Harry had given James a much needed lesson in respect.

****

At midday the five millers headed up the hill to the house, James with Harry by his side leading the way. It had been a full, hard morning of learning the logging business, but he'd taken to it. He'd experienced a rush as James released the water above the dam to flood over its zenith and turn the giant wheel that powered the equipment. His muscles had willingly helped chain the big logs to be drawn up a ramp into the range of the whirling saw. His vocabulary had been enlarged with terms such as scaling, slabs, deal, and planking. He'd learned some of the logs were missing their outer coat because hunters had taken it for a substance they called tannin that lay between the bark and wood. They used it to tan deer hides and often came in search of it at the camps where the Fowlers were logging.

I could get used to this life…good, honest labor, a stable home, a beautiful woman…

He broke off his thoughts right there. *Remember who you are, Harry lad. Remember who you are.*

The walk from the mill was a silent one. The entire morning had been lacking intercourse except for

James's shouted directions to his brothers and explanations and orders to Harry. The roar of the water and whine of the saws had rendered any unnecessary conversation too much of an effort. But now, unlike the wordless walk to the mill that morning, the lack of conversation felt comfortable, companionable. James and his brothers had seen that he could work, that this man their stepmother had brought home from the docks had physical strength, tenacity, and the desire to learn. Were they on the way to accepting him...at least partially?

He hoped they were. He'd enjoyed the camaraderie of working with these strong, capable young men, none of whom shirked hard labor or made any complaints about it. He'd even liked the smell of saw blades hot from whining their way through logs and the clean forest scent of freshly cut lumber.

The cold east wind sweeping down the stream from the wilderness along its upper reaches washed a shiver over his hot, sweating body as they crossed the bridge and headed up the hill toward the house. A warning not to get too comfortable, at least not just yet?

****

At the house, Maggie had dinner ready. A large roast had spent the morning turning on the spit while a pot of potatoes and carrots hung boiling on the crane. The other children were already at their places around the table by the time Harry and his fellow mill hands had washed up to join them.

"I'm sorry there's no proper tea, Mr. Wallace," Maggie apologized as they sat down. "And the bread is unsalted." She ducked her head and began to cut up meat and vegetables for Eppie, seated once again on her lap. "As I've said, we've run out of a few things."

"And no credit until the logs are sold." James's words smacked of fury as he cut into his meat, and he added, almost under his breath, "Thanks to Carmody, the bastard!"

"James, I told you I'll not have such language in front of the children!" Maggie's green eyes flashed as she glared at her stepson.

"Well, he is," he mumbled as he returned his attention to his plate.

"The food is fine, Mrs. Fowler." Harry cut into his vegetables. "In fact, it couldn't taste better."

"Thank you." Her demeanor softened. "If you hadn't confessed to being a Highlander, I'd swear you were Irish, fresh from kissing the Blarney Stone."

"Did you know legend has it the Blarney Stone is really Scottish in origin?" He glanced around the table. The two oldest girls and Samuel looked up at him.

Interested. Good.

The three older boys continued to focus on their food. "Some people believe the Blarney Stone is half of the original Stone of Scone upon which the first King of Scots sat for his coronation in 847. They say that in 1314 Robert the Bruce presented it to the Irishman Cormac McCarthy as a gift for Irish support in the Battle of Bannockburn, the greatest victory in the Wars of Scottish Independence."

He glanced down the table and saw that Maggie had paused in feeding Eppie and was listening with rapt attention.

"You must pay attention when Mr. Wallace tells us such tales of your parents' homeland," she said. "Your heritage is important."

"How will that help us fight off an Englishman like Joseph Carmody?" James muttered.

"It will inspire pride." Maggie returned to feeding Eppie. "Although I'm not Scottish, your father and mother were, and I plan to raise you in the traditions they represented. We've been fortunate to find a man like Mr. Wallace who can help in achieving that goal. Now to other matters. The privy must be cleaned, and soon."

I'll attest to that fact. With a slight grimace, Harry recalled his visit to the facility earlier that morning.

"It's Samuel's turn." Robert grinned. "I did it last time, and now he's old enough to be working in the mill, he's got to do all the jobs we do."

"Ah, Robert…" The boy's voice reflected his distaste for the chore.

"I'll give you a hand." Harry buttered a slice of bread and looked over at the lad. "I'm a dab hand at cleaning privies."

"I find that hard to believe," James sneered. "Those fancy clothes you were wearing didn't look like privy-cleaning gear."

"No, they're not." He ignored the nastiness in the comment. "But I wasn't born into fine clothes. I had to do my share of unpleasant chores as a lad. Now, Samuel, as soon as we finish our meal, we'll get to it. James, we'll need to borrow the team for an hour or so."

****

"How's that?" Harry stood aside proudly when Maggie came to inspect his and Samuel's work two hours later.

"You moved the entire privy," she exclaimed.

62

"Why…?"

"Easier and less unpleasant to dig a deep hole, have the team drag the building over it, and bury the previous location." He grinned at her amazement. "Now Samuel and I must be getting the team back to the mill before James comes to fetch them. Come along, lad. Our work here is done."

He touched his forelock to Maggie as he led Bonnie and Prince past her.

"You are quite an amazing man, Harry Wallace." Her words following him broadened his grin.

"I'm delighted you think so, Mrs. Fowler, although I hardly see relocating a privy a few yards to the left as an amazing feat."

As man and boy walked off toward the mill, Samuel strode by Harry's side, shoulders back, head held high. Catching a glimpse of him from the tail of his eye, Harry suppressed a grin.

Seems I've made a wee bit of headway with this young lad. Moving that privy will be well worth the effort if I have.

****

"Oh, ye'll take the high road,
And I'll take the low road,
And I'll be in Scotland afore ye…
For me and my true love will never meet again
On the bonny, bonny banks of Loch Lomund."

Maggie entered the barn in the twilight that evening and stopped at the sound of a male voice, coming from Scotia's stall, singing the sad words in a fine tenor. *Harry?*

As he continued to sing, she moved to lean on the boards of the mare's stall to listen.

When he saw her, he paused and rested his forearms on the animal's back to look over at her.

"Sorry about that, mistress. Ye must excuse my caterwauling." It was a warm evening, and he'd removed his shirt to work. As he moved around the horse, she saw for the first time the broad muscular chest and the long scar running down his right side.

"Ah." He followed her gaze and rubbed a hand slowly up and down the mark. "An old wound. Nothing to concern yourself about."

"A battle scar?"

"Aye."

He returned to brushing Scotia.

"You have a fine voice, but that is a very sad song. You sang it almost as if…"

"Almost as if?" He moved to the mare's neck, brushing with long, gentle strokes.

"Almost as if you were telling the story of a personal experience."

"Perhaps I was. But not to concern yourself about. Dusted and done."

He continued with the grooming.

"Harry, were you a soldier? Is that how you got that wound? Did you leave a sweetheart behind in Scotland? Did…"

"Lassie, lassie." He ducked under the mare's head and came to face her squarely. "I'm willing to help you and your family. If that includes doing battle with that bastard Michael Kelly and his boss Joseph Carmody, I'm right ready to do that, as well. But I will not answer a passel of questions about my past. You must either take me at face value or send me on my way."

She looked at the strong-bodied, handsome man in

front of her, then up into those wonderful blue eyes, and melted. She didn't care if he'd been a soldier or a highwayman, or if he'd left a lover behind in Scotland. She only knew she wanted Harry Wallace, or whatever his name was, with her and her family for as long as she could hold him.

****

The next morning when Harry and the boys were working at the mill, he caught movement to his right and glanced outside to see Maggie waving to him and the boys. Dinnertime. They'd been so engrossed in their work they'd lost track of time. Harry grinned and raised a hand to tell her he got the message, then yelled to the boys, "Food."

After they'd paused the operation and joined her in the sawdust of the mill yard, Harry's acute hearing caught a sound. He froze to a halt.

"Horses." He looked toward the top of the hill opposite the house.

Over a half dozen riders appeared on the rise. Their leader, a well-dressed man on a big grey horse, held up a hand to halt the group. Like a band of warriors surveying the scene of a proposed battle, they loomed over the valley.

"Joe Carmody." James's words hissed like released steam.

"Let me handle this." Harry stepped to the forefront.

At a sign from their leader, the riders advanced down the hill, walking their horses, spreading out to form a semicircle about the six in the mill yard. Harry saw pistols stuck in several belts, while the one riding nearest Carmody, a man he recognized as Michael

Kelly, carried a musket across the front of his saddle. Trepidations he couldn't afford to entertain welled into his mind.

Sweet Jesus, why today of all days did Maggie have to come down to the mill? He and the boys could face this group in a fight, but he couldn't allow her to be injured. The children needed her.

"Good morning, Mrs. Fowler." Joseph Carmody rode close in front of her and halted his restless, pawing stallion. Harry admired the way she didn't back away from the dancing hooves, even as his heart hammered an angry tattoo at the man's audacity.

He took a moment to peruse the newcomer and take his measure. Joseph Carmody was a man well into his fifties, with thick but neatly trimmed grey sidewhiskers jutting out from beneath his hat. His clothes had the fine cut of a gentleman's. He'd probably once been a formidable specimen, tall and well muscled, but middle age and soft living had left him stout and double chinned. Nevertheless, he exuded the air of one in absolute command, a leader not to be denied or disputed.

"Do I have the pleasure of addressing Mr. Joseph Carmody, magistrate of this fine county?" Forcing an affable grin across his face, Harry stepped between Maggie and the stallion. He caught the animal by its bridle with his left hand and held his right up to the animal's rider. "Harry Wallace, at your service, sir. However, your horse is far too close to my betrothed."

"Your betrothed?" Michael Kelly sneered. "Maggie? Bloody hell, man, she's been a widow barely more than a month. And a tavern wench before that. You must have a taste for whores."

Chapter Six

In a split second Michael Kelly was wrenched from his horse, the musket flying from his hands, and sent sprawling into the sawdust of the mill yard by a fist to his jaw.

"You will apologize to Mrs. Fowler." Harry reached down to jerk the man half upright by the front of his shirt and loomed over him, even though he was aware the other riders, aside from Joseph Carmody, had surrounded him and, seen in his peripheral vision, a couple had drawn their pistols.

"Apologize? Like hell!" Kelly tried to lunge upward, but Harry's foot sent him sprawling again.

"Come, come, now, Michael." Joe Carmody urged his horse forward to part the two men. "We came here to negotiate, not fight." As Kelly staggered to his feet, nursing his jaw and fumbling to retrieve his musket, the entrepreneur turned to Harry. "A pleasure to meet you, Mr. Wallace." He extended his right hand.

Harry hesitated, then brushed sawdust from his own and accepted the offer.

Start out with honey, and save the vinegar for when it's needed. And not expected.

"Mrs. Fowler." Joseph Carmody turned his attention to Maggie. "My shopkeeper, Angus Harper, tells me you've been having difficult economic times of late." His smile was placatingly sly. "Consequently I've come to make you a generous offer. I'll pay you a fair price for your mills—I'm prepared to allow you to keep your farm. I realize you need a place to raise the children. I'll even go so far as to give your older boys work in the mills. As for your eldest girls, my house can always use another servant or two. That will leave you with only one to provide for."

"My children should work for you?" Maggie stepped forward, white-knuckled hands clutching the sides of her shabby woolen dress. "I'd as soon sell them into slavery! Get off my land, Joseph Carmody!"

"Ah, well." The big man turned his horse back toward the trail leading to the village. "No one can say I didn't try to negotiate this matter peacefully and equitably. Come along, men. Michael, brush the sawdust from your pants and mount up. A pleasure to make your acquaintance, Mr. Wallace." He touched his hat brim in Harry's direction.

"Mr. Carmody." Harry made the gesture of touching his forelock.

"You and me are not finished." Kelly paused in mounting his horse to glare at Harry. "Not by a long shot."

"I never thought we were." Harry's words were even as he let a sarcastic, challenging leer cross his face.

"Aww!" Kelly yanked his mount's head around and followed the others up the hill.

As the riders disappeared over the crest of the hill, Harry turned to look at Maggie and the boys. Their expressions bore the results of the tension the last few minutes had produced.

"Go along, boys." He slapped an arm around the

shoulders of Robert, who was standing closest to him. "Dinner is spoiling."

"You were great, Mr. Wallace." Robert said, his expression bright with admiration. "We're not going to let that miserable old bastard take away our home, are we?"

"No, we're not, but mind your language in front of your mother."

"Yes, sir."

"Now go along with your brothers. I've something to say to her."

"Yes, sir."

"Oh, and, lads…" Harry put a hand on the bridge's weatherbeaten railing. "This bit here needs mending. It's near rotted clear through."

"We'll get to it when we get to it," James paused only long enough to mutter before the four boys headed up the hill. Pausing in the bridge's centre, Harry took Maggie's arm.

"A wee word, if you please, Mrs. Fowler."

"Of course. And thank you," she said, her voice soft. "You certainly gave Joseph Carmody something to ponder. But…betrothed? A fancy description for a woman who was bold enough to propose to you."

"Then it's time I put things right." He dropped on one knee in front of her, in the valley that was to be their home, between pond, mill, stream, farm, and forest. "Maggie Fowler, will you do me the honor of becoming my wife?"

Her expression enigmatic, she paused, looking down at him, green eyes widening.

Is she going to change her mind and say she's not about to wed a lout who fights like a street brawler?

"Yes, Mr. Wallace. Yes, I'll marry you." A smile brightened her features. A warmth started in his chest.

"Harry. Call me Harry. What's your christened name? No one was ever baptized Maggie."

"Margaret."

"Verrae well, Margaret." He stood and gathered her into his arms. She looked up at him, green eyes wide and apprehensive. Slowly, carefully, he lowered his head to put his mouth over hers. She didn't try to pull away but met his kiss unflinchingly, although with an utter innocence that startled him.

Good God, has the woman never been kissed by a man?

Perhaps not, but she was letting him know she was ready to learn. He carefully let his tongue probe between her lips, and she admitted him. He felt a slight tremor run through her body—not, he guessed, of fear but of excitement, anticipation. As her response relaxed and welcomed him, his body reacted in tune.

Pull away, man, pull away while you still can. Give her time. Don't spoil what might be.

He ended the kiss and looked down at her with a slight grin. "Enough for now, lassie. Dinner's spoiling."

"Yes." She met his gaze with sparkling eyes. "Yes, it is."

His arm about her shoulders, they headed up the hill together. The boys had already vanished into the house.

At the door, she paused as he reached to open it for her.

"Mr. Wallace…Harry, you're sure about this?" As she looked up at him he saw trepidations mirrored on her face. "Seven children, and our troubles with Joseph

70

Carmody, and…"

"Yes, I am sure. Verrae sure." He brushed a kiss against her temple. "Now let us get to that food. Your husband-to-be has a ragin' appetite."

"Of course." She slanted him a smile that set his innards stirring before she went inside.

The innocent lass has no idea that kiss has left this Highlander hungering for more than food.

He brushed sawdust from his shirt and poured fresh water into the basin on the table by the door to wash up.

Chapter Seven

What had she done? After the men had returned to their afternoon's work at the mill, Lizzie and Bella had gone upstairs to tidy the bedrooms, and Eppie was down for her nap, Maggie sank into the rocker in front of the fire and wet her lips. She'd accepted the proposal of a man she barely knew, a man whose bearing and fine clothes branded him as a London dandy even though he now wore the rough outfits of her former husband and frequently lapsed into a Highland brogue. A man of the world at best, a rogue, perhaps even a highwayman at worst.

And that kiss! Never had she experienced anything like it. True, it was her first real kiss from a man, but it had sent a vast array of sensations she'd never imagined coursing through her body. In those moments he'd made her feel beautiful and desirable and a woman to the core.

Being kissed by a man had never been something she'd wished to occur. She'd been grabbed by enough drunken louts who'd tried to force their mouths over hers, when she worked in the tavern, to make the act repugnant at best.

Those disgusting encounters had been nothing like what she'd experienced in the arms of this stranger, this man she'd propositioned right off a ship the minute it touched land. Just thinking about it now as she sat in the rocker by the fire made her want to hug herself in the erotic joyfulness of it.

With an effort, she forced herself out of her titillating thoughts. *Wake up and face reality, Maggie Fowler. Harry Wallace is a man who's probably learned the art of seduction from any number of worldly ladies. Don't fall under his spell.* She drew a deep breath and sat up straight. *I mustn't let anything like that happen again. It could lead to God knows what, and I've already promised the man he would be free to leave once James is of age.*

The thought of where it could lead nevertheless intrigued her. Thoughts of more kisses, of arousing caresses that could lead them into that bed where Eppie now napped, of Harry's making love to her... experienced, knowledgeable Harry, who no doubt knew any number of ways to pleasure a woman. The possibility that he'd been an outlaw and had probably bedded more than his fair share of ladies should have driven from her mind any idea of taking him as a lover and a true husband, but still...

She remembered when she'd found him singing that heart-wrenching song in the barn as he groomed his mare. Stripped to the waist, he'd presented a wonderful spectacle of what a man should be...even with that long, mysterious scar running up his side. Her breath had caught in her throat. Handsome of face and magnificent of body, Harry Wallace could make most any woman's heart flutter, she'd decided.

So far he'd appeared to be a decent man, a man who worked hard and kept a respectful distance...until that marriage proposal and that unforgettable kiss. Yet her instincts told her he would continue to respect her wishes, that if she repulsed any future advances, he'd accept her decision.

With a sigh, she brought her daydreams to an end. *Yes, I will marry you, Harry Wallace. After that, we'll just have to wait and see which way the wind blows us.*

She got up from her chair and tiptoed into the bedroom where Eppie slept to peruse herself in the crazed old mirror above the chest of drawers. Her face, darkened by outdoor work, was hardly that of a refined lady, while her hair, caught hastily back into an untidy queue at the back of her head, needed washing and brushing. And her hands… Chapped and reddened, they were not the hands a man would seek to hold, definitely not what he would want to kiss. She turned sideways and glanced over her shoulder at her image.

I'm not ugly of face, and my figure is decent…no fat or falling. Perhaps if I did something with my hair and put a bit of ribbon under the bosom of my other dress, I might look a bit more attractive.

A second thought struck her, and she let her shoulders sag. *What difference does it make? Once again, I'm marrying for convenience, for the children. I'm not like a regular bride…and I never will be. I'm a worker, a mother, and that's all.*

She squared her shoulders as she looked down at the little girl sleeping in the bed.

Stop feeling sorry for yourself, Maggie Fowler. How can you feel anything but blessed when such an angel has been given into your care?

****

"Margaret, are you ready?" Harry came into the house, freshly washed and wearing a well-cut black coat, snow-white shirt, tan breeches, and gleaming knee-high boots, a bouquet of small, pinkish white flowers in his hand. He'd eschewed the idea of a cravat, deciding it wouldn't do to look too formal or fine, given what he guessed would be Maggie's limited means to dress up for her wedding.

"Hush!" Bella put a finger to her lips. "She's only just gotten Eppie down for her nap."

"Oh, aye." He lowered his voice and put a finger to his own lips. "Is your mother about?"

"I'm ready."

He turned to see her standing near the top of the stairs, and his breath caught in his throat. *What has the lass done to herself? Shining curls piled on her head, with apple blossoms intertwined, dress cinched in under her bosom with a bit of emerald ribbon… Good God, she's the loveliest creature I've ever seen.*

"You're staring, Mr. Wallace." She proceeded down the stairs to pause at the bottom to smile at him. "Did you not think me capable of tidying up for my wedding?"

"No, of course not. That is…" Bella and Lizzie giggled at his stumbling words as he crossed the room to take her hand. Turning it palm up, he pressed its centre to his lips and was gratified when he heard a quick, soft intake of breath escape her lips.

Ah, Harry, boy, you still have a bit of charm left.

"These are for you." He straightened and held out the flowers. "The leaves are a bit brown spotted, but they are the best I could find for the occasion. Their scent is intoxicating."

"Mayflowers." Bella and Lizzie came forward to inspect the bouquet. "They must be the very first of the season."

"Thank you, Harry." Her smile dazzled him, made him acutely aware of even white teeth and soft pink lips. *Sweet Jesus, man, keep a cool head. You're marrying in name only. Keep that in mind.*

"Come along." He offered his arm. "Bonnie and Prince are waiting."

"Take good care of Eppie," Maggie called softly back over her shoulder as he urged her out the door. "If she wakes before I return, tell her I'll be home soon…maybe that I've only gone to the mill."

"Don't worry. You mustn't feel you have to rush," Bella replied, and both girls giggled.

Do these lassies know what the physical side of marriage entails? Are they thinking Margaret and I might…? Bloody hell, don't let them make me blush.

His hand beneath her elbow, he guided her out to the wagon. A strong May sun had melted the snow and was beginning to dry up the puddles left behind. All in all, Harry decided, it was a glorious spring day. A perfect day for a wedding.

"Should you be needing a shawl?" he asked as they crossed the yard.

"Harry, this dress is made of wool and has long sleeves, and it's a beautiful day. No, thank you, I won't be needing a shawl."

Beside the wagon she paused and smiled up at him. His body stirred in a way it had no right to. Stifling physical urges, he put his hands around her slim waist, hoisted her onto the seat, then vaulted up beside her. He clucked to the team and they started off at their usual shambling trot.

He couldn't resist the urge to glance sideways at her from time to time. Buggar all, she was beautiful, chestnut curls framing a heart-shaped face with long-lashed, emerald eyes and soft pink cheeks. And her figure. His next look slid lower to the profile of her breasts prominently displayed by the ribbon holding her dress in beneath them. Forcing himself to divert his attention back to the road ahead, he clucked the lagging team into a more energetic trot.

For a time they drove in silence. Finally she spoke.

"It's a perfect day for a wedding, is it not, Mr. Wallace?"

He glanced over at her and caught the teasing smile she slanted over at him. Beautiful, yes. There was no denying Margaret Fowler-soon-to-be-Wallace was beautiful, but more than that she had courage and spirit—and the desire to be as bride-like as her limited means would allow.

A sudden desire to see her arrayed in fine clothing, to be able to allow her the leisure to see to her hair and other feminine trappings, engulfed him. He shook the reins over the team's backs in an effort to belay such meanderings. When her stepson came of age, he'd be leaving. This wasn't the time to be letting his imagination run amuck.

"Harry, you can change your mind." She startled him with the remark a few yards farther down the road. "I'll understand."

"Whit?" He halted the team to stare over at her. "Are ye daft, lassie? I never dither. Once I've set my mind to something, I do it. Is it perhaps you that's looking to renege?"

"Definitely not." She lowered her gaze to the bouquet in her hands. "It's just that this will be a legally binding union, and if you ever want to marry again, there will be all manner of proceedings to go through to free yourself, I would think."

"Aye, well, I'm not the kind of man to go marryin' helter skelter, so we'll not worry about a second marriage until we get this one under our belts." He clucked to the team, but as the wagon jolted forward an explosion erupted from the trees beside the road.

"Bloody hell!" Searing pain erupted in his left shoulder. "Get on, there! Bonnie, Prince, move!" He flapped the reins, but the team, terrified by the noise, were already off at full gallop. Maggie lurched against him, and he was glad. She hadn't been thrown. But, sweet Jesus, his arm hurt.

Her hands grabbed the reins, yanking them from his grip. Freed from driving, he clasped his right hand over the wound.

"Whoa, whoa!" she yelled once they were a good quarter mile away from the site of the incident. "Bonnie, easy girl. Good boy, Prince." Gradually they came to a trot, tossing their heads, sweat darkening their coats.

"Whoa, whoa," she repeated, this time her words, soft and soothing. Shortly they shambled to a full stop.

"Harry!" She wound the reins around the whipstand and swung to him. "How bad is it?"

"A scratch, nothing more." He clutched the wound and tried to keep from grimacing. It smarted.

"Let me see." She reached to remove his coat. He helped, shrugging out of it as best he could. "Now your shirt." Her words were calm and controlled, but he felt a tremor in her hands as she began to unbutton it.

"I chust need a bit of cloth to bind it up," he bared his teeth as she eased the garment from his shoulders.

78

"Can't appear at our wedding a bloody mess."

"It doesn't look all that bad." She wet her lips. "But it needs cleaning and bandaging." She swung down from the wagon and held up her hands. "Let me help you down. There's a spring a few yards into the trees over there. I'll wash the wound and wrap it up."

"I'm not a damned invalid." He ignored her offer and, naked to the waist, lowered himself to the ground. The impact brought a grunt of pain he didn't manage to suppress. She shot him an annoyed look. *Foolish, proud man,* he guessed were her thoughts as she gathered up his shirt and coat.

"Come along." With the clothing over her arm, she started into the bush. "It's not far."

He followed her, annoyed to catch himself stumbling a couple of times. *Cursed weakling. I must be getting old. I've had a lot worse than this scratch and not turned into a staggering idiot.*

"Here." She indicated the spot where clear water bubbled out of the bank. "Clean yourself, and I'll see what I can do with these." She held up his shirt and coat. "There's another spring over there. I'll give them a wash."

She strode off into the bushes. *Annoyed by my refusing her assistance back at the wagon. Ah, well, she'll get over it.*

The shock of frigid water on his skin made him flinch, but he washed the wound until it was clean and its cold temperature had stanched most of the bleeding. He was splashing more water over it when he heard a slight movement and looked up to see her beside him, his damp shirt and coat over her arm, a white garment he recognized for what it was dangling from her hand.

She dropped his clothing, knelt beside him, and began to wrap the other item around the ragged tear.

"Sweet Jesus, woman, you can't go using your pantalets as a bandage!"

"What would you suggest I use?" She continued her task of dressing the wound. "I don't imagine you'll be stripping off your undertrousers, not here in the woods, not before we're properly married."

He caught the twinkle in her eyes at the last statement. Slowly a grin curled his lips. *This is one brave lass, joking after what we've just been though.*

"I never should have told that bastard Joseph Carmody we were getting married," he muttered. "I all but invited this."

"You didn't realize how vicious he could be." She scrambled to her feet. "Now, Mr. Wallace, if you're feeling up to it, we'd best get on our way to visit the vicar." She scooped up his clothing and held the two items up for his inspection. "I've managed to wash away most of the blood. You can barely see it on the dark cloth of your coat. If you put it over the shirt, all that anyone will see is an ugly tear on the sleeve." She held down a hand to help him to his feet.

He looked up at her, taking in her previously carefully arranged hair. The wild ride had loosened many of its pins. Errant curls straggled about her face and down her back. Most of the apple blossoms had been blown away. He thought she'd never looked more beautiful. This time he accepted her offer, then followed her back to the wagon.

Bloody hell, the woman very nearly lost another man…this time even before he managed to marry her.

Chapter Eight

"So this is where your minister lives." Harry looked at the small, neat house beside the equally small church on a little island in a river a few miles from their farm. Accessible only by a short bridge, it appeared a place of peace and serenity. He breathed deeply, hoping some of its atmosphere would envelope him after what had just happened.

He'd again donned his shirt and coat, from which Maggie had managed to scrub most of the blood. Now only the dampness of the fabric and the tear in the left arm remained as outward evidence of the attack.

"A right bonny place." He turned back to her and held up his right hand to help her from the wagon.

I wonder what the guid reverend will think if he discovers the groom-to-be has his wife-to-be's pantalets wrapped around a fresh bullet wound.

"It is that." She'd paused to bend and pick up the mayflowers that had scattered about her feet when the attack occurred. Some were broken from their stems, others trampled in the couple's efforts to control the terrified team. When she looked up, he was startled to see tears in her eyes.

"Margaret, whit…?"

"Those bastards. They ruined my flowers and…" She put a hand to her curls. "And all the work the girls did arranging my hair—ruined! I swear I'd kill Joseph

Carmody if I could get my hands on him at this moment."

"Such language for a bride." He battled to make light of the situation before it moved him too deeply. "I know where there are more of those flowers. And"—he assisted her to the ground—"I'm a dab hand at putting ladies' coiffures back in place. Here, hold a moment."

He suppressed a grunt as he raised the hand of his injured arm to aid his right in using the remaining pins to refasten her hair.

"There." He stood back. "Almost as good as new, except for a few missing apple blossoms."

"I'll not go asking where you gained such skill, Mr. Wallace." Touching her restored hairdo, she slanted him a sly smile that banished the tears. "It is our wedding day, and we mustn't quarrel about what is past."

"Aye." He hesitated, then made a decision. "Margaret, there's something I must tell you before you decide to continue further today. You already know my family and I were victims of the Highland Clearances. In fact, I'm the only one who survived. My father, mother, and sister all died as a result. I could do no less than avenge their deaths by becoming a rebel for Scottish rights."

"Harry, I'm so sorry." She put a hand on his arm. "I would have expected you to do no less." She didn't flinch at his admission. "Although I'm English, I'm poor English. I know what oppression and injustice look like."

"There's more." He sucked in a deep breath and fastened his gaze on her face. "I became a highwayman. I robbed the wealthy English and used my takings to further the Scottish cause. I was forced to flee to this country after very nearly being snared in a cleverly constructed plot."

"But no one here knows of your past…except now myself?" She didn't blink.

The woman has more tenacity than I've ever seen in any female…except perhaps Iona…and Annie.

"No one that I'm aware of."

"Then it will be all right." She squared her shoulders and met his look straight on. "You'll appear as respectable as the next immigrant. That is, unless you take up your former career, in which case I'll be forced to have James and his brothers truss you up and throw you aboard the next outward-bound ship. Now let's get on with it."

"Verrae well." She started to move away, but he put a hand on her shoulder. "This will be a marriage in name only, for as long as either or both of us choose to keep it that way, as we agreed. Tonight I'll sleep in my small cell, and you'll sleep in the master bedroom with Eppie and Pig. I'll not trouble you. Trust me. And as for this"—he indicated his wounded arm—"the less said the better…at least until we discover if this new vicar is a comrade of Joseph Carmody."

She looked up at him, green eyes evaluating him as completely as if he'd been any commodity she was considering acquiring. "Agreed," she replied finally. "It's just that…"

"Just that what?"

"This is the second time I've been married this spring, and the other one ended…" She turned her gaze to the ground. "William was a good man. I feel I'm failing to do his memory justice by not donning widow's weeds and mourning him properly."

"Margaret, this is a tough, wild country. To hesitate can mean disaster. You've got seven children and a nasty enemy. You're doing what must be done."

"And we have a new minister." She squared her shoulders and headed toward the manse. "I've not met him, but perhaps he'll be less judgmental than the last old blighter, who strongly suggested William reconsider marrying me."

Suppressing a grin at her description of the previous clergyman, Harry followed her.

"Good morning." The man who answered her knock on the door was a big man, tall and broad-shouldered, with a tangle of fiery red curls. The welcoming smile on his wide, good-natured countenance froze as he stared at the pair. Harry's breath clumped in his throat.

God, it can't be. But it is…

Chapter Nine

Shock rendered him speechless, and for a few seconds the minister appeared to suffer the same fate. Then the clergyman recovered himself.

"Well, well, do come in." He stepped aside to let them enter and held out his hand. "Edward Morgan, minister of this parish, at your service, Mr...?"

"Wallace. Harry Wallace." Staring and astounded, Harry managed to accept the clergyman's greeting and followed Maggie inside. "And...and this is my intended, Margaret Fowler."

Good God, I'm stuttering. But this man, this minister...

"Your intended?" Harry caught amusement in Edward Morgan's voice. The minister apparently was better at recovering from surprise than he was. "Well, well."

"Yes, my intended." Harry cleared his throat and squared his shoulders. "We've come to be married."

"Indeed? Well, then come in, come in. My wife's in the parlor, just through there. Go along and introduce yourself." The minister indicated the direction to Maggie. "She'll be delighted to have company. I'll have a word with your future husband, and then we'll join you."

Maggie preceded the men down the narrow hall, but the clergyman caught Harry by his wounded arm as he started to pass him, causing a flinch. "Sweet Jesus, Hamish, is it really you?" he hissed.

"Harry Wallace, if you please, Reverend…is that how I'm to address you?" Harry faced his companion's astonishment with a sly grin.

"Mr. Morgan…Edward Morgan."

"Ah, a fine English name for a man of the cloth." Humor tugged at Harry's innards as he began to get the wind back into his sails, and a gush of pleasure suffused him.

Damn, but it was good to see Lachlan again, whatever he was calling himself.

"Yes, a man of the cloth, to be sure." Edward Morgan grinned. Seeing that Maggie had vanished into the parlor, he grabbed Harry into an embrace that crushed him and made him grimace as pain glanced up his left arm. "God in heaven, Hamish, but it's guid to see you!" he muttered into his ear.

"Aye, and you as well, but this isn't the time or place to be discussing such matters." He spoke in equally muted tones and winked at the minister as they stepped back from each other. "The ladies will wonder what is detaining us. And I'm Harry Wallace, please remember. My wife-to-be knows me only as such."

"Ham…Harry, do you think that's wise? To begin a marriage without telling the woman the truth?"

"It is to be a marriage in name only. The lady wants our arrangement to appear respectable to the community, but it will not be consummated."

"Ah." Lachlan stood back and looked Harry squarely in the face. "And do you think you'll be able to live up to such an arrangement, my fine laddie? She is a pretty little thing."

"If that is what Margaret wants, so shall it be. Now let's get on with it. The ladies will become suspicious of what is keeping us."

"Oh, aye. We'll find another opportunity to talk and better explain our circumstances. You seem to have torn the arm of your coat." The clergyman looked down at Harry's ragged sleeve. "If past experience has made me wise, I'd say there's a bit of a bloodstain about it. Do you care to tell me about it?"

"Quite a story. I'll explain after we've met with the ladies."

The man who'd identified himself as Edward Morgan nodded and led the way down the hall to a closed door, which he pushed open.

"You're in for another surprise, laddie." He grinned over at Harry.

In the small, neat room a beautiful woman with hair dark as a raven's wing looked up from the baby she held in her arms. Eyes as blue as a summer's sky widened and her lips parted as she saw Harry.

Sweet Jesus, it can't be. But it is... He stifled the impulse to draw her to her feet, to take her into his arms, to tell her how very, very glad he was to see her again...her and her husband.

"Mrs. Morgan, I'd like you to meet Harry Wallace. This is my wife Mary." Before anyone else had an opportunity to speak, Edward Morgan stepped to his wife's side to make the introduction. "And I believe you've already met Margaret Fowler, his intended."

"Yes, indeed, Mrs. Fowler has informed me she's here to be married." Mary Morgan looked up at Harry, and a smile that held more than a hint of humor crossed her face. "Verrae guid, Mr. Morgan, verrae guid."

"You're Highland, Mrs. Morgan?" Harry was enjoying the interplay. "Your words suggest no less."

"Aye, that I am. I came south to the north of England to visit a relative and met this man who was to be my husband. And married the enemy." Her blue eyes sparkled as she smiled up at him.

"A fine, romantic tale," Harry said. "But now to the business for which we came. We've children waiting at home."

"Children?" Mary Morgan's expression mirrored her surprise.

"Yes, seven, to be exact. Margaret was married to William Fowler, a widower, who died and left her with a hearty group of stepchildren."

"Ah, yes, I've heard about your tragic loss." Edward Morgan's forehead furrowed. "Your husband was buried just before I arrived at St. Stephen's. I'm so very sorry."

"That's why I hope you'll understand what we're about to ask of you. William's children need a father, and I need a partner in the several enterprises in which my late husband was involved. Therefore..." She paused and looked up at Harry.

"Therefore"—he took up the request as she faltered—"we want to be married today."

"Mrs. Fowler, are you quite sure?" The minister cast a penetrating gaze on Maggie. "You've been widowed but a short time. How long have you known your...intended?"

"Long enough to know he's a good man, a man who will stand by my children and me." The words came out in a gush.

"And you, Mr. Wallace. Are you quite sure you

want to take this step? It's a most serious one, I assure you."

"I do, Minister. Now if you'll chust be gettin' on with it. We don't want to leave the bairns alone any longer than necessary." In his desire to hasten the proceedings, Harry lapsed into his Highland accent.

"You're understanding this will be 'til death do you part?"

"Oh, aye." Harry cast Edward Morgan a sly wink behind Maggie's back. "What with ye bein' a man of the cloth and all."

"Mrs. Fowler, your bouquet is lovely." Mary Morgan laid the baby in its basket and came to smile at Maggie. "Flowers in this country at this time of year are rare."

"Yes." Maggie cast a smile up at her husband-to-be with an excellent imitation of a besotted bride, Harry thought. "Mr. Wallace is most romantic."

"Aye, well, it's grand to meet a man who knows what ladies desire." Edward Morgan stopped speaking abruptly and stared at Harry's arm. "Mr. Wallace, it appears you're bleeding from that rent in your coat. You've injured yourself. Ladies, if you'll excuse us, I'll take Mr. Wallace into the kitchen and tend to his wound before he says his vows."

****

"Well, well, Lachlan." Harry grinned at the minister the moment the kitchen's plank door closed behind them. "The last people I expected to see were you and Iona...or should I say Mr. and Mrs. Edward Morgan."

"And why might that be, Hamish?" The clergyman poured water into a basin. "We always talked of coming to this place, with its inviting name of Riverhaven, if we had to flee our enemies in the Highlands."

"I didn't know you and Iona had fled." He gritted his teeth as the other man eased the coat from his arm. "We got so widely separated after that last raid I had no idea where you had gone."

"That's true. We were lucky to escape with our lives. Highland rebels are being hunted down like vermin." He removed Harry's shirt and unwound the bandage beneath. "Good God, Hamish! Are these your intended's pantalets?"

"Aye, well, we were a mite short on cloth to bind it up." He refused to watch as Edward carefully placed the garment on a chair.

"Buggar all, Hamish." Edward Morgan burst out laughing. "You never cease to astonish me. Coming to get married with what I fancy is a bullet graze on your arm, bound up in a lady's undergarment."

"It's no laughing matter, Lachlan Cameron. Margaret has a vicious enemy in the person of one Joseph Carmody. Are you acquainted with the man?"

"Aye. The big toad in the puddle around here. Owns most of the valley and apparently won't be content until he owns it all. After your Margaret's holdings, is he, the greedy bastard?"

"I'd be mindin' my language if I were you, Mr. Morgan, if it's a man of the cloth you're professin' ta be."

"You're right, but hear me out, laddie. If you're about to involve yourself in this woman's troubles, don't let your guard down for a single moment. This Joe Carmody and his bunch can be a ruthless lot, not above harming women and children to get their way."

"Do you think I don't know about the man and his greed? I'm no fool."

"Ah, Hamish, don't go getting your tail in a knot. This moment brings back memories of our devil-may-care days in the Highlands. Memories of riding like the wind with a troop of redcoats far behind us, laughing at their bumbling efforts to stop us. And you aping that posh aristocratic accent that made the English think you were one of them when needs be. Ah, what days, eh, Hamish, lad? You and me and Iona and Brodie. Tell me, where is Brodie? I'm assuming he escaped with you." He dipped a cloth into the basin, twisted the excess of water from it, and began to wash Harry's wound.

"Brodie is dead." The words came out sudden and stark before he could stop them. He'd needed to tell someone, to share the pain, and now he could. Edward Morgan's fingers froze in cleansing his injury and clamped onto his shoulder with painful force.

"Sweet Jesus! Brodie...dead. I thought...I thought..."

"That he was, for all his wild and crazy ways, invincible. I know."

"How? Shot?"

"Captured, possibly hanged, hopefully not cut to pieces by bayonets."

"Dear God!" The clergyman's ruddy complexion paled, and he stood rigid until he glanced down and saw blood trickling from Harry's wound. Moving like a man in a trance, he went to a drawer, opened it, and pulled out a length of linen. "Dear God!" he muttered again as he made a bandage of it around the other man's arm.

"I heard Fox scream, and when I managed to

glance back, I saw that big red stallion falling, shot. I knew Brodie was done for. There could be no going back, not against an entire regiment. They got our friend and if I know anything about those redcoated bastards, they probably hanged him on the spot…if the fall didn't break his neck."

"I cannae believe it." The minister knotted the bandage so tightly Harry flinched again. "Brodie. He'd suffered so much already. Iona will be devastated. Harry…" He touched his friend's bare shoulder. "Allow me to tell her after your wedding, tonight when we're alone and I can soften the blow with a wee dram."

"Of course."

"Now." Edward Morgan stepped away from Harry and rubbed his hands together. "We must return to the ladies…and get you married, Mr. Harry Wallace."

****

As they boarded their wagon, newly wedded, and headed back to the farm, she voiced the thought he'd suspected might be occupying her mind.

"You and the Morgans seemed surprised to meet," she said. "Almost as if you'd known each other before today."

"You have an active imagination, Mrs. Wallace." He used her new name for the first time and was startled at the sensations it caused, none of which he could define or comprehend. It set his innards rolling and his heart thumping irregularly. "Right now we have more immediate concerns. We have to settle into married life with as little upset to the children as possible. The younger ones won't question our not sharing a bed, but the boys…"

"Were made accustomed to that situation during

my brief marriage to their father." She wet her lips and looked off into the trees lining the road. "William was a gentleman. We barely knew each other when we married. He…was allowing me time to become accustomed to the situation. I slept in the room you now occupy, he in the bed in the other room, with Eppie on the trundle mattress and Pig on the floor beside her."

"You mean your marriage was never consummated?" He halted the team abruptly to look over at her.

"No." The word came out barely above a whisper.

"Well…well." He sucked in a deep breath and flapped the reins to re-start the team.

"I'm not averse to sharing a bed with my husband." She stared down at her hands clutched in her lap. "But it must be a husband…" Her words trailed off in confusion.

"A husband you know and love and trust." He clucked to the team and flapped the reins again, sending them forward at a shambling trot. "I understand. Don't be concerned. I can be as much of a gentleman as William, for as long as you choose."

I hope, he added silently, casting a quick glance at the pretty young woman on the wagon seat beside him. *I've been celibate for months now, and sleeping a few yards away from this lovely creature who is supposed to be my wife won't be easy. I never was cut out to be a monk.*

Chapter Ten

"That was a fine breakfast, Mrs. Wallace." Harry smiled down the table at her the following morning. "All that would make it better would be a cup of tea."

"Indeed." She stood, taking Eppie, who'd been in her usual place on her lap, up into her arms. She placed the child on the rug by the hearth with her ragged doll and turned back to him. "Hot water?"

"No, thank you, my dear." He furtively watched the children seated at the table as he used the endearment, but they offered no indication of its effect. They knew he'd slept alone in the small room the previous night, and the older ones must have understood what that meant.

"Now, I've been thinking." He stood and looked at the downcast heads of the three eldest boys and the upturned faces of the other children. "Now that your stepmother and I are wed, I believe it's time we established a manner of address. You called your birth parents Papa and Mama, and so it shall remain, but you must have names for Margaret and me. I'm hoping you'll see fit to call us Father and Mother. That will in no way diminish your parents' importance in this family but will give us a decent way of speaking to each other. We'll take a vote. All in favor of calling us Father and Mother, raise your hands."

No response as the clock ticked, the fire crackled.

Then, slowly, Bella raised her hand. Lizzie hesitantly followed suit a moment later, then Samuel, and finally Robert.

"Aye, well, then, good. Dusted and done. Now with that bit of family business attended to, it's to work, everyone. I'll be riding into the village this morning." He turned to Maggie. "You've said you wanted to find a ship awaiting a cargo of lumber. I'll look into the matter."

"Harry…" Her forehead furrowed as he headed for the door.

"Yes?"

"There's no need, not just yet. We don't have a shipload ready, and no captain will be willing to contract for anything less."

"I realize that, my pet." He addressed her warmly in front of the children, and returned to place a kiss on her forehead. "But it does no harm to check out the situation."

"Very well." She sucked in a deep sigh. "Be careful."

"I will."

"Yeah, be careful." The sneered response came from James. Harry ignored it and strode out of the house.

As he headed for the barn to saddle his horse, he felt more admiration for the woman he'd married welling in his gut. She hadn't tried to stop him, had understood it was something he had to do. She recognized his free-wheeling spirit and wasn't about to tie him down.

She'd have been a good partner in the Highlands…like Iona. But the two oldest lads? Now there was a challenge.

****

In the village he tied Scotia to a hitching post in front of the mercantile, released three sacks from behind his saddle, and strode inside with them in hand. He'd forgone the impulse to dress in his own good clothing. Better to go looking as exactly what he now was...husband to mill and farm owner Margaret Wallace.

He saw a big man behind the counter and strode forward, right hand extended in introduction.

"Mr. Harper, I believe." He offered a hearty greeting. "I'm Harry Wallace. I understand you're in charge of this fine establishment."

"Aye. And what might I do for you, Mister Wallace?"

"My wife, the former Margaret Fowler, came in a few days ago seeking supplies. At the time she had no coin with which to make her purchases. Now"—he reached into a pocket of the woolen work pants he wore and pulled a small cloth bag from it. It clattered as he threw it onto the counter—"we do. I think you'll find more than sufficient there to cover the cost of our needs." He swung the three sacks he carried over the counter. "I'd like sugar, salt, and tea. We'll be needing more items, but I'll wait until our lumber has been sold."

"Ah, I thought I heard your voice." A door at the rear of the room opened, and Joseph Carmody strode out, Michael Kelly close behind him. The entrepreneur was dressed in a fine coat and breeches, his waistcoat and cravat of grey silk. "Did I hear you correctly...you're now married to Maggie Fowler?"

"Yes, happily so." Harry faced the entrepreneur and waited.

"You do know she was a tavern wench before she married Fowler, gossip has it, for his holdings?"

"I know my wife is a hardworking woman who took on the responsibility of seven motherless children when, I suspect, few others would."

"Ah, yes, a veritable saint, our Maggie."

At Carmody's smirk, Harry's hands knotted into fists at his sides, but he restrained himself. *Not the way to go about this, Harry lad, not the way at all.*

"And now you're looking to make purchases for this new family of yours, are you, Mr. Wallace?"

"Yes. This is a mercantile, is it not?" Harry struggled to suppress a sneer. He would have to behave himself. Margaret and the children needed those supplies. "As you can see," he picked up the money bag and rattled it. "I have coin to pay."

"Ah, yes, coin." Carmody came to stand three feet in front of him. "Coin. I wonder just how you obtained those coins, Mr. Wallace. You fight as a man of much experience, yet I cannot believe a soldier would have such wealth. Makes a person wonder if perhaps you didn't come by it honestly."

"You will have to prove that, sir." Harry turned back to Angus Harper. "Now if you'll be so good as to fill my order, I'll be on my way."

"Mr. Wallace won't be needing those supplies." Joseph Carmody's hand shot out to stop the shopkeeper as he reached for the bags. "We'll not do business with a suspected highwayman. And don't go plotting how you'll once again take on my man Kelly here, Mr. Wallace. I've no doubt you'll throttle him on every occasion you think it necessary to do so. I must warn you, however. If you do it again, as magistrate I'll be forced to call in the militia. You'll not so easily fend them off, and on my orders they'll not hesitate to throw you in shackles aboard the next outward-bound ship. Then where will that leave that pretty little peahen and her seven chicks?"

Harry flexed his fingers, willing them not to be fists as he fought to contain his outrage.

"Your store, your right to choose your clientele…I suppose." Harry picked up his purse and shoved it deep into his pocket. "Good day to you, Mr. Carmody…Kelly." He touched his forelock, snatched up his sacks, and strode out of the store.

"Not so tough, are you now, you bastard!" Michael Kelly roared after him. "Got you over a barrel, haven't we, where that doxy and her brats are concerned."

****

"Did you find a ship?" Maggie rounded the beehive oven to confront him as he trotted Scotia into the dooryard. Beside her, on the oven's shelf, four loaves of golden brown bread sat cooling. His stomach rumbled at the sight, reminding him he hadn't eaten since breakfast.

"None in port." He swung to the ground, aware of her eyes on the empty sacks behind his saddle.

"I suspected as much." She turned back to the bread. As she slid it onto a wooden tray, he guessed she understood the real reason for his ride to the village and was answering in turn. "Joseph Carmody keeps everything for himself. But, Harry…" Carrying those tempting loaves, she paused and glanced back over her shoulder at him. "I appreciate your effort."

The smile with which she favored him before continuing on into the house shot straight into his chest. *She's one amazing woman, my wife.* The last word warmed him, gave him a startling sense of pride, as he led Scotia toward the barn and the first raindrops of what would be a downpour slapped him in the face.

Chapter Eleven

Harry eased sock feet onto the floor, stood, and quietly pulled on his pants and shirt. In the midnight moonlight streaming in through the small window above his bed, he gathered up his boots and coat and the bag that held all he'd need in the days and journey ahead, checked the lock on his trunk, and adjusted its key on the chain about his neck. Then he moved like a shadow out of the cubicle and into the main room.

With his hand on the bar of the door, he paused. He couldn't leave like this, not without seeing her one more time. Walking as though on egg shells, he moved to the door of the bedroom and peered inside. In the shadowy room, he saw her, chestnut hair spread out across the pillow, the little girl snuggled against her side, angelic with her golden curls and cherubic face. On her quilt by the bed, Pig raised her head. Harry put a finger to his lips to signal the little animal to silence. Seeming to understand, she obeyed and settled back into her bed.

He stood staring at them a moment longer. Maggie stirred in her sleep, drawing the child more securely against her and sighing softly.

They'll be fine. He squared his shoulders. *Carmody knows better than to try anything while he believes I'm still here.* But a nervous tick rattled his gut as he turned away.

He eased the bar from the door and went out into the yard. The beehive oven greeted him, cold and empty. In a few hours she'd be urging the boys to get the fire started to be ready for baking. The earlier it started heating, the better. He bent to gather up kindling.

Ah, hell, a few minutes more wouldn't matter.

Chapter Twelve

"He's gone." James banged the plank door shut behind him as he strode into the kitchen and crossed to the hearth. Grasping the stones above its opening, he stared down into the languishing breakfast fire and gave the fender a kick. The scowl on his face made thunderclouds look friendly.

"Are you quite sure?" Maggie turned from washing dishes and wiped her hands on her apron. Eppie sat on the floor near her feet, playing with her raggedy doll, Pig beside her. At James's noisy entrance, both looked up, and Eppie's little face contorted into a prelude to tears. "His trunk is still in his room."

"No doubt full of more of his fancy duds, worth nothing to us."

"Calm yourself." Maggie knelt to gather Eppie into her arms. "You're frightening the baby." She gave the little girl a comforting squeeze, stood, and went back to her chore. "I hardly think a man who was planning never to return would take time to light a baking fire. I noticed he'd left the beehive oven heating when I went to the privy."

"What is it about him?" He swung to face her. "Do you want to trust him just because he's what a goodly number of women would term handsome? And he's sure enough got a way with words. Don't you understand? He left because he didn't get you into his bed! That's the only reason he'd have for marrying someone like you!"

"James Fowler, mind your tongue!" She swung to face him, anger and hurt gushing through her. "You know how difficult it is to get anyone to work for us, let alone fight for us. You didn't see him on the wharf the day he arrived. He and his mare took on Michael Kelly and his crowd with nary a second thought. And we agreed to have a marriage in name only. We barely know each other, after all. Harry will come back, you wait and see."

She knelt to comfort Eppie, who again appeared about to burst into tears.

"Yes, well, I'll do just that…wait and see. In the meantime, I'd best get back to the mill. The boys will be needing my help. Sorry, Eppie. James isn't angry at you." He paused to give the child a reassuring smile.

He left with less vehemence than he'd entered. Hoping she'd managed to quell at least some of his resentment against Harry Wallace, she went to the bottom of the stairs and called, "Bella, Lizzie, have you finished tidying up there? You'll have to do the barn work. The boys are busy in the mill and"—she thought about the heating oven—"I have baking to do."

****

Maybe he isn't coming back. Maggie checked the meat roasting on the spit over the fire and turned to the cupboard to begin peeling potatoes for their evening meal. *Perhaps James is right. Oh, God, no! I can't believe it. He agreed to the terms of our marriage, and I never led him to believe there'd be anything more. Still, it's obvious from his clothes and talk, when he wants to play the highborn Englishman, that he's a sophisticated man, a worldly man, a man who's probably known many beautiful, refined women, who's probably enjoyed...intimate relations with more than a few. And he is so very handsome. And it has been over a week. I don't know how much longer I can go on defending him to the children. Perhaps it is time I allowed James to break open that trunk, perhaps...*

Another thought struck her. Harry had disappeared after his unsuccessful trip to the village. Had he aroused Joseph Carmody to violence? Had Harry, like William, become another victim of the entrepreneur?

Oh, dear God, no!

"Lizzie, Bella, mind Eppie," she called up the stairs. "And take care of the dinner on the fire. I have to go to the village."

****

As she drove the team toward Riverhaven, her fear and outrage cooling, she decided storming up to Joseph Carmody with accusations wasn't the way to proceed. No, much better to begin calmly, logically, and see what developed from there.

As she reined Prince and Bonnie to a halt at the steps of Joseph Carmody's big white house, she was annoyed to see Michael Kelly sprawled on a chair on the veranda near the main entrance. He didn't get up, merely pulled his mouth into a sneering grin.

"Well, well, if it isn't Mrs. Fowler—or is it Mrs. Wallace—or some other name by now? You surely have a way of procuring men and then getting rid of them in short order."

"I've come to see the magistrate," she said. She climbed down and tied the team to the hitching rail.

"I doubt he has time for the likes of you, Maggie."

He pulled himself up in his chair, the smirk widening.

"Michael, did I hear a wagon?" Joseph Carmody came out of the house, then turned to Maggie. "Well, well, Mrs. Wallace." He came to the top of the steps and smiled down at her. "This is a surprise. And quite possibly a pleasure? Have you come to accept my offer to buy your enterprises?"

"Definitely not." Squinting up at him, Maggie wished the sun wasn't in her eyes and they faced each other on level ground. "I've come to report my husband missing."

"What? That fine young man you sequestered fresh off the first ship that docked at my wharf this spring? I find that hard to believe." He stuck his thumbs into the pockets of his waistcoat, puffed out his chest, and cast a knowing wink in Michael Kelly's direction. The man gave a scoffing laugh.

"Mr. Wallace disappeared over a week ago." Fighting to remain calm, she continued, "Is it not the duty of the district magistrate to investigate such problems?"

"Under reasonable circumstances, yes, it would be." The man continued his self-righteous stance above her. "But Harry Wallace, in spite of his fancy horse and clothes, is a vagabond, a man of the road, quite possibly a highwayman wanted in the Old Country for any number of nefarious crimes. Therefore, it would hardly behoove me to expend time and resources searching for such an individual. Like a stray dog, he's probably just run off…after the next creature in heat."

The man's crude words coupled with Michael Kelly's snigger broke her vows to remain cool.

"You have no proof that my husband has been

anything other than an honorable gentleman! Your refusal to assist in searching for him leads me to believe he probably met the same fate as William. I know you're not above doing murder to get what you want!"

Fingers trembling with anger, she untied her team and climbed to the wagon seat.

"That's a serious accusation, young lady!" Joseph Carmody yelled after her. "And you've made it in front of a witness!"

Too outraged to care, she flapped the reins and sent Bonnie and Prince into their shambling gallop back toward her home. Once out of sight of the village, she slowed the team to a walk as unpleasant possibilities suffused her mind. Both Joseph Carmody and her own stepson had attributed Harry's disappearance to sexual needs. Were they correct? The idea haunted her. When he'd kissed her, he'd demonstrated that he was not inexperienced in the art of making love. Had she been wrong to expect a healthy, virile man to live chastely with a woman he'd taken as his legal wife?

Chapter Thirteen

The sounds of hooves charging up the hill and men's voices yelling shattered Maggie's thoughts. She swung away from the cupboard, where she'd been preparing food, toward the window at the front of the house—to see a cloud of smoke rising above the trees from the direction of the mills. Something that felt like her heart banged into the back of her throat. Hoofbeats pounding up the hill sent her running out onto the veranda. In the dooryard, at the bottom of the front steps, was Eppie, dressed in her little trousers and shabby coat, hunkered down making a sand castle.

Three horsemen, whooping and urging their frothing mounts to full run, bore down on the child. The little girl looked up, blue eyes widening in horror. Her mouth opened in a silent scream.

"Oh, dear God, no!" Clutching up her skirts, Maggie lunged forward, tripped and went sprawling down the steps.

Then, a miracle. From under the veranda, Pig dashed into the path of the riders, knocking the child out of their way. As the first horse thundered into the yard, there was a shriek and a squeal. Pig flew through the air to drop into the grass on the far side of the yard. And lay still.

"Bastards!" Maggie scrambled to her feet and staggered through the prancing horses to the fallen child. Dropping to her knees, she gathered the little girl into her arms. "Miserable bastards! Look what you've done!" she screamed, clutching the silent, staring Eppie.

"Now, now, is that any way for a mother to talk?" She recognized Michael Kelly as he cavorted his half-crazed horse around her, a stench of rum hanging about him. "But then, you're not really a mother, are you? You're the local tavern whore who'll take in anyone, even a highwayman, just to have a bed warmer. And you can't even keep that bastard around."

"Get off my property!" Against her breast, the child had begun to shudder violently.

Suddenly, seemingly out of nowhere, a rider on a big sorrel horse burst up the hill, yelling and wielding a sword above his head. He charged his mount among the invaders, slashing one from his saddle with the weapon, kicking another's animal with his boot. The mare shrieked and reared. The third man, Michael Kelly, caught in the centre of the melee, fought to control his bucking gelding.

"I'm getting the hell out of here!" the first to be assaulted yelled, scrambling back into the saddle of his dancing horse. "The bastard's crazy!"

"Aye!" the second swung his mount about and headed off down the incline at full gallop.

"Ah, to hell with it!" Michael Kelly roared. "Blitherin' cowards." He turned his horse and kicked it into a run behind his companions as they fled down the slope, across the bridge, and up the road toward the village.

"The wee lassie." The newcomer leaped from his horse, letting it race off into the barnyard, and knelt beside Maggie and Eppie. "Is she…?"

"She's alive, but I don't know how badly she's been injured. I have to get her into the house. Thank you." Maggie looked at the man who'd come to their rescue and hoped the gratitude she was feeling in her heart showed in her face.

"Ah, well, just in the right place at the right time." A tangle of sandy curls surmounted a handsome face that had dissolved into soft lines of compassion and concern as he spoke. He got to his feet, sheathed his weapon, and held out his arms as Maggie stood. "Here, let me help you."

"I don't think…" Maggie started to protest, startled almost as much by his change into kindly demeanor as by his entrance in the guise of marauding barbarian.

"Come, lassie." He spoke softly, his Scottish inflection reminding Maggie of her late husband's voice…and Harry's. "Let Brodie carry you."

To Maggie's surprise, Eppie who normally spurned strangers, went into his arms without protest.

As they started toward the back door of the house, James, Geordie, Robert, and Samuel, dirty and breathless, came running, stumbling up the hill.

"We would have been here sooner, but those cowards set fire to the sawdust pile," Robert gasped, his face, like his brothers', streaked with soot. "We had to get it out before the mill caught."

"Eppie…?" His face grey and taut, James moved forward to stare down at his small sister in the stranger's arms.

"She'll be all right, I think. But Pig…" A sob caught in Maggie's throat as, with a jerk of her head, she indicated the inert little animal. "She saved Eppie's life. And," she forced herself to continue, "this man, he saved both of us."

"Brodie MacMillan's the name. Now, we'd best be getting this small lassie inside and into a warm bed." He started again toward the back door of the log house.

"Take care of Eppie." James spoke to his stepmother but cast Brodie MacMillan's back a suspicious glance. His voice shook. "We'll do what has to be done…out here."

Bella and Lizzie, who'd been in the barn, came running up, eyes wide, faces pale.

"Those men…" Bella stared from the stranger and Eppie to Maggie.

"I'll explain later." Maggie reached to open the door for the man who'd identified himself as Brodie MacMillan.

When the man paused to wait for admittance, Eppie turned in his arms and saw her pet.

"Pig!" She screeched her first word since her mother's death. "Pig!"

She fought to scramble out of Brodie's arms, but he held her fast against his chest. "Dunnae greet, lassie," he cooed in words and tone so soft and gentle, so much like William's they amazed Maggie. "Dunnae greet."

"We have to see to supper, Eppie," she forced herself to add, fighting back tears of anger and sadness as she hurried to hold the door for them. "James will take care of Pig."

"Pig, Pig, Pig!" The child's screams echoed out into the chill air of the bleak spring afternoon.

As Brodie MacMillan carried the shrieking child inside, a pain, brutal and hard, invaded Maggie's chest.

Joseph Carmody, I hope you rot in hell. If someone

doesn't kill you soon, I will.

****

A half hour later, Maggie returned to the kitchen. Eppie had sobbed herself to sleep in their bedroom. Now she faced the children, who, with the exception of James and Geordie, who'd gone to take care of Pig, sat at the table with drawn faces. Brodie MacMillan sat in one of the rocking chairs by the fire. He was bent forward, elbows on his knees, hands clasped between them, staring at the floor. He looked up as Maggie returned.

"The wee lassie?" His words reflected the depth of his concern.

"She'll be all right." Maggie sank into the chair opposite him. "But Pig…"

"Pig died saving Eppie." Bella, her face paler, her expression more gaunt than that of any twelve-year-old child's should ever be, spoke softly. "She's a hero. Her and Mr. MacMillan." Her blue eyes swam with tears.

"Yes, they're both heroes. But how do you know his name?"

"While you were tending the wee lassie, we introduced ourselves." A small grin quirked Brodie's mouth. Rolling his shoulders, he straightened up and leaned back in the chair. "You've a fine family here, mistress."

Tired, weary. The man has had a long, hard ride, yet he found the strength to fight for us.

"We'll see to supper." Bella stood and nudged Lizzie to her feet.

"Thank you, girls." Maggie forced a smile, hoping the gratitude she was feeling radiated from her expression. "I'd appreciate a few moments of respite."

She took the opportunity to peruse the man seated opposite her. Although dressed in the rough homespun of a working man, Brodie MacMillan wore knee-high boots of a good cut, and his sword belt now hanging on a peg by the door was of fine leather. *A fighting man, a man who needed strong boots and equipment to do his job. Another rebel highwayman like Harry Wallace? And, if so, how did he find his way to this remote farm?*

"Look who is here." Grinning, James shoved open the door and held it wide for Geordie to come in carrying...Pig. Although only one eye was open, it blinked.

"Lizzie, Bella, run upstairs. Get pillows and quilts." Maggie was on her feet, issuing orders to the girls. "Oh, Pig, dear Pig." She went to lay a gentle hand on the heaving side.

"She's got a bunch of cuts and a bunged-up eye, but she'll live," Geordie said, laying the animal on the bed the girls had rushed to make for her. "Rest and soft food should do the trick. Takes more than a bunch of bandits to kill a hero, isn't that so, Mistress Pig?"

The little animal mustered a soft, snuffling snort before closing her good eye in sleep.

"I think she deserves a name, a real name." Maggie patted the rough bristles of the animal's head as she pulled a quilt over her. "I think she should be called Precious because she saved our precious baby. What do you think?"

She looked up at the children surrounding her.

"I think it's perfect." Lizzie was the first to speak. Bella nodded in agreement.

"Kind of a silly name for a tough little critter," Samuel muttered with a grin. "But I guess females like that kind of thing."

"Precious it is, then." Maggie stood, put her hands on her hips, and smiled around at the group. "That is, unless Eppie decides otherwise…now that she's talking again."

"We'd best go back to the mill." James turned to his brothers. "We have to be sure that fire has been all-out extinguished. A blaze like that can play dead, only to erupt again."

"Would you be needin' a hand?" Brodie MacMillan started to rise.

"No, thank you, sir." James spoke respectfully. "But I will be grateful if you'd stay here with the family in case…"

"Oh, aye." He reseated himself. "I hardly think that rabble will return, but I'll do as you suggest."

The four boys filed out and headed down the hill. A small wail erupted from the bedroom, but as Maggie started to respond, Bella put a restraining hand on her shoulder.

"Lizzie and I will tend to Eppie."

"Mr. MacMillan, I must thank you once again for your rescue today," she said, once the children had gone into the bedroom. "But I cannot resist asking, what brings you to our isolated farm? We're not on the way to anywhere."

"I'm seeking a friend." He looked over at her, eyes narrowing. "He came out from the Old Country weeks ago, and I have reason to believe he may be in this area. We often spoke of emigrating to this village called Riverhaven. Today, after I arrived, I spoke to a dock worker who told me such a man had arrived some time ago. He told me he'd taken up with a woman named

Maggie Fowler, who owns mills and farm about ten miles distant. But since I don't see him about, I'm assuming he's moved on."

"Can you describe this friend for me?" *I'm not about to go giving out information to this man, even though he seems a decent person. The thickness of his accent brands him a recent arrival from Scotland. God knows what his real reason might be for wanting to find Harry.*

"Tall, with dark curling hair, broad shoulders… and, they tell me, handsome enough to catch any woman's eye." The twinkle in his own made Maggie glance away. "Perhaps most distinctly, he rides an unusual mare…charcoal grey with silver mane and tail. You haven't been seeing him about, have you, mistress?"

"You say you are his friend?" Maggie took the chair opposite and looked directly into eyes as blue as a summer's sky, as blue as Harry's.

"Aye, his boon companion. We've ridden many a road together."

"He was here." Maggie took a leap of faith. "He left over a week ago. I don't know where he is at present."

"Ah." Brodie MacMillan stood and rubbed his palms on the hips of his breeches. "Typical Hamish. The wanderlust has always tickled his feet."

"Hamish?" A cold flash dashed over her. "The man who stayed here called himself Harry Wallace."

"Harry Wallace." Brodie MacMillan chuckled. "Aye, that sounds like him." Then he sobered. "You say you have no idea where he is or when he'll return?"

"No." She stifled the impulse to substitute "if."

"Verrae well, then. If you'll permit me, I'll stay on a couple of days and wait for him. You'll not find me a great nuisance. I'm willin' to work for food and shelter for the Fox—that's my horse, Fox—and me. Your barn will suit us right down to the ground for sleeping. Or maybe," he continued, rubbing his chin, "I should bed down in your mill...in case those villains decide to return."

"That's kind of you, Mr. MacMillan, but I'd not expect you to sleep in such uncomfortable surroundings. I'm sure you put something close to the fear of the Lord in them this afternoon and they'll not be returning any time soon." She gave him a quick smile.

"Aye, well, I admit I do a fair to middlin' imitation of a wild man." His lips curled, the corners of his eyes crinkling. "Usually scares the hell—excuse me, ma'am—out of the likes of those cowards. If you think I've run them off for a time, then I must admit a night in the comfort of your barn would be most welcome, to both the Fox and me. I'll be up with the sun, never fear, and at the barn work." He stood and headed for the door.

"Another pair of hands will be welcome, Mr. MacMillan." She also got to her feet. "We'll be expecting you to take supper with us."

"That's most kindly of you, mistress. I'm grateful. And Fox will appreciate a night out of the elements with a full belly and lots of water."

"You call your mount Fox? An unusual name."

"Ah, perhaps for some, but not for such a lad." He cast her a grin that made her want to trust him. But there was that Scottish burr coloring his every word, and she'd just been deserted by another who spoke in the same manner. "His coat is the same color as a red fox, and he can be just as sly and clever as one. More than once he's saved my neck when…"

He stopped abruptly, then continued, "But enough storytelling. Now, so you won't think me taking too great advantage of your good will, as soon as I put my horse away, I'll see to your stock."

"That would be most appreciated, Mr. MacMillan. The children have had a hard day, as you've seen. They'll be grateful to find the barn work taken care of."

"I saw your operation as I rode here. A fine-looking outfit." He headed for the door. "Not an easy venture for a woman alone with seven children to take care of. I hope Ham-, er, Harry has been of some help."

A small shiver of apprehension washed over her. *Taking inventory?*

"That he has. Supper will be in an hour, Mr. MacMillan."

"It will be a pleasure and an honor to share it with you and your family, ma'am. I haven't had a decent home-cooked meal in a dog's age. But I would like to be knowin' your name. Your bairns have introduced themselves while you were tending the wee lassie. They used the surname Fowler. I assume you'd be sharing it?"

"No, I wouldn't. Do please excuse me, Mr. MacMillan. In the excitement, my manners lapsed. I'm Maggie Wallace." She held out a hand.

"Wallace? A relative of this man Harry Wallace?"

"His wife, sir."

Astonishment appeared to freeze the man in place. Then a broad grin broke over his face.

"Well, I'll be damned! Er, excuse me, Mrs. Wallace—darned. Ham-, Harry married. Good for you, mistress. It's not before time someone captured the lad. Congratulations. You've done what many a lassie before you has failed to do."

As he opened the door to leave, she heard a wagon coming up the hill. Her breath caught. Had she been mistaken to trust the agreeable Brodie MacMillan? Was this perhaps his reinforcements arriving?

Chapter Fourteen

"Hamish!" Brodie MacMillan's exclamation of pleasure banished the thought as he strode outside. She followed close behind, to see Harry drive a team of Percherons hitched to a loaded wagon into the dooryard. Scotia was tied to its rear, along with a black horse and a palomino paint pony.

He's back. The realization sent a flood of joy coursing through her body. But driving a wagon and team? Where had he gotten the outfit and its contents? The memory of Michael Kelly's branding him a highwayman flashed back. Surely he couldn't have gone robbing and plundering?

"Brodie, you son of a gun! Bloody hell, Brodie. I thought you were dead!" Harry jumped down from the wagon seat, a grin splitting his face as he and Brodie MacMillan embraced with all the alacrity of long-lost friends. "Sweet Jesus, laddie!"

"Ah, it will take more than a few redcoats to finish off the likes of me."

Who are these two men? What am I getting into by involving myself with them?

"Well, well." Harry finally held the newcomer out at arm's length and looked him up and down, his face bright with pleasure. "I never thought I'd see this day. Bloody hell, but it's good to see you, you crazy devil."

"And you as well, but I'll not go givin' you

demeanin' names." Brodie grinned back at him.

"Here I thought I was the one to be giving gifts this day." Harry's delight seemed boundless. "When all the time the best gift in the world was waiting for me right in my own dooryard."

"Aye, well, like a bad smell, I'm dreadful hard to get rid of." Brodie slapped him on the shoulder.

"Enough of this." Harry sucked in a deep breath and turned back to the wagon. "The animals are weary. We've come a good distance today. They need food and water. We'll tell our tales later." He held out an arm to Maggie. "Come here, Mrs. Wallace, and let me introduce you to my best friend and trusted comrade Brodie MacMillan. Brodie"—he drew Maggie to his side as she joined them—"meet my guid wife, Margaret Wallace."

"I've already had the pleasure. And the surprise. It's for sure and certain then? You and this lovely lassie are married?"

"Ye're casting your eyes on Mr. and Mrs. Harry Wallace, laddie." Harry made no attempt to hide his Highland accent.

"Mr. and Mrs. Harry Wallace." Maggie caught the wink the new arrival cast at Harry. "Oh, aye. Well, it's a pleasure to meet you both. And"—he held out his right hand to Harry—"Congratulations, Harry Wallace. You've chosen well."

"Thank you. I've no doubt on that score. Now help me unload the wagon, and we'll tend to these weary beasts and then get inside. I'm sure Margaret has supper ready. We'll tell our stories after the bairns head off to bed. You must have met them also by now."

He turned to Lizzie and Bella, who'd followed

Maggie and Brodie outside at the sound of the wagon. The boys were coming up the hill from the mill, Samuel leading the way, Robert walking close behind him, the two eldest lagging at the rear.

"What do you think of Goldenbug?" He addressed the girls as he pointed to the yellow pony. "Think you can ride her and take care of her?"

"Is she ours?" Lizzie spoke directly to Harry for the first time, her eyes wide and bright.

"Aye, yours and Bella's and Eppie's."

"She's beautiful." Bella came down the steps to put a hand on the pony's neck. Lizzie followed close behind, eyes round and bright.

"And this dark beast is for you lads." Harry went to slap the black gelding on the rump and turn to the boys. "I figured young men of business need a faster way of getting about than a pair of Clydes. He's named Midnight because there's nary a speck of white on him."

Maggie couldn't contain the smile that tugged at her lips as first Samuel and then Robert went to examine the creature.

"I get first ride," Samuel was quick to declare as he took the animal by its halter and lowered its head to rub its snout.

"Now, no squabblin'." Harry was smiling, too, when she looked over at him. "First you lot will care for these beasts, this team included. They'll be spending the night. They've had a long journey and need food and water. In the morning I'll return them to the minister, from whom I borrowed them."

Harry went to the heads of the team and led them around to the rear door of the house, the others following. "Now," he instructed the boys who'd followed, "unhitch these gallant beasts and those from the rear, take them to the barn, and see to their needs. We'll leave the wagon here to be unloaded. We won't make them wait any longer for well-deserved rest and nourishment."

Samuel immediately took charge of the black gelding, the girls of the pony.

"Robert, I'd be pleased if you'd see to Scotia," Harry addressed the other lad. "Perhaps you can let her have a gallop in the pasture before you stable her. She's been spoiling for a romp."

"All right." Struggling to conceal his delight in being given the care of Harry's prized mare, the young lad untied her from the rear and started toward the paddock with her prancing behind him.

With a few muttered words, James, with Geordie following his example, moved to unhitch the team.

After they'd led the animals off to the barn, Harry pointed over the side of the wagon. Maggie saw several barrels and a couple of trunks.

"Tea, sugar, molasses, salt, and a collection of other things you mentioned you were running low on." He climbed into the driver's seat to swing into the back and indicate the barrels.

"But how did you come by the minister's wagon and team?" Maggie had to have at least the rudiments of an explanation.

"I rode Scotia to the village, where I borrowed his wagon and horses. I knew ours couldn't be spared."

"But all this…I won't be able to repay you for some time…not until I've successfully shipped a vessel-load of lumber."

"I'm your husband, you may recall. It's my duty to support our family. Now come on, lad." He had turned to Brodie. "I'm assuming you're looking for work, and there's plenty of it around here. So get a move on and put your back to unloading this wagon."

"Aye, milord." Grinning, Brodie made a mockery of touching his forelock. He vaulted into the wagon's cargo space and began rolling barrels on their rims toward the backboard. "And you might lend a hand, too, squire. I'm not about to strain my back in your service."

****

"I'd best head on down to the barn and make certain the children are making out well with the beasts," Brodie said, once the contents of the wagon had been deposited inside the log house. "New horses, no matter how well trained, can act up on finding themselves in strange surroundings."

"Aye, I'd be grateful if you would, lad." Harry nodded to Brodie, and when their gazes met, Maggie caught something beyond her present ken in the looks.

These men understand each other, share some kind of deep secret. I wonder if they'll ever feel safe to share it with me.

"Well, aren't you going to open them?" Harry stood, grinning, beside a trunk after his friend had gone out. "No mystery about the barrels…sugar, molasses, salt, and the small one, tea. But these," he gave one of the other containers a shove with a booted foot. "Now, they could be filled with surprises."

He took a pair of keys from his pocket and unlocked first one, then the other.

Looking inside, Maggie suppressed a gasp.

Clothing. Pretty clothing. Women's clothing. Gowns.

"Oh, Harry, what have you done?" She looked up at him, astonished.

"Nothing shameful, I hope." He grinned at her. "Go ahead. Take a closer look."

Reaching inside, she withdraw a dress, a pretty yellow dress that would fit Bella. Next came a blue one in Lizzie's size. There followed two others for each of the girls and an exquisite pink one perfect for Eppie. Tied around it was a long length of matching ribbon.

As she stood admiring it, Eppie came out of the bedroom. Except for a bruise on one cheek, she looked unscathed by the attack. Seeing Pig on the hearth, she flew to the animal and fell on her knees beside the little animal.

"Pig," she whispered. "Pig!"

She started to gather her into her arms, but Maggie stopped her. "She's a bit sore, darling. Best let her rest. And look." Maggie held the dress up to the child, happiness all but overwhelming her. "Look what Father has brought you."

Eppie ignored her, lowered her head, stuck her thumb into her mouth, and returned her attention to Pig.

"What happened to the pig?" Harry for the first time became aware of the little animal lying near the hearth.

"She was injured…in the attack…and Eppie saw it happen. You must forgive the child any seeming lack of attention to your gift at the moment. She's still recovering."

"Attack? What attack? Sweet Jesus, Margaret, what has been happening in my absence?" His face furrowed with concern, he grasped her by the shoulders.

"Were any of you harmed? I'm assuming Joseph Carmody and his louts were the perpetrators?" He released her and slammed the fist of his right hand into his left palm. "If he's hurt anyone…"

"No, no, we're all well." She put her hand on his arm. "Fortunately, your friend Brodie arrived in time to drive them off. But the boys did have a struggle to put out the fire at the mill."

"Fire at the mill? Sweet Jesus, woman, this tale gets darker and darker!" He sank down onto her chair at the table and stared up at her. "Perhaps you'd best tell me the entire story."

****

"And so we all survived, even Pig, thankfully for Eppie's sake." She finished the account.

"Of course. That wee beastie means the world to her. Will she…the pig…be all right?"

"The boys think so. We can only hope and pray."

"Brodie and I will be looking into the matter directly, have no fear." He stood. "Now what about the wee dress…do you think it will fit? Is it a fittin' color for the wee on'?"

"It's beautiful, and a lovely shade." His concern touched her. "It's just that she's never seen anything like it. And right now all she can think about is her pig. Give her time. And thank you." Her voice softened. "But how? Where did you get all this?" She spread out her hands to indicate the largess.

"Riverhaven isn't the only settlement in this province." He grinned. "By asking a few questions when I was in the village, I learned of others where I might purchase what our family needed." He shrugged. "All it took was a few directions and the borrowing of the minister's team. And I was lucky. The place had an excellent seamstress, haberdasher, and shoemaker. The pony and gelding I bought along the way."

"You've been too generous."

"Not a bit of it." He looked embarrassed by her praise and changed the subject. "It was purchased with coin intended to aid victims of the Highland Clearances, and I'm convinced William Fowler's children and their stepmother qualify. More importantly, did I just hear Eppie speak?"

"Yes. Only the one word, but it's a start."

"Guid, verrae guid. Now get back to emptying these trunks."

She reached inside once more and pulled out a soft linen gown of emerald green. Its size dictated it could only have been meant for her.

"To match your eyes, lassie." The words were soft, so soft she glanced at him in surprise. It was the first real compliment he'd ever given her. "Is it all right?" The last came out shyly.

"Oh, my, yes. It's perfect. I've never had such a pretty gown. Thank you." She held it against her breasts and looked at him, hoping the sincerity of her gratitude was apparent.

"You needn't unpack the rest right now," he said. "It's simply more clothes for the children, the boys included, and few pairs of boots and shoes. Oh, and a pair of satin slippers for the lady of the house. And a couple more gowns. But right now I hear Brodie and the others returning. We'll discuss the purchases later."

"Harry, you'll have to forgive James and Geordie any lack of enthusiasm tonight." She put a hand on his arm. "They've had a hard day, what with the fire at the mill, and the raid."

"I never thought the man would have the temerity to attack this place. Somehow he must have found out I was not here."

"Yes, he must have." Recalling her visit to the entrepreneur's home, she realized that she, in her outrage against Joseph Carmody, in her desire to blame him for yet another death, had invited the raid on the unprotected family.

Fool! Your hot head will get us all murdered if you don't learn to control yourself. I can't bring myself to tell Harry...not just yet, at least. He'll think me the worst kind of idiot, and he'd be quite correct.

"Well, let me assure you, it won't happen again. I'm home and intend to stay."

"Until the next time you get the urge to take off." James, who'd entered the room with the others in time to hear Harry's last sentence, twisted his mouth into a sneer.

"Nothing of the sort, laddie." Harry ignored the slight. "I'm not about to go deserting my family. I simply left to get supplies. I thought I'd warned Carmody off...at least for a time."

Behind James, Geordie issued a derisive snort. Maggie saw Brodie, bringing up the rear, observing the situation, blue eyes keen and penetrating.

"That will be quite enough, boys." Maggie couldn't contain the reprimand. "Harry has brought you gifts you'll enjoy no end. He deserves respect." She indicated the clothing and barrels.

"What are we owing you for all this?" James wasn't about to let the subject drop.

Still leery, still not ready to accept the man and his

generosity.

"Hard work, and loyalty to your mother and me." Harry startled her with his bold words. "We've a farm and business to run. Sniping at each other and disagreeing at every turn will do little to advance either. I've married your mother and agreed to stay as long as this family needs me. You'll find I'm a man of my word. What happened this afternoon proves we'll need every hand available to manage it. Do we have a truce?"

He held out a hand to James. The clock ticked. A stick in the fire snapped. Maggie held her breath. James set his mouth in a hard, thin line, squared his shoulders, and finally, after what she thought might have been the longest hiatus she might ever experience, accepted Harry's offer.

A silent sigh of relief whispered up through Maggie's body.

"Now us lads had better head outside and wash up." Harry addressed the group as the handshake ended. "We're none of us fit to sit down at the fine meal Mother has prepared."

He put an arm around Maggie's waist and pulled her close to plant a kiss on her temple before leading men and boys outside to the washstand.

"It's guid ta be home, lass," he murmured in her ear.

Chapter Fifteen

"Look at me, I'm beautiful!" Lizzie whirled about the crowded kitchen in her new dress. The family had finished supper and settled down to enjoy Harry's gifts. Now the girls, arrayed in their new clothes, danced around in delight. All except Eppie. She sat stubbornly on the hearth rug, one arm around Pig's shoulders, thumb stuck in her mouth. She'd refused to put on the little pink dress or in any way show her delight at the purchases.

"Come, lassie." Brodie turned in his chair and smiled at her. "Bring that pretty little pig over here and join the fun. Look!" He picked up a pink ribbon lying on the table among the other clothes. "This is for your hair, but I'm thinkin' you might want to share it with your friend."

Still she hung back. Pig looked up at the child, snuffled, then struggled to her hooves. For the first time Maggie could recall, Precious the Pig left the child's side, in order to limp over to Brodie. Holding up her snout, she nudged the man's hand.

"Aw, well, then." Brodie bent and began to wind the pink ribbon around the pig's neck. "It seems your friend is ready to get dressed up." He made several circuits around the animal's neck with the silk, then tied it in a wide bow beneath her chin. Pig let out what sounded like a contented sigh.

"See?" Brodie looked over at the little girl. "Precious wants to be pretty. Now, what say? Will you let your mother dress you in this lovely little gown?"

He held it out to Maggie. Eppie paused for a moment, staring at Pig. Still sucking her thumb, she marched into the bedroom.

"I'm guessing she's about to try on that wee garment." Brodie grinned at Maggie. "With your help, of course, Mrs. Wallace."

Maggie, astounded by the changes this newcomer seemed to be able to effect with the child, nodded and followed her.

Five minutes later they emerged, Eppie resplendent in the pink dress, her hair brushed into long, golden ringlets down her back.

"Now, there's a proper young lady." Brodie grinned as the other two girls paused in their enjoyment of the gifts to stare in amazement.

"Eppie, you're beautiful," Bella breathed.

"You are kind of pretty," Samuel admitted, looking at his sister.

"And just for being so good, your father has something special for you." Brodie jerked a thumb toward Harry, who sat in the rocking chair by the fire. "If you'll go and climb up on his knee, I'm thinking he'll be more than happy to give it to you."

The child turned to look at Harry, started to put her thumb into her mouth, then stopped as Pig hobbled toward the man, noises that sounded like pleasure issuing from her snout. She paused beside him, sat, and allowed him to scratch behind her ears. She murmured her pleasure in the gesture.

"Go along, lassie." Brodie's words were soft and

encouraging.

Slowly she edged toward Harry. All the others in the kitchen paused to watch the drama unfolding before them as she approached the man, finally stopping at his knee.

"I've a wee gift for you, Eppie," he said softly, and Maggie recognized the anxiety, the outright fear in his gentle words. This big, tough man was afraid of rejection by a small, blond three-year-old. He reached down on the floor beside his chair, took up a small sack, and handed it to her. "Look inside."

Slowly, cautiously, the child did as he requested. A single glance and she thrust her hand deep inside and pulled out a doll—a petite, exquisite, china-faced doll dressed in satin and lace. Her eyes widened as a small gasp escaped her lips. She stared at the gift, then clutched it to her chest, rocking to and fro.

"I think your father deserves a thank you." Brodie's words were softly encouraging.

The child looked up at Harry, eyes bright with joy, then, still clutching the doll in one arm, held up the other. Maggie felt tears stinging her eyes as Harry recognized the invitation and carefully hoisted the little girl onto one knee while Pig snuggled against the other. When Harry looked at her over the child's head, she saw such joy mirrored there she had to swallow hard to manage the lump in her throat.

"This has been quite a day." Grinning, Brodie stood. "And down in the barn, among my belongings, I have just the thing to put the icing on it. Mrs. Wallace, while I'm gone, perhaps you'll do us the honor of putting on that pretty dress your husband has bought for *you*."

With a wink at Harry, he strode out into the lengthening shadows of the May evening.

****

By the time he returned, Maggie had complied with his suggestion. Coming out of the bedroom as he entered, she blushed as all eyes turned in her direction.

"You look beautiful, Mother." Bella, the first to speak, stumbled out the word, and Maggie felt her heart swell.

"Thank you, Bella." Trying desperately to stifle a blush as she caught Harry's undisguised admiration, she turned to Brodie. "And what have you got there, Mr. MacMillan?" She gestured to the elongated case he'd laid on the table.

"Ah, just something to bring a bit more fun to this evening." He opened the case and drew out a fiddle and a bow. Tucking it under his chin, he tapped his foot a few times, then began to play a jig.

"Come on, come on, you lot." He was tapping his foot in time to the music. "Dance."

Soon the younger children, Eppie and Samuel included, were hopping around the kitchen, while Robert slowly relented his stern stance and began to clap time. James wore an expression of bored indifference, but to Maggie's surprise Geordie's face held evidence of rapt attention. He appeared entranced by the music. There was a softer side to this boy who'd always seemed to live in James's shadow, perhaps only reflecting his older brother's stubborn defiance. Had Brodie MacMillan and his music made a dent in Geordie Fowler's armor? She could only hope.

Brodie kept up the pace until the young dancers began to show signs of weariness. Pausing, he gave them the opportunity to sink onto benches at the table or onto the floor by the hearth.

"Now, it's time for Mother and Father to show us their style." He grinned at Harry and Maggie, who'd been sitting to one side in the rocking chairs, watching the children's antics.

"Oh, no, I hardly think…" Maggie began to protest, but to her surprise, Harry stood and drew her to her feet and into his arms.

"Can you manage that disgraceful new dance called the waltz, maestro?" Harry looked down into her eyes with a gaze so intense her protests swirled away in a cloud of blue.

"I'd be a poor musician if I've not kept up with the newest tunes." Grinning, Brodie drew his bow smoothly across the strings and eased into the softly lilting strains of a waltz.

"I…I don't think…" Maggie stood stock still.

"Of course you can." Harry's words were soft, reassuring. "Just let yourself go and follow my lead."

At first she stumbled, tripping as she tried to match her movements to his. Then, as realization dawned, she abandoned the effort and allowed herself to do as he'd requested. Her eyes locked into his as they moved rhythmically over the plank floor in harmony. The moments dissolved into sheer magic. She forgot the children staring at them from the sidelines. She forgot all but the sweet, sensuous sound of Brodie's fiddle and Harry's magnetic, blue-eyed gaze. His arm about her waist, his hand in hers, she floated around the kitchen in the backwoods log house, her heart throbbing to the beat of the music.

What is this? Can this be…what some call falling

in love? Oh, my, whatever it is, it's wonderful!

Maggie Wallace, who'd only known hard work all her life, gave in to the most breathtaking moments she'd ever experienced. This handsome, worldly man was gazing down at her with a smile at once sensuous and filled with caring.

Never let the music end.

But it did. Harry bowed gallantly over her hand.

"A pleasure, Mrs. Wallace," he said, his words carrying all the eroticism of a caress, his gaze suggesting there could be much more to come when she was ready.

"A pleasure, indeed, Mr. Wallace," she replied, and dropped an awkward curtsey.

Was that the proper thing to do?

With an effort she turned back to the children.

"It's been a full day. We'd best all be off to our beds. Thank your father and Mr. MacMillan, and let's be gone."

****

They were alone in the chairs in front of the fire. The children were in bed, even Eppie, exhausted by the excitement, her doll clutched in her arms, Pig on the mat beside her bed. Brodie had retired to the barn.

"Fancy a wee dram?" He went to the dresser where he'd left a bottle, picked it up, and glanced back at her.

"Thank you, but no." She sat by the fire, clutching a tin mug in her hands. "This tea is exactly what I need. I did miss it so. Thank you again, Harry, for getting it."

"Ah, yes, an English lady should never be parted from her tea." A sense of satisfaction warmed his innards as he reached for a cup and poured a generous measure of whiskey into it.

"Hardly a lady, but I do agree." He turned in time to see her casting him a shy grin. "An Englishwoman does enjoy the brew."

Now it was time. He placed his drink on the dresser and went into his cubicle. From a haversack, he removed a small, delicately fashioned crystal bottle.

"For you." He advanced back across the kitchen and held it out to her.

Eyes wide, she stared up at him.

"Scent." He urged it into her hand when she failed to reach for it.

"Are you saying I stink?" Her lips hardened into a thin line, her eyes narrow as she glared up at him.

"No! No, no, no." Startled by her response, he stuttered. He'd never encountered anything like it when he'd given such a gift to other women. "Not at all. Definitely not." Then regaining a semblance of control, he continued, "It's a gift for a lady. And"—he softened his tone—"you are most certainly a lady, Margaret Wallace. You deserve to be treated as such."

He watched as suspicion and embarrassment dissolved from her expression. She lowered her gaze to the sparkling bottle. "It's beautiful," she said, her words shaking.

"Open it." He became eager for her response now that the misunderstanding had been cleared away.

"How?" She turned it over in her work-reddened hands. "I don't want to break it. It must have cost a fair penny."

"Allow me." He took it from her and carefully removed the stopper.

He handed it back to her, and she raised it to her nose.

"Oh, my!" she breathed. "It's what heaven must smell like."

"I'm not sure about that. But it is a popular scent with the ladies in the Old Country."

"Oh, yes?" Suspicion tinged with teasing reflected in her eyes as she looked over at him. "And how you'd be knowing that, I fear to ask."

"Then don't. What happened thousands of miles away is past and gone. Just be happy I have the knowledge to purchase something appropriate for my lady wife."

"Very well." She touched her finger to the top of the bottle and made to dab it on her wrist.

"No." He stopped her. "Not your wrists. Behind your ears. Just a touch."

"My, my." She fluttered her eyelashes as she did as he suggested. "Your knowledge of scent and where ladies should apply it is amazing, Mr. Wallace. Too bad your cleverness doesn't include how to run mills."

"Ah, but now that's taken care of." He fetched his cup and sat down in the rocker opposite her. "My friend Brodie is one of the best millwrights you'll find anywhere. He'll have your mills humming like never before."

"Ah, yes, your friend Brodie MacMillan. Strange he would show up here looking for you, all the way from Scotland." She eyed him suspiciously. "Almost as if it had been by some preconceived plan."

"In a way it was." He took a drink and leaned back comfortably. "Back in the Old Country, Brodie and I heard about this village called Riverhaven, a place whose name suggested sanctuary. Sometimes, when we were in our cups, we'd talk of going there someday, of making a life in this new land. It was only logical that Brodie would follow me here."

"But why now? Why would you not come together? Why…"

"Enough questions for one night." He stood and rotated his shoulders. "I've had a long drive today. I'll be off to bed. Good night, Mrs. Wallace." He bent and planted a kiss on the top of her head. "At the moment you not only look like an angel in that dress, you smell like a piece of heaven. That's too much temptation for a man to bear."

He strode into his small cubicle and pulled the curtain shut.

Bloody hell, how long can a man be expected to live in the same house with such a woman and continue the habits of a monk?

****

"Hamish!" He came out of deep sleep to hear his name being hissed through the open window above his bed. It was a warm night, and he'd left it open.

"Brodie?" He struggled up on an elbow.

"Aye. Pull on your britches and come out here."

Soon Harry, dressed in boots, pants, and shirt, had joined his friend in the moonlit dooryard.

"Whit the hell do ye want?" Still dazed by sleep, he lapsed into his brogue.

"Come on down to the ice house." He slapped his friend on the back. "I've a wee surprise."

Inside the structure, Brodie waited until their eyes had adapted to the darkness, then led Harry to the back. He brushed aside a thick layer of sawdust to reveal two sacks.

"Whit…?" Harry stared as his companion bent,

opened one, and held up a bottle.

"The finest malt whiskey you'll find anywhere," he said proudly. "Two sacks full, carefully wrapped in horse blankets to keep from breaking."

"You didn't bring these with you. You barely had more than the clothes on your back and that fiddle. Brodie"—his voice dropped apprehensively—"you didn't take to your old ways? We always said when we got here, no more."

"Aw, just for a weak moment, Harry. Just as a small recompense. Here, take a swig." He opened a bottle and handed it to his friend.

Harry hesitated, then took a hearty drink. "I have a feeling I'll be needin' it. Now, how did you come by this bounty?"

"I took a wee ride to that monstrous big house on the edge of the village, the house I learned on my arrival belonged to the illustrious Joseph Carmody." He accepted the bottle back from Harry and helped himself to a generous quaff before continuing. "I didn't feel we should let the incidents of today pass without some reparations. So I eased myself into the manor and raided the pantry of the best of the man's brandy, wine, and whiskey. Then I took myself out to the barn and released a rather rude-mannered grey stallion and a pair of carriage horses. And somehow his two fine milkin' cows managed to escape and get into his kitchen garden. After that, I lighted a wee fire against the door of the man's ice house. Oh, not enough to burn it down, just enough to signal he'd been robbed, and melt some of his precious ice."

"Sweet Jesus, Brodie! The man's the local magistrate! He'll be arrestin' us at dawn!"

"On what evidence? Have you forgotten so quickly, Hamish, we're experts at coverin' our tracks, at leavin' not a trace? In fact, I left proof that someone else was responsible."

"Who? How?" Harry accepted the bottle back into his hand and took another swig.

"This afternoon when those useless bastards tried to run down your wee on', one of them must have dropped his knife, the initials M K carved into the bone handle. I found it on my way to the barn. I left it on the pantry floor." His tone implied he was grinning.

Harry couldn't resist joining in his humor. Although he doubted Joseph Carmody would believe his right-hand man responsible, certainly it was a trick worthy of Highland Harry and Brazen Brodie at their best.

"Aye, well, you got away with this once, but niver, niver, do it again, agreed?" he forced himself to sound severe. "This is a new land and a new start. We won't be resortin' to thievin' again, no matter what."

"Aw, Hamish…"

"Brodie, respectability means the world to Margaret." Sincerity deepened his voice. "Promise."

"Aye, well, if it means so much to you and your lass, Hamish, I promise. But, damn, it felt good…takin' stuff from a bastard like that…like we used to do."

"I'd best be gettin' back to the house." Harry handed him the bottle and turned to leave the ice house, but paused. "By the way, how did you know I'd be sleeping in that little room and not with my wife?"

"It was in your eyes, brother." Brodie leaned against a beam. "When you danced with the lassie. All the unfulfilled longin' stood out clear as day. And"—

his caring tone turned to humor—"I saw your trunk in that cubbyhole. It wasn't hard to figure out."

Chapter Sixteen

Harry turned as James nudged him. The whine of the saws and rush of water made verbal communication next to impossible in the mill. His eldest son jerked his head toward the mill yard. With a sinking feeling, he saw Joseph Carmody, with his usual companions, by the sawdust pile. Although the entrepreneur's hat was pulled well down over his forehead, Harry had no trouble recognizing the scowl disfiguring the man's face or understanding the reason for the visit. The big man was mounted on a nondescript brown mare, too small for her rider. Apparently the grey stallion hadn't yet returned home or been found.

He heaved a sigh, signaled to Brodie and his sons to shut down the operation, and headed out to face whatever the man had in store for him. After Brodie's actions in the night, he'd been expecting the visit but had been hoping against hope it wouldn't happen.

"Wallace, I've come with a warrant to search your premises." Joseph Carmody wasted no words in greeting. He pulled a paper from his coat pocket and waved it in Harry's direction.

"On what grounds?" Harry walked up to the man and stood at his stirrup. Confront an enemy dead on. Never let him see the least hint of fear or retreat.

"On the grounds that someone robbed my house and barn last night." Outrage colored his words. "On the grounds that I strongly suspect either you or your friend"—he indicated Brodie—"guilty of the offense." He looked at the four young men standing back, watching silently. "I can't seriously suspect your boys. This was the work of well-seasoned blackguards, and both of you fit the description."

"Although I resent your accusation, I won't protest." Harry stepped back and spread out an arm to indicate the mills and farm. "Search away, but bother my wife and daughters and, by God, you'll know what retaliation really means."

"You're a bold bastard, I'll give you that, but if I find so much as a single bottle of my liquor here, be prepared to find yourself in my jail cell awaiting transport to a more permanent institution. Michael, take the house. The rest of you, spread out and search the barn and mills."

****

"Harry, what—" Maggie started as Michael Kelly strode into the house where she was making pies with the three girls. Her husband followed, close on the man's heels.

"This lad has a warrant issued by Joseph Carmody to search our home, Maggie." He scooped up Eppie and drew the other two girls to his side with his free arm. "Let him do it. He's under the misguided impression that we robbed Mr. Carmody in the night and are hiding the booty."

"Robbed?" His gut tightened as he saw Maggie's expression turn bellicose. *Don't, Margaret, don't. Just let the bastard have his way.*

"Yes. But once he's had a good look around he'll realize how very wrong he is." He shot her a warning look.

"Search." She shrugged and spread out her floury hands. Relieved, he saw that she got the meaning and intended to follow his lead. "We've nothing here that isn't our property."

"Fine." Michael Kelly began to rummage through the cupboards, flinging wooden dishes and tin mugs to the floor.

Harry could only be glad they had no fine china.

****

As they rode away an hour later, Harry stood by Brodie's side in the mill yard and watched them go.

"Old bastard," Brodie muttered.

"I was just about to call you the same…without the 'old' in front of it." Harry swung on his friend. "Sweet Jesus, Brodie, they tore the place apart. We're just lucky they overlooked the ice house."

"Stupid buggers. They think anything of value has to be in the house or barn. At any rate, I suspected they'd come today, so I moved the booty to a hiding place down by the river."

"Aye, well, they made a right mess of the house. The barn I haven't seen yet. So now I'd suggest you get yourself on up there and help Margaret and the girls set things to rights. And"—he lowered his voice so the boys heading up the hill to survey the damage couldn't hear them—"you're never, never, never to let the family know what you've done."

"Do you think I'd be so daft? Bloody hell, Harry!"

He turned and started up the hill, but Harry caught him by an arm.

"And you're to promise me you'll never do anything so daft again."

142

His only reply was a shrug, and a quirk of his friend's mouth.

Chapter Seventeen

"Angel mine, you must try not to do that." Maggie knelt and gently took the finger from Eppie's mouth. She and the little girl were alone in the kitchen the following morning, all the others having gone about their tasks. The child's face began to contort, ready to cry, but Precious shuffled up to her, and in a moment both her arms were about the animal's neck.

"Maybe you can break that habit." Maggie spoke to Precious as she looked down at the pair, hands on her hips. "At least when she's hugging you, she can't do it."

She was placing a plate of scones on the table when Brodie MacMillan stepped inside, whistling. He broke off short when he saw Eppie sitting on a hand-hooked rug near the hearth, Precious in her arms.

"Hello." His handsome face broke into a broad grin. "What have we here? Two pretty ladies?" He moved closer, hunkered down in front of them, and held out a hand. Precious stuck her snout into the offering. "Ah, good little piglet," he said softly, and scratched the animal behind an ear. Precious responded with a sighing grunt. Eppie took her thumb from her mouth, and the tension in her small face slid away. Maggie watched, afraid to let the delight she was feeling overwhelm her.

"Do you think your mother would be allowin' us a

couple of those fine scones she's just baked?" A gentle smile lighted up his face as he took the chair at the end of the table. "If ya think she might, I'll head back outside and wash up. I've been seein' to the horses' hooves, and my hands could use a cleanin'. Your good man has given me a bit of leave from the mill to tend to the job," he finished, addressing Maggie.

"I'm sure there's a few to spare with our farrier." She smiled over at the man. "Tell me, Brodie, is there nothing to which you cannot turn your hand?"

"Aye, a great many things." He stood and slanted her a surprisingly shy grin. "I've no fine manners like Harry can demonstrate when needs be."

"A skill that is, but scantily needed in this country. I think knowing the work of a millwright and that of a blacksmith much more important."

"Aye, well, perhaps. But when it comes to wooing the ladies…" He broke off, ducked his head, and headed out the door. "I'd best be washing up before you change your mind about sharing some of those scones with me."

The door banged behind him. Maggie was left to ponder his words, words he had left unfinished. What had he been about to say? That Harry had been skilled at wooing the ladies? If so, who? And had there been more than one? And—oh, bloody hell, what did it matter? They weren't truly married. It little mattered to her, did it?

****

"If you'd care to climb up on my knee, I'll be happy to share one of these lovely scones with you and your pretty friend." Brodie had come back inside, the extent of his ablutions obvious in the damp curls on his forehead. Seated at the end of the table, he addressed Eppie.

Maggie bit back the comment that they didn't feed Precious from the table. This moment was too important, could be too easily broken.

He held out welcoming hands to assist the child, who hesitated, then raised her arms that he might pick her up.

"Well, there now, lassie." He settled her comfortably on his knee and broke a scone in two. "Which wee piece do you think your friend would like? One with butter or one without?"

Again a hesitation, but this time a shorter one before a small hand pointed to the butter dish in the middle of the table.

"I agree." Brodie MacMillan balanced the child on his knee, buttered the biscuit piece, and offered it to Pig, who, like her mistress, hesitated only briefly before taking it and munching contentedly.

"Now we'll just be buttering the rest for us, don't you think?" His arms reached around the little girl and past her to take up the second piece and smear it with the buttery knife. After she'd accepted it and was chewing contentedly, he broke another scone apart, prepared it in a similar fashion, and popped a section into his own mouth. He made an exaggerated display of smacking his lips.

Maggie's heart skipped a beat as Eppie for the first time since she'd known her, for the first time since her mother's death, Maggie suspected, let a shy little smile tremble on her lips. No matter who this man really was or what his past, Brodie MacMillan had a way with children, and no mistaking.

"Now I'd best be gettin' back to the barn. Thank you for the scone, Mrs. Wallace. Delicious." He gave Eppie a quick kiss on the forehead before placing her on the floor and standing.

"Mr. MacMillan?" His name stopped him at the door.

"Aye?"

"My name is Maggie. Harry calls me Margaret, so take your pick, but I'd like you to call me by a Christian name."

"Verrae well." He grinned. "If my friend chooses to call you Margaret, then so shall I. And I'd be honored if you'd dispense with the 'Mr. MacMillan' and call me Brodie."

"Brodie it is. I'll be seeing you at dinner…Brodie."

He touched his forelock and went whistling.

He appeared a happy man on the surface, but Maggie couldn't help feeling there was a deep and abiding sadness behind those keen eyes. When the moment was right, she'd ask Harry.

Chapter Eighteen

"Tomorrow being Sunday, we'll be heading to the kirk." Harry made the announcement at the breakfast the following Saturday, then glanced around the table to catch the reaction. "I've a desire to hear this new minister preach."

He saw Brodie seated at the end of the girls' bench, Eppie by his side, duck his head and return to his oatmeal. He wouldn't press him on the matter. He understood. Furthermore, he hadn't explained about Lachlan and Iona. He preferred to save that for a surprise when they could meet face to face.

"Mr. Wallace." Maggie addressed him. "A word, please." She stood and headed for the back door. With her hand on the bar, she paused and looked back, raising her eyebrows when he hesitated.

"Of course." With a sigh and a shrug, he stood and followed her outside.

"Harry, I know your idea is well intentioned and that the children should go to church," she began, once they were far enough from the door not to be overheard. "But…" She paused and looked off toward the barn, fingers rubbing the folds of her woolen work dress.

"But?"

"I took them the week after their father died." She returned her gaze to him, emerald eyes filled with pain. "The minister and the congregation… That is, we were, in fact, shunned. No one acknowledged our presence, and when I tried to approach people, they turned their backs on me. Harry, they view me as an opportunist, a tavern wench who married a man with considerable holdings and then…"

"And then?" he pressed as she once again looked away.

"Killed him." She swung back on him, pain coloring her expression to such an extent it made him hurt with rage for her.

"Bloody hell, how could anyone think such an outrage? You took on the care of this lot as few women would! I cannot believe people would…"

"Harry." She placed a gentle hand on his arm. "We can't change what people think. We must just learn to live with it as best we can."

"Hell and damnation, no, we won't!" He caught her by the shoulders and swung her to face him full on. "My wife and children are respectable members of this community. We'll all go to church and be accepted, you wait and see. This new minister is cut from a very different length of clerical cloth." His words softened over the last sentence. "And where the bellwether leads, the flock follows. Now come along." He caught her by a hand and began to draw her back toward the door. "There's a lot to do to be ready for the morrow. There's clothing to prepare, children to bathe, horses and harness to clean… The Wallaces will arrive in all their glory at the kirk on the Sabbath, and no mistake."

She pulled back for a moment. Then, as he turned to look at her, he saw a smile slide slowly across her lips. "Verrae well, laddie," she aped his Highland accent. "We'll put on a fine show, dunnae be afeerd."

The mill fell silent as the day turned into a turmoil of bathing and clothes preparation. Harry's room was turned into a bath house as buckets of water were heated on the hearth and carried behind the curtain for each of the children to bathe. In the main room, Maggie, Bella, and Lizzie smoothed wrinkles from the finery Harry had brought.

Just before noon, Harry decided he'd never have an opportunity to use the tub. Gathering up a piece of soap and a length of toweling, he headed down the hill. Beneath the bridge, hidden from the house, he doffed his clothing and waded into the waist-deep water barely moving now that the great wheel had been shut down. He ducked his head and came up, blowing water as he rubbed soap into his hair.

Ten minutes later he waded ashore and stood for a moment letting the breeze and May sunshine dry his naked body. Feeling strong in body and refreshed in spirit, he began to sing a Gaelic song he'd learned as a lad.

"Harry..." Her voice made him turn full on to face her as she came down the bank behind him.

For a moment they stood staring at each other. Then she swung away, confusion obvious in her bowed head, her faltering speech.

"I...I'm sorry," she stammered. "The boys said they saw you leaving the dooryard and heading toward the mill. Then I heard you singing, and..."

"No need to apologize, Margaret." Picking up his shirt, the irony of her embarrassment struck him. "We are, for all appearances, man and wife. What was it you were wanting?"

The last held a slight teasing he couldn't resist.

"Dinner. Dinner is on the table, if you've a mind to come." Grasping up her grey skirts, she scrambled up the incline to the path leading to the house.

Harry chuckled. Then, as he bent to pick up his undertrousers, a groan replaced his mirth as he saw his body. Fresh from the ice-cold water of the pond, he was hardly an inspiring sight.

Chapter Nineteen

"Ye've got a fair to middlin' gloss on that harness, laddie." Harry walked into the barn after the noon meal to find Brodie brushing down Prince with vigor. He paused to admire the gleaming leather straps and brass. "As fine an oilin' job as ever I've seen. And I've never seen that mare looking better." He ran a hand over Bonnie's sleek, glossy coat.

"You said you wanted your family to shine at church tomorrow." The millwright paused and leaned against the gelding's rump.

"Aye, well, yes." He crossed his arms on his chest. "It's important to Margaret."

"Your blushing bride. She is a beauty." Brodie put a hand in the centre of the horse's haunches and pivoted around behind the animal's hindquarters to face his friend.

"Aye, well, she may be blushing just a wee bit more than usual right now."

"Bloody hell, man, what did you do? I know you're no stranger to women, but your wife is a country lass. Some of your skills…"

"It's not my skills that may be distressing her." He turned and walked into Scotia's stall, where he became involved in removing a tangle from her mane.

"Well, what then? You're not totally ugly, you keep yourself reasonably clean, and God knows you can lay on the blarney when..." Brodie followed him and leaned over the wooden barrier at the mare's side.

"Margaret saw me naked this morning...after I'd been bathing under the bridge." He interrupted his friend's listing of his qualifications.

"And why might that deter... Bathing under the bridge you say? In ice-cold water?"

"Aye."

"And you turned to face her?"

"Not intentionally. I came out of the water and...she was there."

Brodie stared at him for a moment, then burst out laughing, finally doubling over in his mirth. When he got control of himself, he managed to choke out, "I'm taking it your charms had been severely diminished?"

"God damn it, you great fool, of course! And she saw it...all."

"Ah, hell, lad, I'm sure she'd be willing to give you a go anyway. She's young and inexperienced and probably wasn't even aware of your...shortcomings." Then he sobered. "Any road, didn't you tell me you'd agreed to a marriage in name only?"

"Things have changed." He came out of Scotia's stall and faced his friend. "I'm thinking I want to make this a real marriage, to be a real father to all those bairns, to stay and help them run the farm and mills."

"Then forget about what just happened." Brodie clapped a hand on his shoulder. "And get on with courting her."

"Courting? Brodie, I wouldn't know where to start."

"Buggar all, Hamish, you've seduced women for years. It was part of your work. Just apply your charms this time and mean it."

"Mean it?"

"Let your heart take charge." He turned to go back to his job of grooming the Clydesdale. "I'm sure Margaret, for all her innocence, is woman enough of the world to know that in a nice warm bed things can blossom." He glanced back over his shoulder at his friend, wiggling an eyebrow, eyes twinkling.

"Argh!" Harry guffawed and strode out of the barn, leaving Brodie grinning and whistling.

****

The first Sunday morning in June dawned bright and clear, with a tender breeze and warmth that boded well of approaching summer weather. Harry, in his best clothing, waited patiently in the driver's seat of the wagon while the children, one by one, each in their new clothing and looking as if they'd been scrubbed to within an inch of their lives, climbed aboard. The team with their well-groomed coats and cleaned harness made a handsome pair, even if they weren't carriage horses and they were pulling a work-worn farm wagon.

Then Maggie stepped out of the house, and his breath caught in his throat. She paused for a moment on the back doorstep, Eppie by her side, to open the frilly green parasol he'd bought to match the green dress she saved for special occasions. Her chestnut hair, peeking out from beneath a straw bonnet trimmed with emerald ribbons, curled softly against her cheeks.

She took Eppie by the hand, the little girl looking like a china doll in her frilly pink dress and little satin slippers. The only flaw in the perfection of the picture mother and daughter presented was Precious the Pig standing beside the child, pink bow and leash neatly in place.

But it wasn't really a flaw, was it? Harry quirked a grin. Somehow he couldn't imagine his life without seven children, a beautiful wife, a pet pig, and—he glanced at Brodie adjusting the team's harness—a man who was his brother in all but blood.

"Margaret, you're looking more than beautiful this fine day." Brodie came from the horses' heads as she crossed the yard to the wagon. He lifted her up to join Harry. "Harry, you're one lucky devil."

"That comes as no surprise, my friend. I'm not blind."

"Are you sure you won't come with us?" Maggie, from the seat beside Harry, looked down at him, concern furrowing her forehead.

"Someone has to mind the place, Margaret." He grinned. "Dunnae greet. I'll do well with a bit of peace and quiet."

"If you're certain."

"Certain sure."

He picked Eppie up and carried her to the back where the other children waited, Precious trotting along beside them. There he hoisted first the little girl and then the pig into place and stood back, a grin on his face.

"Ye're the right picture of a fine family," he said.

"Brodie…" Harry understood the effort all this must be costing his friend.

"Move along, Harry, move along." Brodie waved them away. "You'll find the place safe and sound when you return."

"I want to make an announcement before we go." Harry swiveled on the seat to address the children.

"Brodie MacMillan has been my brother in all but blood for some time now. Therefore, I will be grateful if, from now on, you'll address him as Uncle Brodie."

Brodie's lips twitched as he batted his eyelids. "Right kind of you, Harry," he muttered. He turned to the children. "And you lot. I'd be honored to be called your uncle…if you'll have me as such."

"Well, then, good. Dusted and done." Harry flapped the reins over the backs of the horses and headed them down the hill. "Farewell, Uncle Brodie. We'll be home at noon and expecting you to have a meal on the table."

****

As Harry turned the team into the churchyard, he couldn't help wondering what kind of reception he, Maggie, and their unusual family would meet. Sitting up proud and straight beside him, she was the most beautiful woman he'd ever seen. Behind him, seven children sat on the board seats along both sides of the conveyance, Pig on the floor between them. How they planned to get Eppie to go into the church without the little creature he couldn't imagine, but he'd leave that up to his wife. She seemed to have a way with everything regarding the children.

Aware of the stares they were attracting, he drove his team to a shaded place beneath the pine trees that surrounded the small church, jumped down to tie them, then assisted Maggie to the ground. One by one the children followed, all but Eppie, who was too small to master the distance. Harry strode to assist her and found her waiting, Pig clutched to her side.

"Pig can't come into church, darlin'," he tried to be gentle as he faced stubborn blue eyes and a protruding lip. She shrugged away from his reaching hands. "She can stay here with Bonnie and Prince. She'll be fine."

He reached out again, only to be met with a shriek of defiance as she backed beyond his reach.

"It's all right, sweetheart." Maggie was by his side. "You can bring Precious."

"Bloody he—" he began.

"Harry, please watch your language in front of the children." Maggie lifted first the pig and then the child to the ground. "Come along, Eppie dear," she said, handing the pink ribbon leash to the little girl.

He hesitated, staring after his wife as she walked, shoulders back, head held high, with the little girl and the waddling pig toward the church, the rest of the children strung out behind them. His mouth quirked as he shook his head ruefully and followed.

Good God!

****

If he'd thought Maggie would shepherd her family unobtrusively into one of the back pews, he was sadly mistaken. Instead, she marched up the aisle to the bench at the front of the church and preceded the children down its length to settle herself at the far end. The girls and Precious managed to fit into the pew with her, but Harry and the boys had to take the seat behind them.

Murmurs from the other parishioners came to his ears, a mixture of surprise and dismay, he gathered. Maggie must be hearing some of the remarks, because she sat up stiff and proud, focusing her gaze on the altar. Harry stifled a grin. *It will take a lot more than a bunch of catty old biddies to deter his lady.*

Edward Morgan entered the front of the church and took his place on the raised platform. After a brief introductory prayer, he took a pair of spectacles from his pocket, adjusted them on his nose, looked down on the newest members of his congregation seated directly in front of him, and cast a welcoming smile over them.

"Members of my flock, this morning I want you to join me in welcoming a miraculously formed family to our midst…the family of Harry and Margaret Wallace. They've chosen to take on the laudable task of raising William and Jane Fowler's seven children. We must all support them in any way that we can. God bless you both, Harry and Margaret, and of course your family." He smiled down at them again, this time over his eyeglasses, directly at the pig. "Which of course includes the four-legged members."

Precious chose that moment to snort and snuffle.

"You're very welcome, Miss Piglet." The clergyman was all out grinning now and, catching Harry's eye, winked. "Now let us proceed with the service with the singing of a favorite hymn, 'God, You have brought us to this place.'" The minister again looked over his spectacles, but this time it was at Harry. "It will hold special significance for some of us."

Harry wet his lips as he stood with the congregation and returned Edward Morgan's gaze with a rueful glance. Halfway through the first verse, his attention strayed to the back of Maggie's head, to her slender neck with soft curls escaping beneath her bonnet. A sensation struck with such a force that for a moment he nearly staggered. It enveloped him like a warm bath, a perfect summer day, a dram of Scotland's best whiskey, and a whole lot more he couldn't begin to describe. As she half-turned in his direction to quiet a squirming Eppie and he saw her in profile, the realization of what it was hit him like a lightning bolt.

Sweet Jesus, I love her! Bloody hell! After all these years of romancing English ladies, I'm in love...with the mother of seven children. Good God, it feels...I don't know...wonderful and terrifying and...all I want to do is live with it forever.

Overwhelmed, he stared at her in amazement. She must have sensed his gaze, because she glanced back at him and smiled before returning her attention to Eppie and the singing. A surge of happiness such as he'd never before experienced rushed through his body and soul. He loved the woman, and together they'd make a life...if she'd let him.

After the service, Edward Morgan stood at the top of the church steps, his wife Mary at his side with their child in her arms, to shake hands with the male members of the congregation as they filed out and to exchange a few words with the ladies. Harry led his family out as Maggie had ushered them in, and paused to wait for his wife as the children acknowledged the clergyman before dashing off toward their wagon.

"A fine sermon, Mr. Morgan." Harry had to struggle to suppress the twinkle he felt burgeoning in his eyes as he addressed the minister.

"Thank you, Mr. Wallace." The returned pleasantry brought a smugly wise expression over the clergyman's face. "Delighted you approve."

"Mrs. Wallace." Mary Morgan stepped forward toward Maggie and spoke loudly enough for the retreating members of the congregation to hear. "My husband and I have been remiss in not paying your family a visit. Would tomorrow afternoon be convenient?"

"It would be most convenient, Mrs. Morgan." A smile lighted up Maggie's face as she replied. "We can have tea." She glanced proudly up at Harry. "Can't we, Mr. Wallace?"

"Yes, Mrs. Wallace, you most certainly can have tea," he replied with a solemn nod, hoping his eyes weren't twinkling at her pleasure.

Let those old cows take that in to chew with their cud. The Wallace family has just been given the stamp of approval by the clergy. And now they also know we do have tea in spite of Joseph Carmody and his blockade.

As he took Maggie's arm to guide her to the wagon full of frolicking children, he saw one of the older women grasp her husband's arm and pull him away from where he'd been staring at the newly accepted Mrs. Wallace. A shaft of jealous pride shot through him.

Damn, but I have a beautiful wife. Let the old bugger drool.

****

"Lachlan." As James loaded the family aboard the wagon for the return trip to the farm, Harry went back to the church, to where the minister stood alone on the steps watching his congregation depart.

"Edward…Edward Morgan," the minister corrected him. "What can I do for you, Mr. Wallace?"

"Bloody hell, if that's what you want." Confusion made him snap at the clergyman. "Mr. Morgan, then. A strange thing just happened to me. It came over me like a great wave during the service as I chanced to look at my wife. I feel the desire to share it with someone I trust."

"Oh, yes? A huge chill, a major belly ache, a seizure of gout?"

"Aye, make sport of me." Catching the teasing gleam in the other man's eyes, Harry felt instantly foolish.

"No, no, of course not, Mr. Wallace. Please go on."

"I…suddenly knew I loved my wife."

"Ah, you had an epiphany…like Saint Paul on the road to Damascus."

"Aye, perhaps something like that. But you've no need to go talkin' like a biblical scholar."

"I do when it's a spiritual moment one of my parishioners is describing and asking my advice about."

"And your words of wisdom would be?"

"Get down on your knees at the first opportunity and thank the Almighty. There's many a man would give much to be in your place." He placed a hand on Harry's shoulder. "Now go and drive your family home. Rejoice in the wonderful revelation our Lord has seen fit to bestow upon you."

"I'm not a religious man, Lachlan. You know that. I don't believe in miracles and the like."

"Aw, yes. The old Calvinist belief in the Lord helping those who help themselves and all that type of thing. Very well, then. Just be thankful to whatever force in the universe saw fit to give you a wonderful woman like Margaret Wallace, and act accordingly."

As Harry drove home, he had to struggle to avoid glancing over at his wife. He loved her. But had he any right to expect her to care for him in return? They'd struck a bargain, a business arrangement, in fact. He couldn't tell her how he felt. He couldn't go mucking up what he'd agreed to. She deserved better than an outlaw for a husband. The thought made something inside sink like a stone and lodge deep in his gut. No, he had no right to expect her to care for him as anything more than a helpmate and protector.

****

Maggie came down the stairs after making certain the girls had hung their new dresses up properly and tidied their bedroom. She found the table cleared of dinner dishes and the children seated on both sides, slates and pieces of chalk before each of them. Most surprising of all, Harry sat in his place at the head wearing *spectacles.*

"Please." He held out a hand to indicate her usual place at the end of the table. "Lessons are about to begin. Since we don't work on the Sabbath, it's an excellent opportunity. I brought back from my recent purchasing expedition the means to get some learning done."

She glanced from her husband to Brodie rocking by the fire, an amused grin on his face. He nodded and also indicated her place. "Best take a seat, Mrs. Wallace. The schoolmaster is about to begin his lessons, and I don't think he'll tolerate tardiness."

Still in a state of surprise, she sat down as Harry stood and went to several slates fastened together and propped against the dresser. On them were a series of markings she recognized as letters—not words, she guessed, just letters.

"Now, let's begin." Harry, his white shirt open at the throat, looked deadly serious, even if those spectacles made Maggie want to chuckle. "Brodie has put these slates together to form what is known as a blackboard. It was invented in Scotland in 1801 by

James Pillans, only one of many helpful items devised by our people. Take pride in the fact. On this blackboard, I've put letters—the letters of the alphabet. I want you to try copying them, one at a time. It's important. They're the basis of your learning to read. All of you." The last three words carried a command as Samuel squirmed on his bench.

There was a slight rustle of something Maggie branded discontent. Sunday afternoons had always been free time for children who worked hard all week. This wasn't their idea of playing or relaxing.

She looked down their ranks and hope trickled into her heart. Robert was staring at the letters, his brow furrowed in concentration. Pulling in a deep breath, she recognized interest. One captured by learning, only six more to go. Well, two, she decided on reflection. Margaret Wallace definitely wanted to become literate, as well.

****

"Why do you call your horse Fox, Uncle Brodie?" Samuel asked. He was an ardent equine fancier and spent every spare minute with the horses, Midnight in particular.

It was beautifully warm after supper that evening. The family had gathered on the front veranda, the children seated on the steps and railings, Maggie and Harry in the rocking chairs they'd brought out from beside the hearth.

"Well, laddie, he's clever as a fox and just about as swift. There's not a whole lot he can't do…if I ask him just so." He grinned down into the boy's bright interest. "Watch this." He straightened up from where he'd been leaning against a post and walked to the bottom of the steps, Samuel by his side. Putting two fingers to his lips, he emitted a sharp, clear whistle.

Within seconds the stallion, which had been confined in the pasture behind the barn, came thundering across the yard to join them.

"Bloody hell!" Samuel's words of astonishment burst out. "Mother, Father, you should have seen him clear the pasture gate…like he was flying!"

"Samuel Fowler, mind your tongue!" Maggie was quick to reprimand and shoot an accusatory glance at Harry. "You must not go repeating everything you hear in the mill yard."

Harry shrugged, a grin curling his lips. His mouth formed the word "sorry" toward her, and then he turned to watch Samuel and Brodie petting Fox Fire as the stallion nuzzled the man.

"Can you teach me to ride like you, Uncle Brodie?" The boy rubbed the horse's nose. He looked up at the man, eyes bright. "I want to be able to jump fences and streams and go fast as the wind."

"Aw, now there, laddie, there you must appeal to your father." Brodie looked up at Harry, eyes crinkling at the edges in good humor. "No one in all the Highlands could ride like your father. He and Scotia could outrun the wind, it was said."

"Father?" Samuel looked up at Harry. "Will you?"

"Surely, laddie, surely. But first we'll have to teach Midnight some tricks. Scotia and the Fox have had a lot of training. It takes time and patience. Do you think you have a fair share of both?"

"Yes. I'll work as long as it takes. I want to be like you and Uncle Brodie. Show me what Scotia can do…please?"

Glancing over at Maggie, Harry saw first pleasure, then apprehension wash over her expression in fast succession. He understood.

"Not tonight," he said. "We'll have no fighting horse displays on the Sabbath. Tomorrow evening will be time enough."

He glanced over at Maggie. She gave him a nod and smile of approval.

Chapter Twenty

Harry came into the house the following afternoon to find a white embroidered cloth on the plank table, neatly set with tin mugs, a milk pitcher, a bowl of sugar, and a plate of scones. Maggie, in one of the plainer dresses he'd bought her, an unadorned sunflower yellow gathered under the bosom with a ribbon of dark gold, was fussing about the room, moving furniture and dishes about.

"No need to be nervous, lassie," he said, identifying her agitation. "Everything looks just fine."

"Still." She stood back to survey the table, running her hands down her dress front. "I should like everything to be perfect. These tin mugs and wooden plates hardly seem fitting for a visit from the minister and his wife. I wish I had china cups and saucers."

"The cloth looks bonny." He stood back to admire its snowy length.

"I found it tucked away in a trunk in the girls' room." She drew a deep breath. "I assume it was part of Jane's trousseau. I don't think she'd mind my using it for such an important occasion."

Harry sat down in one of the rockers by the hearth. "This visit means a great deal to you, doesn't it?"

"Oh, my, yes!" She returned to her fussing, readjusting the dishes. "It means we've been accepted into the community, you and me and the children. It means…" She hesitated, glanced over at him, then returned to her work.

"It means?" He raised an eyebrow in question.

"It means respectability." She turned to him and paused. "Harry, you may as well know. Back in England, my father was a drunkard who lost the hovel of an inn his father had left to him. He, my mother, and I were forced to emigrate with little more than the clothes on our backs and with creditors at our heels. I don't doubt he failed to pay our full passage to the ship's captain, who probably had every right to seize our belongings on our arrival. He probably finessed the man into taking us aboard on some vague, wild promise of future payment. He could be quite convincing when it was necessary. I want never to relive those shameful days."

He'd suspected her past hadn't been an easy one, but this! In her own way, Margaret Wallace was a fugitive, too…a fugitive from degradation. The knowledge only further warmed his heart toward her.

"Well." He stood. "I'd best be heading back to the mill. Busy day. The lads need every hand on deck."

"Oh, no!" She blocked his leaving. "As the man of the house, you must be present for the minister's visit. It's only proper."

"Is it? Well, then, I'd best hie me into my room and put on my best bib and tucker." He let a smile curl his lips. *Man of the house.* It had a nice ring to it.

****

Harry repressed a smile as Maggie poured tea and handed around a plate of her carefully baked scones. She was a lady presiding for guests at her own tea table. Glancing over at Edward Morgan, balancing a small plate on his lap and a steaming mug in his right hand, Harry caught his wink and sly smile, and the moment was sullied. What was he, so-called Harry Wallace, doing, sitting here pretending to be the respectable head of a household, father of seven fine children, when he was nothing more than…

"She's so pretty." Maggie crossed the room to smile down at the Morgans' baby in her basket at her mother's feet. "You've been blessed, Mrs. Morgan."

"That we have." Mary Morgan smiled down at her little one. "I never thought I'd see the day when Edward and I would be party to such happiness. And"—she glanced up at Maggie—"I'm sure that in time you and Mr. Wallace will share a similar joy."

"Oh…yes…of course." Maggie turned and headed back to fetch the teapot on the hearth. "More tea, Mrs. Morgan?" She shot a short, furtive glance at Harry, her uneasiness obvious.

"Yes, thank you. It's a fine brew." Mary Morgan extended her cup. "It comes from an excellent blend, I reckon."

The conversation lagged.

"Mr. Morgan, how about our taking a wee stroll down to the barn and leaving the ladies to chat?" Harry stood. "I'd like you to meet our new hand."

"Certainly." Drawing a deep breath, the minister stood and placed mug and plate on the table. "Always interested in meeting a new parishioner."

As they crossed the yard, the clergyman cast a suspicious sideways glance at Harry. "Why do I get the feeling there's something unusual about this new hired man?"

"Maybe it's because I've got a roguish twinkle in

my bonny blue eyes?" Harry grinned and headed into the barn. "Anybody home?" he called out.

Brodie straightened from checking Fox Fire's hoof to confront Edward Morgan.

"Bloody hell, as I live and breathe! Brodie MacMillan!"

In three strides the two men were together, embracing, laughing.

"Brodie!" Edward Morgan's voice broke over the name when he finally held the other man out at arm's length. "Hamish told me you were dead."

"He thought I was...until I turned up on his doorstep a few days ago. Damn, Lachlan, but you look fit. Tell me, how did you come here? And what of Iona?"

****

"And now you see before you the proud father of a beautiful lassie and husband to the love of his life." Lachlan finished his story a few minutes later. "I've been blessed."

"Aye, blessed indeed." Brodie's words were soft, muted.

"Bugger all, Brodie." Lachlan Cameron's happy expression dissolved into one of pained remembrance. "I'm sorry. I shouldn't have said..."

"Forget it, laddie." Brodie turned away and went back into his horse's stall. "It was a long time ago."

"Still..."

"Enough of sad memories." Harry stepped into the void. "We're back together again and on the way to solid, respectable lives."

"Aye." Edward Morgan grinned. "What say we take a stroll down the trail along the river? We need to talk…somewhere we won't be overheard."

The three men set off down the path behind the barn to where the river returned to its normal flow after servicing the mill. Once out of sight of the farm, the clergyman sat down on a tree stump and grinned up at Harry and Brodie.

"I can't tell you how good it makes me feel to see your ugly faces again," he said.

"Aye, and yours as well, Lachlan." Harry sank to the ground beside him and clasped his arms around his knees, while Brodie leaned against a tree. "It appears we all took most seriously our half-assed plan to come to Riverhaven if things got too hot for us back home."

"Indeed we must have, seeing as how Brodie showed up here as well. It would be a grand reunion we'd have, if only…"

"If only our necks might not all fit into nooses were our true identities to become known." Harry's mouth quirked. "Even that of your beautiful Iona."

"And that would be a tragedy, to be sure, especially with our baby daughter involved. You must come and see her, Brodie…when the time is right." Lachlan Cameron glanced at the man, then down at his hands.

"I'll do that." Harry heard the catch in his friend's voice, and a sick sense of remembrance rose up through his body and soul. "When the time is right."

"Now tell me, laddie." The minister looked over at his friend. "How did you manage to escape? What happened?"

"Well, after we were set up for capture by the Lady Annabelle Spencer, we managed to get away, pursued by redcoats she'd had lying in wait for us. It was raining and snowing, the road slick, the worst night heaven ever devised." He turned his gaze up into the branches above his head for a moment before continuing. "About a mile from the manor, one of those bastards managed to hit Fox with a lucky shot. He slipped and went down. I can still hear the poor beast's screams." Brodie paused for a moment. "I thought they'd killed him. I freed myself from the saddle and dove into the trees. It was dark as pitch. I knew if I tried to run they'd find me. So I took a chance and threw myself flat on my belly under some foliage." He sucked in a deep breath. "The fates must have been on my side, because they rode right past me and continued on after Harry."

"The fates or the Guid Lord," Lachlan murmured.

"Aye, call it what you will." Brodie muttered, then went on with his story. "After they'd gone, I went back to the road and found the Fox lying on his side but still alive. I managed to get him on his feet and lead him a distance into the trees. It took time, but the gallant beast finally recovered, and we later made our way here."

"Until the day I die, I'll always hear you yellin' for me to go on, to get away." Harry lowered his head and stared at his hands. "Guid God, I should have gone back. I shouldn't have assumed…"

"It was the only thing you could think." Brodie looked over at him. "When a man's horse goes down in the pursuit, it's reasonable to believe he's doomed. I won't have you harborin' regrets on that score…or any other, brother."

"Verrae well." Harry cleared his throat and turned back to the minister. "Right now Brodie has a full-time job managing the mill and the passel of children Margaret and I have foisted upon him." He tried to lighten the moment. "We've given him the title of 'uncle' since he's become a part of this family and has always been a brother to me."

"I like it." Brodie came out of his reverie and grinned. " 'Uncle Brodie.' Aye, I like it."

"Now, tell me, how did you pair come to end up here? I thought we'd never be together again after we got separated that night."

"Believing Brodie dead and myself in serious danger of being apprehended, I gathered up my belongings and a bit of booty." Harry took up the tale. "Then Scotia and I headed for the coast and the first ship we could find headed for the safety of Riverhaven."

"You took a great chance bringing that mare with you." The clergyman leaned back and stared up through the trees dappling sunlight down on them. "She's easily identified."

"I couldn't leave the lass behind. She's saved my life so many times, waited for me in the cold and snow and rain, was wounded on two occasions."

"I understand. But, Hamish, to arrive here and take up with the widow Fowler within hours…"

"She made me an offer the moment I stepped off the ship. I had no plan, no idea of what I'd do." He cast his companion an amused, sideways glance. "I couldn't imagine there being much work for a highwayman in this country. So I decided to see what she had to offer."

"And marriage was part of it?"

"Aye. She claimed that was the only way she could be assured of my loyalty, of being certain I wouldn't take up with Joseph Carmody and his crowd. It's no true marriage, Lachlan, you know that, what with you pretending to have the power to join us in holy matrimony. Furthermore, we do not share a bed. It's purely an arrangement that at the present suits us both."

"I see." The minister steepled his fingers and looked down at them. "And Brodie, how chanced you here?"

"Once the Fox recovered, and realizing I was alone, I sat down and thought about what I should do next. Going back to continue the fight would be useless. Harry and I had been about to give it up after that one last adventure. We'd planned to go to Riverhaven as soon as it was complete. I decided that Hamish, left on his own, would head for it. A visit to the docks where we spoke of reuniting to head for the New World confirmed the fact. I learned a man of his description and with a very distinctive mare had boarded a ship bound for that destination. I followed. Now tell me of you and Iona."

Edward Morgan heaved a sigh and rubbed his boots in the moss at his feet. "Iona and I rode the hills as much outlaws as you and Hamish, you remember, Brodie. She was the best companion a man could have, brave and strong and loyal. We were careful of not getting in the family way, you understand. But then one day, a little over a year ago, she discovered she was pregnant. Although the child was unplanned, that did not mean it was unwelcome. We decided the only thing to do was to come to America, where the wee on' could be born in safety and security. Like you and Hamish, we remembered Riverhaven, and so we set out."

"And took up the identity of a clergyman."

"Aye, and took up the identity of a clergyman." He looked over at Harry. "I'm not sorry, Hamish. All those years of running before the law, of never having a roof over my head, of never being able to be a true husband to the woman I love…they're behind me now. Let the young lads take over the fight for freedom. We did our bit. More than our bit. What about you? Have you found a way of life that suits you, that will suit you for the rest of your days?"

"We should rejoin the ladies." Harry ignored the question, stood, and squinted up into the sunshine. "Margaret will be disappointed if you don't get a chance to sample more of her scones."

Chapter Twenty-One

"Father, you said you would." Samuel came to stand beside Harry as he finished his dessert of rhubarb pie.

"Said I would what, laddie?" Harry, muscles aching from a full day's work, looked up into the boy's eager face.

"Sunday evening you said you'd show us what Scotia can do, how she's trained as a fighting horse."

"You did promise." Maggie flashed him a smile as she helped Bella and Lizzie clear the table.

"Aye, that you did." Brodie threw his leg back over the bench where he'd been sitting and stood. "In fact, I think we both said we'd give a display of what our beasts can do." He grinned at Harry. "Or are you getting too old and stiff to do a bit of fancy riding after a wee day's work?"

"Wee day's work!" Harry swallowed the last of his tea and stood. "Come along, everyone. You're about to see your father and his mare make your uncle look like a lady who's never ridden except in a carriage."

Twenty minutes later, as he and Brodie put their mounts through their paces as fighting animals and obedient riding horses, Harry managed a glance at his family watching from beside the barn as the pair capered about in the field beyond the structure. For the first time, he thought he saw a glimmer of interest, maybe even respect, in the expressions of the two oldest lads. In a flurry to further impress, he directed Scotia into one of her highest leaps and kicks. The smattering of applause from the girls and Margaret didn't please him half as much as James's nod of approval.

"You're wonderful, Father!" Samuel rushed up to him when the display ended and Harry and Brodie had brought their horses to a blowing halt before their audience. "Please, oh, please say you'll teach Midnight and me to do those things."

"I'll try." Harry dismounted and patted Scotia's arched neck. "You have to realize horses are like people. Some are more athletic than others, and some shouldn't be pushed beyond their capabilities. We'll test Midnight and see what he's up to. Then we'll decide how he's to be trained. Agreed?" He held out his hand.

"Agreed." Samuel grasped it with alacrity and pumped it.

Glancing over at Maggie, he caught her subtle wink and soft smile of approval. It did a lot to soothe away the aches in his back and shoulders.

Maybe I am getting too old for fighting and all that goes with it. Maybe it's a good thing I met Margaret and decided to settle down. Bloody hell, I'm stiff. But there's more I should be teaching my lads aside from fancy riding.

The next evening he and Brodie took the oldest three boys off in the wagon. He told Maggie they were going to look over a new stand of timber for next winter's cutting, but he saw suspicion mirrored in her expression. Sometimes he feared she could look right into his soul.

Two miles from the farm, he halted the wagon, jumped down, tied the team securely to a tree, and waited until the others had joined him on the ground.

"Come here," he ordered the three young men. "Take these." He held out a pistol case to each from behind the seat. "Your uncle and I are going to teach you to shoot."

"I can shoot." James refused the offer of weapons. "I've brought down moose and deer, and more than a few birds. Father taught me."

"Aye, I've no doubt you're a dab shot with that great, antiquated musket that leans against the hearth." Harry pulled his spectacles from his pocket and began to load one of the weapons under the watchful eyes of the other boys. "But these are fighting tools. You're all old enough to help out in a fight with Joseph Carmody and his hooligans, should the need arise. To do that effectively, you have to learn to shoot a pistol. Once you're proficient, your uncle will give you a bit of instruction in using a sabre." He'd finished loading the weapon, cocked it, aimed, and fired, hitting a branch a few yards away.

"These things are only accurate at close range," he said waiting for the smoke to clear. "So you have to wait until your enemy is near. You can't afford to go wasting a shot. It takes too long to reload."

"And are Carmody and his men supposed to wait until you get your spectacles on, as well?" The corner of James's mouth lifted in a half-sneer.

"Now just a damn minute!" Brodie whirled on the lad, eyes flashing with anger.

"Easy, lad." Harry admonished his friend. "We'll get nowhere squabblin' amongst ourselves." He turned to his eldest stepson. "No, James, those blackhearts won't wait while I fumble with my spectacles. That's where you fine lads come in. As well as shooting, you'll be helping reload, a vital task in any fight."

"Do you think we'll have to fight an actual battle, Father?" Robert's face had grown pale under its tan, his eyes wide.

"I'm hoping not, son." He put a reassuring arm across the boy's shoulders. "But it's always best to be prepared. Now, James." He turned to his oldest son. "What say? Want to have a go at besting me in hitting that branch dead centre?"

"The ball goes in first, then the powder?" James began stuffing the weapon.

"Aye, and mind how much you use. You don't want to go blowing your head or hand off."

Behind James's back, Brodie grinned and made a thumbs-up signal.

"Gettin' there, Harry boy, gettin' there," he muttered into Harry's ear as he passed him on his way to instruct Robert and Geordie.

"And you're not to go telling your mother what we've been up to." Harry handed James his powder horn and spoke to all three boys. "We don't want her thinking we're about to be attacked. This is just a precautionary measure, mind."

Robert and Geordie nodded. James gave a grunt Harry hoped meant acquiescence.

****

"Where are you going?" Maggie strode across the dooryard to confront the two men mounting their saddled horses. It was late June, and the pond was devoid of logs, while stacks of squared deal and boards stood in the mill yard ready for sale. Harry was dressed in his gentleman's clothing, Brodie in a clean outfit, his sword hanging in its sheath at his side.

"We have enough lumber ready to make a cargo or more." Harry patted Scotia's neck as she cavorted, ready for a run. "We're going to Riverhaven to find a ship to transport it."

A sudden breeze caught his coat and flashed it open to expose the pistol stuck in his belt.

"You're armed." She frowned up at him. "You're expecting trouble?"

"Best to be prepared, Margaret." Brodie cast her a roguish grin as he adjusted the sword he was wearing.

"We're not leaving you unprotected." Harry calmed Scotia and brought her to a standstill. "James, Geordie!" he called, and the two young men emerged from the barn, pistols stuck in their belts. "The boys are armed and know how to use the weapons."

"No!" The word snapped out. "No, you'll not go putting our boys in the way of gunfire."

"Rest easy, Margaret." Harry looked down at her. "I've instructed the lads to shoot over the heads of the horses of anyone who threatens this place. From what I've seen, those beasts of Carmody and his crew are not accustomed to combat or gunfire. That's all it will take to send them off at a full run. We'll be back no later than midday. Ten miles for these fine animals is but a short run." He patted Scotia again, and the mare snorted and pranced.

"She's as eager to be off as Fox." Brodie grinned, swinging his dancing stallion about. "Let's give this pair the run they've been spoiling for, Ham...Harry." He stumbled over the name, headed his snorting mount down the hill, and set off at full gallop, with a war whoop, toward the bridge.

"You'll have to excuse Brodie, Margaret." Harry grinned ruefully down at her. "He can be a bit of a lad at times."

"And yet he has such a way with the children."

"Aye, well, he has a few good qualities." He touched his hat brim, then leaped his mount in pursuit.

What were these men before they arrived in Riverhaven? The question that hung in her mind once again came to the fore as she watched them vanish over the opposite hill. Good men, it appeared, ready to come to her aid and that of her family, with the ability to care for her and the children, but with mysterious pasts that had included their becoming accomplished warriors. And the wealth Harry apparently had at his disposal? Where had it come from? Why did he find it so easy to ape an aristocratic English manner of speech when he chose to? Would she ever know the answers about the man who was her husband and about his affable best friend?

Chapter Twenty-Two

At first the two men raced their horses at full gallop down the trail that led to the village of Riverhaven. They and their mounts needed this freedom. While he and Brodie might enjoy life on the farm with Margaret's family and in the mills with her stepsons, both men had been warriors, their horses accustomed to hard running and wilder times.

When they slowed first to a canter, then a trot, and finally to a walk, side by side, Brodie looked over at his friend and grinned.

"Ah, laddie, that felt guid, dinnae?"

"Aye, but we're farmers and businessmen now, mind. Once we get to Riverhaven, we must behave as such."

"Aye. No more Highland Harry or Brazen Brodie."

"We left those identities in Scotland, my friend, along with the shadow of the noose."

"And a good thing it is, too. I was getting right weary of runnin' and hidin'. Livin' with you and Margaret and the bairns and workin' in the mill has soothed my soul. Especially havin' the wee lassie about."

His voice dropped over the last sentence. Harry shot a furtive glance at him and saw his friend's head droop.

"Brodie, you know how sorry I am about Annie

and your wee on'." He brought his mount to a halt and turned to face his companion. "You know the guilt I'll always carry because of what happened to them. If you hadn't taken me in when I was wounded, if you hadn't hidden me in your mill, those soldiers never would have invaded an innocent place like your home. Small comfort that I'd left by the time of the raid. It was because of me that they came, that they threatened Annie to make her tell them where I'd gone."

"You're no more to blame than myself, Hamish." Brodie pulled his stallion to a stop, wet his dry lips, and looked across at Harry, eyes moist. "I shouldn't have ridden out on business when I knew those redcoated bastards were in the district."

"But you and Annie and the babe she was carrying were innocents. If you hadn't sheltered me…"

"Enough. It's past and done. Now we've Margaret and her brood to care for." Brodie forced a shaky grin. "Let's get on with it. Let's see if two rogues can become successful men of business."

He winked, raised one corner of his mouth in an attempt at a grin, and whirled his high-spirited horse about to send it racing off down the trail toward the village. After a moment's hesitation, Harry clucked to Scotia and sent her off in pursuit.

As they rode into the village, Harry recognized one of the ships tied up at the wharf.

"That's the vessel I arrived here aboard," he told Brodie as they halted their horses at the edge of the wharf. "I think Captain Charles Duffy is just the man we need to approach to sell our wares."

The two men walked their mounts out over the planks of the deserted pier. No loading or unloading of vessels was underway, the area denuded of lumber, the usual export of the region. At the gangplank of the *Avon Queen*, Captain Duffy sat in a chair, smoking his pipe.

"Good morning, Captain." Harry dismounted in front of him. "A fine one, is it not?"

"Well, good mornin' to you, Mr. Wallace." The captain got to his feet and held out a hand in welcome. "I hope all has gone well with you since you disembarked my vessel."

"Very well, thank you." Harry was careful to contain his Highland accent. "This is my friend Brodie MacMillan. We've come to see if you're interested in a cargo of prime lumber...planks and deal of excellent quality, cut and graded."

"You've got my attention, sir. There's been a dearth of such. It seems most of the saw mills in the area haven't yet produced enough this spring to fill a ship, and the owners aren't ready to throw their lots together to manage such. Am I to understand you have enough to warrant loading my *Queen*?"

"Aye, that we have." Brodie's enthusiasm showed in every word as he got down from his horse and came to stand beside Harry. "The Fowler mill has been workin' at full capacity, with an able-bodied crew. We're ready to haul enough finished lumber to this dock to fill the holds of your fine vessel and more."

"There's only one problem." Captain Duffy took another puff on his pipe and squinted up at the taller men in the early morning sunlight. "Joe Carmody will not allow you to load from his docks. I've been warned not to touch a single stick of Fowler lumber. But..." His weathered face creased into a cunning expression as he lowered his voice and leaned toward the two men. "There is an old dock a few miles downriver, falling into disrepair. However, a skilled mariner such as myself might just be able to bring his ship alongside. If a couple of enterprising men were to arrive there under cover of darkness tonight with a few wagonloads of prime cuttings, they might just find a vessel waiting to load. Especially," he continued, "since this old seadog owes one of them his ship and cargo."

"A couple of enterprising men will be waiting, Captain." Harry winked and nodded. "Just give them directions."

Ten minutes later, as Harry and Brodie rode back toward the farm, Brodie turned to his companion.

"Whit did the good captain mean about owin' you his ship and cargo? What were you up to durin' the voyage to this place?"

"A wee skirmish with a wee band of pirates...or privateers, as some of that lot now call themselves. Nothing worthwhile spinnin' a tale around."

"Ah. I'm puttin' the pieces together in my head. You were the only man on board who had any skill with a pistol and sword...probably with his boots and fists, as well. One good deed does deserve another. Now we'd best be gettin' back to the mill. We've a fair amount of work to do."

"I'll go with you as far as Lachlan's house." Harry put Scotia into step with Fox. "We'll be needing two wagons to haul our wares to that dock. I'll just be borrowin' his...again."

****

Harry stood on the rotting dock and watched the heavily loaded *Avon Queen* slide silently out into the river's tide. The moon was down, and in the light of the few stars still visible in the predawn hours, the ship looked more black ghost than reality. He hoped Captain Duffy wouldn't forget his order for a set of fine china. And books. Books that would help him teach the children. Especially Robert, who had shown a deep desire to learn. He'd asked Captain Duffy to try to find a copy of *Robinson Crusoe*. The boy was bound to like that adventure. Much better than dull sentences on a blackboard. And a new hunting musket for James. And a list of other items for the family who'd worked so hard to make this outgoing cargo possible.

Drawing the back of his hand across his sweating forehead, he turned to the silhouettes in the darkness behind him, three humans and two teams harnessed to a pair of wagons.

"Well done, lads," he addressed the trio of Brodie, James, and Geordie. "A good night's work."

"Aye, and with a good profit to show for it," Brodie replied. "It was right decent of Captain Duffy to pay us now. A lot of ship's masters would have made us wait until he'd sold the lot and come back."

"The man's no fool." Harry pulled in a deep breath that swelled his chest. "He knows he'll make a roarin' profit in the Old Country, what with them cryin' out for lumber just now. Furthermore, we saved him the cost of Joe Carmody's loadin' fees."

"Ye're right." Brodie's Scottish accent came out strong as he returned to the wagon he'd been driving, the one borrowed from Lachlan Cameron, and pulled a flask from beneath the seat. "I think this calls for a wee dram. Of the good stuff."

In the darkness Harry couldn't see his friend's face,

but he sensed he was grinning over the fact that the "good stuff" had come from his raid on Joseph Carmody's stock.

He pulled out the stopper and took a swig, hesitated, glanced at Harry, who gave him a slight nod, then handed it to Geordie. "Ye've worked like a man this night, lad. You deserve a drop."

Geordie glanced at Harry, then James. The former hesitated only a moment, then jerked his head in agreement.

The young man raised the flask to his lips, took a swallow, then dropped the container to his side, choking, coughing, and spitting.

"A wee sip, laddie, only a wee sip." Brodie chuckled. "Here." He handed the flask to James. "See if you can master the art."

James looked over at Harry.

"Go ahead. I'll not be tellin' ye'r mother." As James raised the flask to his mouth, Harry continued, "Just take your cue from ye'r brother and no go downin' it like well water on a hot day."

James raised the flask to his mouth and took a careful sip. He drew back, baring his teeth and sucking in his lips.

"Now." Harry rolled tired shoulders as Brodie retrieved his whiskey and took another pull before reinserting the plug. "We'd best be gettin' back. We don't want to be seen by any of Carmody's men with a pair of wagons bearin' the leavin's of loads of lumber in their beds. We may be wantin' to use this secret dockin' again."

He returned to the wagon where Bonnie and Prince waited between the traces, heads drooping.

"Ye've done well, lad and lassie." He paused to rub both horses' heads beneath their forelocks. "Ye'll be gettin' an extra servin' of oats when we get ya back home."

"Harry, you'd best smother that Highland brogue." Brodie followed Geordie aboard the other wagon and let the younger man take up the reins. "We can't ever be sure…"

"Oh, aye…yes. Best to keep that silent. James, you drive. I'm right tuckered."

"All right." His eldest son vaulted aboard and waited while Harry climbed up beside him. Then he clucked to the tired team. Turning them skillfully in the small clearing, the young man headed them down the rutted trail all but obscured by branches, the other wagon following.

"A fine night's work, lad." Harry clamped a hand on James's shoulder. "A fine night's work indeed."

"Thank you…Father." The words coming out of the pitch darkness beside him startled and delighted Harry to the bone.

Chapter Twenty-Three

Harry paused, pulled a handkerchief from his pocket, and mopped his sweating face. Bugger all, but it was hot. He looked around at the others laboring in the blistering heat of the hayfield and, in spite of his physical discomfort, felt a smile tugging at his mouth.

Bella sat on the high seat of the wagon, controlling the team, while the boys and Margaret swung scythes to harvest the crop. Harry and Brodie, like the young lads, stripped to the waist in the heat, had the task of pitching the fodder onto the conveyance. Hard work, but when it was a family chore its difficulty became bearable.

"Get back to work, ya great oaf." Brodie paused to glance over at him. The grin on his sun-bronzed face glistening with sweat belied the seriousness of his order. "There's bound to be a whale of a thunderstorm after this heat, and we want this field harvested before that happens." He looked up at the sky, at the dark clouds gathering off to the northeast, and wiped his forehead with the back of his arm. "And just look at how that great pain in the arse is actin'." He indicated Prince, who was tossing his head and pawing. "He knows there's a storm brewin'."

"Aye, aye." Harry stuffed his handkerchief back into his pocket and hefted his fork. "I'd say this load is ready for the barn. Bella, lass, you can head Bonnie and Prince back home."

"Yes, Father." With a skill he admired, she brought the big team about and started them toward the farmyard. Pride swelled his chest. All of his children were capable and clever. Not only could they master any task required, but they were making remarkable strides in the lessons he taught most evenings before they wearily made their way to bed.

"Well, Mr. Wallace, a good day's work, wouldn't you agree?" His wife had come to stand beside him in her boy's attire. She grinned up at him.

"Aye, a good day's work indeed, Mrs. Wallace. It looks as if we'll have a fair to middlin' harvest in all areas this year."

"Thanks in no small way to you and Brodie."

"Ah, lass, you could have done it without us. You and the bairns are clever and strong enough to tackle any task."

"Is that pride I'm hearing in your voice, Father?" She shot him a smug little quirking of her lips.

"Aye, that it is, Mother. Pride, pure and simple. Now, I see the boys and Brodie are well on their way back to the barn to start unloading. We'd best follow, or that oaf of a Highlander will once again be accusin' me of shirkin'."

****

They'd finished unloading the last of the hay when Lizzie, riding the pony Goldenbug at full gallop, raced up the hill. "Eppie…she's lost! I can't find her." The girl pulled the animal to a halt beside them in the barnyard, her face deathly pale.

"What do you mean?" Maggie dropped her pitchfork and whirled on her. "Isn't she in the house? Why aren't you with her? Who told you to leave her

189

alone and go riding?" Anger bubbled into her words, but Harry stepped forward and put a calming hand on her shoulder.

"Lizzie, where was Eppie the last time you saw her?" He struggled to keep his tone calm, although fear was rising like a riptide in his gut. *Joseph Carmody wouldn't dare take the child, would he? But then, he'd probably had her father murdered. Bloody hell!*

"We were in the kitchen…where you told us to stay." Terror crinkled the child's face as she stared wide-eyed up at her mother. "But it was hot, and Eppie wanted to go picking berries down by the river. She whined and cried until I said we'd go but on Goldenbug. It was too hot to walk that far."

"Oh, dear God! You didn't leave her alone by the river!" Maggie's words choked out.

"We started picking there, but the best berries were back in the woods. There were lots of big berries the farther we went, and I…kind of…forgot Eppie for a few minutes. When I looked around, she was nowhere in sight. I looked and looked." The child's voice rose in desperation. "And I called and called, but I couldn't find her and she didn't answer."

"Come on!" Harry wrenched his shirt from where he'd left it hanging on a peg on the barn door with those of the other male family members. "Brodie, you, James, and I will take our horses and ride out there. James, I'm assuming you know the way to this famous berry patch?"

"Yes, Father." He set off at a run into the barn with Brodie to get their mounts.

"Margaret, you, Samuel, Robert, Lizzie, and Geordie follow in the wagon. And when you get there, for God's sake stick together. We don't need to be searching for more than one member of this family. Bella, you stay here in case she returns. Lizzie, was Precious with Eppie?"

"No, we left her in the house. Eppie said it was too hot to bring her with us."

"Margaret, get Precious and bring her along. She may be able to pick up Eppie's scent."

"Yes, of course. Give me the reins, Bella. You'll stay here as Father instructed." Margaret climbed up beside her daughter. "We'll need to drive fast."

With a nod, the girl relinquished the reins and jumped to the ground as the boys clambered into the back.

Brodie and James strode out of the barn, moving at such a pace the three bridled but unsaddled horses they led had to break into a trot to keep up. Brodie handed Scotia's reins to Harry. He grasped a handful of her mane and vaulted aboard. The other two followed suit, then all three took off at a gallop down the hill. Margaret paused at the house to allow Geordie to fetch Precious, then followed as fast as the team, weary from a long day's work, could manage.

"Is this where you last saw her?" Harry held a prancing Scotia beside the wagon and asked Lizzie as they paused on the edge of the berry patch.

Overcome with tears, she nodded. "And that was where I met the men just before I noticed she wasn't here." She pointed to an area a few yards away.

"Men? What men?" Brodie whirled Fox about, his face blanching ashen at the child's words.

"Two men...two of the men who almost rode Eppie down in the dooryard just before you came. Bella and I saw them from the barn that day." She swallowed hard and wiped her face with the backs of her hands.

"Sweet Jesus!" Harry's expletive was a hot hiss. "What exactly did these men want? What did they say?"

"They asked if we were getting lots of berries. Then they said we shouldn't be picking here because this land belongs to Mr. Carmody."

" 'We'? They spoke as if there was more than you, but when you looked around Eppie wasn't there?" Nausea boiled in Harry's gut. "How did they know there was more than you, unless…"

"Unless they'd seen Eppie somewhere… somewhere off by herself. Bollocks!" Brodie held his stallion in place, ground pawing. "Harry, you don't think…?"

"No, no." A glance at Maggie's white face made him speak an insincere denial. "But we'll take a look over where Lizzie says those riders stopped. If we find tracks, we'll follow them…just to see if they know anything. James!" He swung on the other rider. "You ride down by the river and up along the bank. Eppie loves looking for frogs. She might just be there. Maggie, you and the rest break up into two parties and start searching around here. See what Precious can find. But mind! No one goes off on their own. We don't need to be looking for more than one person." He glanced up at the sky, alive with charcoal clouds scudding in to cover the blue of the late summer afternoon. "And be smart about it. I'd say we're about due for a thunderstorm. Come on, Brodie. Let's get to tracking before rain wipes everything out."

****

"If they've harmed a single hair on Eppie's head, I swear I'll hack them both to pieces!" Brodie rode close behind Harry as the pair followed hoofprints and broken branches left by Michael Kelly and his companion.

"I don't doubt you will, and I'll help." Harry leaned over Scotia's shoulder and studied the marks in the soft earth. "They stopped here for a bit, but I see only men's boot prints, no child's. That's encouraging."

"They could have had her tied over a saddle. They could have…"

"Shut up, Brodie! We'll find her, and if those two bastards are in any way involved in her disappearance, if they've so much as bruised her, we'll both extract fitting punishment. But until we know for certain what's happened to Eppie, we have to keep all morbid thoughts at bay. Agreed?"

"Agreed. Let's get back to tracking. I felt a drop of rain."

Urging their horses ahead, they came out onto a trail. Fifty yards ahead stood the pair they were after. They'd dismounted and were sharing a flask.

"Hah!" Brodie slapped his heels against Fox's sides and bolted forward. As he rode past the startled pair, he leaned down and grasped Michael Kelly about the throat to drag him several yards before dropping the choking, flailing man in the dirt.

"What do you think you're doing, you crazy bastard?" Kelly choked as he staggered about trying to regain his footing and his breath.

"Where's our wee lassie?" Brodie leaped to the ground to grab the man by his shirt front.

"What wee lassie?" Michael Kelly wet his lips and

stared up at him with bloodshot eyes. "I don't know what you're talking about."

"Oh, I think you do." Harry swung to the ground and seized the other man by his vest front, lifting him onto his toes. "You two found my daughters picking berries, and now one of them is missing. You'll tell me where she is, or by God I'll let my friend here have his way with you. And you know from past experience he can be a nasty piece of work when he's angry."

"Aye, he's a lunatic, this one. Near cut me in two with that sword of his." Sweat coursed down Michael Kelly's dirty, bearded face. "God in heaven, man, let me go before you strangle me!"

"If I find you've laid even a finger on that wee lassie, I'll use that sword to remove every appendage from your body." Brodie shoved the gasping man away so that he staggered and fell to his knees, clutching his throat. Harry recognized the gleam in his eyes. Brodie MacMillan was capable of carrying out that threat.

"We don't have her. We only saw one girl...about ten or eleven years old. As we were leaving, we saw her start looking around as if she'd lost something. And that's the God's honest truth." The man Harry held captive blurted, "We wouldn't hurt no child. What do you take us for?"

"Scum in the employ of Joseph Carmody, and a pair of liars." Harry flung the man away so violently he tripped and fell on his backside in the dirt. "You almost rode her into the ground in our dooryard. If we find out you've lied to us, rest assured both Brodie and I will pay you a visit. And Brodie will bring along his sword. It's razor sharp, I can assure you. Now get out of here."

"You think they told the truth?" Brodie asked as he

and Harry watched the pair scramble onto their mounts and make a hasty retreat down the trail as rain began to fall in great, splattering drops.

"Aye. They're scared to death of you and your sword."

"Aye, well, acting like a crazy man at times has its advantages. So where do we look next?"

"Back to the berry patch and see how the others have made out. Maybe Precious has found something. She has a good nose."

Rain was bucketing down when Harry and Brodie returned to the rest of the family. James had come back from an unsuccessful search of the riverbank.

"Precious didn't find anything?" Harry asked the unnecessary question.

"She started deep into the trees over there, but then the rain came and washed away the scent." Margaret put an arm over the back of the wagon seat to rub the pig's head. "She did her best, poor girl."

"What now?" James, water running down his face, held Midnight in check as thunder rumbled.

"You and the rest of the family go home. I don't want any of you getting sick from this drenching. Brodie and I will keep looking. We're accustomed to being cold and wet."

"I'm staying with you." James turned determined eyes on the two men. "She's my sister."

"Verrae well." Harry recognized the futility of arguing with the young man. "But the rest of you— home. Margaret, let Geordie handle the team. You look all in."

"Yes, Mother, let me drive." Geordie took the reins from her hands and clucked to the team. As team and passengers headed down the road, Margaret turned on the seat, her face haggard, streams of water running down from her drenched hair. She mouthed something Harry interpreted as "Please find her." He inclined his head in acquiescence.

As God is my witness, I will...or die trying.

"Come on, lads." He swung Scotia about as the first bolt of lightning cracked open the dark sky. "We've got a lot of territory to cover."

****

It was nearing midnight when the rain ceased and the storm rolled away. A sliver of a crescent moon glided out from behind the clouds, and the air turned cold. In his drenched clothing, Harry shivered and turned to his two companions, their mounts steaming from being overheated in the changing temperature.

"We'll go home and start out again at first light." Much as he hated to abandon the search even for a few hours, he could see no point in further exhausting themselves and their horses by riding through the night. "We must get dry clothes and food, and the horses need to be fed and rested."

"No!" James, shuddering with a chill, snapped the response. "Eppie is out here somewhere, cold and wet and scared. You two can go home, but I'm staying."

"Lad, your father is right." Brodie rode close to the young man and clapped a hand on his shivering shoulder. "We're going in circles right now, too worn out to search properly. We'll sleep a couple of hours, eat, get dry clothes, and head out again. It's the best plan."

James hesitated, looking Brodie squarely in the eyes. Finally, he gave a resigned shrug and turned his gelding down the trail in the direction of the farm.

A short time later, Brodie halted Fox in front of the house and stared at the wagon and team stopped at the house's back door. "Now who can that be? At this time of night."

"God knows." Harry nudged Scotia on toward the barn. "We'll find out as soon as we stable these weary beasts."

****

"Harry, James, Brodie, you're back safe." Maggie got up from where she'd been sitting in a chair by the fire blazing on the hearth, relief brightening her words. A gaunt, middle-aged man and a young woman about Maggie's age also stood from where they'd been seated at the table, steaming mugs in front of them.

"Gentlemen, I'd like you to meet Duncan Green and his daughter Morag. They found Eppie wandering near their farm just as the storm broke. She's safely asleep in her bed now. They waited until the rain abated to bring her home."

A wave of relief so intense he felt his knees weaken swept over Harry. He stepped forward to grasp Duncan Green's hand and shake it vigorously.

"Thank you, sir, a hundred thousand thank-yous," he said. "You can't imagine what this means to us."

"Oh, aye, I think I can." A grin lit up the man's leathery face. "This one here"—he indicated his daughter—"got herself lost when she was just a lass. Fair scared the daylights out of me."

"Well, then you can appreciate the sincerity of my gratitude, sir." Harry crossed the room and reached for a bottle on a shelf. "Might I be offering you a wee dram? I see Margaret has already made tea, but perhaps you'd fancy something a tad stronger?"

"I haven't had a taste of good Scotch whiskey in a dog's age. I'd enjoy it."

"Papa, you know what Mama says about…" The girl made a weak response.

"Aw, girl, your mama never minded my taking the odd sip until she got tied up with that self-righteous Lillian Gardiner. This is most welcome, sir." He grinned at Harry as he handed him a mug.

"Mr. Green, I want you to meet my oldest son James and our dear friend Brodie MacMillan." Margaret made the introductions, and the men shook hands. "Now, all three of you, go and change out of those wet clothes before you catch a chill. James, please be very quiet when you go upstairs. Eppie just now fell asleep in Lizzie's arms."

"Ye'll have to excuse us, Mr. Green." Harry grinned. "The mistress has spoken, but stay and enjoy your drink. I'll be back directly."

He turned to head for the cubicle, but out of the corner of his eye noticed Brodie staring at Morag. The girl was pretty in a shy sort of way. She had hair as black as a raven's wing, large blue eyes, and skin Harry guessed would feel as soft as down. She could have passed for a true Highland beauty. He struggled to keep a smug grin from tipping his mouth.

Well, then, isn't this a nice surprise. Brodie is coming back to the land of the living. "Brodie, man, come along. You'd best get out of those wet clothes."

"Oh, aye." Brodie brought himself back to the moment with a sheepish grin and followed Harry into the cubicle where he kept his clothes. Two weeks previous, Harry had told Maggie that Brodie knew the true state of their marriage. Seeing no further reason for the man to sleep in the barn now that he knew their secret, she had insisted Brodie move into the house and sleep by the hearth.

****

"Ye're abroad bright and early." Harry came into the shadowy barn out of the bright sunlight the following morning to find Brodie cleaning stalls.

"Aye, well, I thought the bairns and Margaret deserved to rest after the night they had. And the fields won't be dry enough to cut hay until midday, after all that rain." He threw a forkful of manure into the barrow and urged Bonnie to one side as he moved into her stall.

"Or perhaps you couldn't sleep, with visions of the fair Morag Green dancing around in your head." Harry leaned against the wall and grinned.

"Ah, ye're daft, laddie." Brodie scooped up droppings and hefted them into the barrow.

"Brodie." Harry stopped him with a hand on his shoulder. "There's no shame in it. Annie has been gone a long time now, and she wouldn't want you to spend the rest of your life acting like a wild man because you feel you buried your heart and soul with her and the wee on' on a hillside in Scotland."

"Sweet Jesus, Hamish, how can you talk so?" He drew himself to face his friend squarely, eyes bright and moist. "I loved that woman more than life itself. And the promise of a wee on'…"

He lurched away from Harry and went into Fox's stall to lean his head against the stallion's arched neck.

Harry let him have his moment, then continued softly, "Brodie, I see how you love Eppie, how you care for all my children and my wife. But that can't be enough, laddie. You need a family of your own. And," he continued, his tone lightening, "if there ever was a Highland beauty to be found outside of Scotland, Morag Green is just that. Oh, I grant she's a bit shy, and it'll likely take more charm than a raw lad like you has to offer to win her, but you can at least give it a try. I'll even give you a few courting lessons." He let teasing come into his words over the last couple of sentences.

"Courting lessons?" Brodie straightened, the beginnings of a grin on his face. "All you'd be capable of is seducing lessons!"

"Ah, well, suit yourself. I'll bet you a quart of my best whiskey you can't get the fair Morag to go for a wagon ride with you in, say, the next week or two."

"Dust off the bottle, my fine lad." Brodie came out of the stall and hit him a light punch in the shoulder. "Dust it off and get ready to pass it on. Oh, and by the way, I think it's high time you did some serious courtin' on your own. I see the way Margaret looks at you. Laddie, that lovely lass is more than ready to become your true wife."

"I'll put your suggestion under consideration." Harry turned away. "Yes, I definitely will think about it."

"You do that, and I'll get the children out of the way for a bit. A picnic, I think. Yes, for sure and certain, a picnic will do it. Just let me know when."

Chapter Twenty-Four

"Lizzie, wait." Maggie stopped the quiet girl as she finished her kitchen chores and headed out to join Bella in the barn. Alone with the child in the kitchen, Maggie knew it was time to have a talk with her.

"Lizzie…" She drew the girl to sit beside her on a bench at the table. The child's eyes were still red from crying over Eppie's loss. "Lizzie, you're not to blame for what happened. Eppie wandered off while you were involved in berry picking. It could as well have happened to me. And she's fine now, just tired. That's why she's sleeping so late."

"But she might have been hurt!" Lizzie's blue eyes were wide with the horror of the memory. "She might have drowned! She might have been eaten by a bear!"

"But none of those things happened." Maggie drew the child into her arms and let her sob out her regrets. When she felt she'd had long enough to vent her feelings, Maggie held her out from her and smiled. "Lizzie, I've been noticing. You're a fine little seamstress. There's still a bit of pink cloth left from the things Harry bought. What about making a dress for Eppie's doll? You could even fashion tiny slippers for her feet. Eppie would love having such things."

"Yes, oh, yes, Mother." The child's face brightened. "I'll do it. I will."

"But first, my darling…" Maggie stood and went

into the bedroom. She emerged with combs and a hair brush. "I'm going to fix your hair." She touched the child's tangled locks. "I've been neglecting your and Bella's training as young ladies. Starting today, we're going to remedy that."

As she was brushing the child's hair, Harry stepped into the kitchen. She smiled at him. Smiled at him from her heart. "Harry," she said.

"Margaret, Brodie has suggested taking the children on a picnic tomorrow. You and I could have a wee time to ourselves. What do you think?"

Her smile widened as she saw a sudden shyness in the handsome, confident man she'd come to love.

"I think that's a fine idea, Harry. A very fine idea."

"Well, then, guid." He ducked his head and turned to go. "I'll tell Brodie."

After he'd gone, Lizzie giggled.

"Now what's that all about, young lady?" Maggie stroked the brush through her long hair.

"Father wants to be alone with you, Mother." She put her hand over her mouth as she giggled again. "He wants to court you, Uncle Brodie said."

"Court, indeed! You mustn't take your uncle too seriously, child," she brushed aside the young girl's words, but she couldn't deny the warm gush of anticipation that had enveloped her at her husband's suggestion.

****

"Come on, you lot." Brodie, perched on the seat of the wagon, urged the children not to dally. "I told you we were going on a picnic, and so we are, so look lively. Bella and Lizzie have enough food for a small army in these baskets, the sun is shining, and the horses are champing at their bits. Climb aboard, and let's be off."

They scrambled into the wagon, James and Robert hoisting the smaller ones into place, then Precious.

"Where are we headed, Uncle Brodie?" Bella asked.

"To a magic land, far, far away," he teased. "Somewhere there are fairies, and pots of gold, and..."

"And maybe a place to swim or dabble your feet in the water." James grinned, bringing them back to earth as he jumped up beside Brodie. "Maybe even fish a bit. Now, let's go."

He looked down at Harry and Maggie standing alone in the yard, hesitated, then nodded.

Harry could only manage a weak grin in return. *Bloody hell, what am I supposed to do now? I know what they're up to, and I'm grateful, but...*

"Come on." James turned his attention back to Brodie. "Let's get this caravan on the road."

As the couple watched the heavily laden wagon drive off down the road into the woods beyond the farm, Harry, for the only time since he'd first made love to a woman years before, felt a flutter of misgivings.

What does she expect? What should I do? Bloody hell, I don't want to distress her, or...

"Harry?" She startled him by turning to him with a bright smile.

"Aye."

"Come." She took his hand and led him back toward the house.

Bloody hell. Is she telling me it's all right? That she's ready...

In the kitchen she astonished him further.

"Harry, I think it's time."

He didn't have to ask for what. But it wasn't right. That farce of a marriage with that rogue Lachlan Cameron presiding…

"Margaret, I…"

"Look, Harry." She came to stand close in front of him and gazed up at him with those bewitching emerald eyes. "We both know the reason Brodie took the children away. And I, at least, am ready to make this a true marriage…that is, if you feel the same way."

"Margaret…"

"Oh, for heaven's sake, Harry." Her smile vanished, and she swung away to stride to the cupboard. "If you don't want to, just say so. Don't stand there sputtering my name."

"It's not that I don't want to." Why were his words coming out sounding like a stranger was mouthing them? "It's just that…we decided this would be a marriage in name only, and…"

"Until such time as we both felt we were ready for more." She rounded on him angrily. "Well, I thought we were. Forgive me. I must have been mistaken."

She started for the bedroom, back stiff, head held high.

"Margaret, I *am* ready." He caught her by the arm and was appalled to see a glitter of tears in her eyes. "It's just that…"

"I'm unattractive, is that it? You find me rough and sunburned and…and a tavern girl pretending to be respectable."

"No, no, no! I find you the most beautiful woman I've ever encountered…both inside and out. And"—his voice softened—"you are the most respectable woman there ever could be."

"Then what is it?" She stared up at him. "Harry, do you have a problem? I saw you by the pond that day." She hesitated. "Would a wee dram help?"

Oh, sweet Jesus! She thinks I'm incapable.

"No, no, no, I'm fine…in that way. It was the cold water, you understand…" *Bugger all. Babbling again. Has the prospect of sex with the woman I love turned me into a blithering idiot?*

"Then I see no impediment." She took his hand. "Harry Wallace, I've fallen in love with you. Now come along."

He was lost. He could no more retreat than if he'd been bound with chains as she led him into the bedroom, as she loosened the laces at the neck of his shirt in the shadows of the chamber with curtains drawn.

Moments later, when he lay naked beside her in the wide bed with its freshly laundered covers, covers he'd seen flapping on the line the previous day, the reason for which he was only now understanding, he could only think heaven must have a lot to offer if it surpassed this moment.

"I love you, Margaret Wallace," he breathed against her hair as she ran her hand over his chest, allowing it to outline the scar along his side.

"Do you, Harry?" She looked up at him, eyes wide with what he saw was hope.

"Aye, lassie, with all my heart and soul. Let me tell you about the moment I first realized…"

But she had no plans for listening. Her mouth covered his, and what he'd demonstrated in that previous kiss she used in good measure, with a passion that aroused him to the quick.

"Oh, Harry," she breathed, sliding her hand down his body. "Oh, my, you certainly don't need a wee dram, do you."

He fingered her breast and nuzzled her neck, and was rewarded with her sharp intake of breath. *Good...good, good, good. So far I'm not doing anything too wrong.*

****

Harry surfaced an hour later as she slept against his shoulder, one arm cast across his chest, his entire body contentedly drained. He gathered her to him, to bury his face in her hair and run his hands down the sleek, damp length of her back. He'd known he loved her before that day, but he'd never known how deeply, how much she'd become his *raison d'etre*.

A soft summer's breeze floated in through the open window, drying the sweat from his body and feeling wonderfully soothing after the heat of their lovemaking. He could lie there forever with Margaret in his arms. And God help anyone who dared harm a single hair on her head. Moving aside errant curls, he planted a kiss on her forehead. If Joseph Carmody ever dared touch this woman or her family, he, Hamish Wallace, would personally see to his demise.

He ran his knuckles down her soft cheek, and she sighed in her sleep and snuggled closer. *Let Brodie and the children stay away just a while longer, please God. Give me just a little more time alone with my wife.*

Then remembrance struck him, and he flinched so hard that she stirred in his arms. She wasn't his wife, not really, not legally, not in the sight of God.

"It's nothing, lassie." He whispered into her ear.

"Go back to sleep. All is well."

With a sigh, she obeyed, and he went back to his unsettling speculations.

Damn Lachlan Cameron and his play-acting the minister. Margaret values respectability above all else. When she finds out… And, to make matters worse, I was her first. Good God!

The euphoria he'd been enjoying vanished into a roiling turmoil. There was only one thing he could do to set things right. He had to find a genuine clergyman and, if Margaret would consent after she learned the truth about Edward Morgan and Harry's failure to tell her of it, they'd be married immediately.

But where would he find a minister? Damn it, he'd have to go to Lachlan at the very first opportunity as fast as Scotia could run, and ask him where such a clergyman might be found.

****

As dusk fell, the wagon pulled by weary horses trundled into the dooryard. Harry, standing on the back doorstep, was waiting to welcome them. He hadn't confessed the true state of their marriage to Margaret. She'd been sleeping so contentedly in his arms he hadn't had the heart to spoil her repose with an upsetting truth. But when she stepped outside to join him, his arm went about her shoulders as if it had a mind of its own, a reflex born of love.

"Well, lass." He looked down at her, feeling as if his face ached with the joy of the intensity of emotion warming his chest.

"Well, laddie." She smiled up at him, the smug smile of a lover playing over her features. "It appears our children have returned."

207

"Aye, our children." His arm still about her shoulders, they walked down the steps and across to the barnyard, where James and Geordie had jumped down from the seat and were going to see to the horses while the other children, looking tired but happy, scrambled from the back.

Robert paused to lift Precious down, and then Brodie, holding a sleeping Eppie in his arms where he sat behind the driver's seat, jerked his head in a come-here motion to the waiting couple. Maggie hurried forward to take the child from him. She kissed the little girl's forehead, glanced another smile at Harry, then headed off toward the house, their youngest clutched to her breast. The younger children surrounded her, their excited voices telling of their day as she kept cautioning them not to wake their sister.

"No need to ask about your afternoon." Brodie grinned at Harry when the older boys had led wagon and team away and the two men stood alone in the soft fading light of the summer's day. "That look the lass cast you tells it all. I'm happy for you, laddie. It's high time."

He slapped Harry on the back, and Harry was startled to feel something like a blush stealing up his neck. *Bloody hell, you'd think this was my first time.* Then another thought, an epiphany of a sort, flooded through him. *Maybe it was the first time…the first time filled with respect and caring…and love.*

"Thanks, Brodie." He looked into his friend's eyes, hoping he'd see all the sincerity he felt mirrored there.

"Ah, laddie, it was nothing. I had a snappin' good time with the bairns. Your makin' me uncle to this brood has been a major gift."

"You may not be my blood brother, but your name means just that, and I'll always regard you as such. When I thought you were dead…"

Harry's voice caught, and he didn't continue.

"All past and best forgotten. Now, come. As soon as this bunch falls into their beds, I think you and me and the lassie had best share a wee dram of celebration. That is, if you dunnae think my knowing about your lovely afternoon together will embarrass her."

"Brodie, she's a clever woman. She knew the purpose of your taking the children away and was ready. Margaret Wallace is too pragmatic, too reasonable a woman to dissolve into blushes behind a fan because our best friend understands the joy we've shared. Now let's help the lads put those horses away. It looks like rain."

****

"Lachlan, wake up!" At midnight Harry stood in the pouring rain pounding on the minister's door. "Man, let me in! It's important."

"Good Lord in Heaven, what is it?" Broad chest bare, wearing only his trousers, the minister pulled open the door on the inhospitable night to face his friend.

"I need your help…now." His words echoed the desperation he was feeling as he wiped water from his wet face with the back of his hand.

"Come in, come in, laddie." The clergyman stepped aside and swept out an arm. "You're soaked to the skin. Come into the kitchen, and I'll build up the fire. But be quiet about it. I don't want you waking the wee lassie. You're not wounded again, are you?"

"No, no, nothing physical. I need your help in quite another matter." He lowered his voice and moved as quietly as he could as he followed his friend through the house.

"Sit yourself down here." His host closed the room's plank door after them, indicated one of two chairs in front of the hearth, and proceeded to add a log to the embers. "A wee dram to chase out the chill?" He went to a dresser and took down a bottle.

"Aye, aye, that would do nicely."

When flames danced before them, and they sat with mugs of whiskey in their hands, the clergyman turned to Harry.

"Now, what is so blessed important that it couldn't wait until morning...or at least until this storm had abated?"

"I slept with Margaret." The sentence came out in a heaved sigh.

"Oh, aye? And the problem is? Never tell me you fear you've made a wee on' and you don't want it. Harry, that would be a great wrong..."

"No, no, not that." Impatience made his words clipped. "You, of all people, must know what's wrong with it."

"Harry, I'm no a mind reader. And I don't intend to spend the night guessing."

"As you well know, we're not truly married. That ceremony you performed was a farce, a joke. Lachlan Cameron, posing as a clergyman, for God's sake! Now I want to make it right. Margaret deserves to be truly my wife, to be respectable."

"So it's posing you think I am, is it?" He stood and went to refresh his mug at the dresser. When he turned back to Harry, he was grinning broadly. "What do you think I was before I joined your jolly band of rogues,

Hamish Wallace? Aye. I was an ordained man of the cloth. You're as married as you can get in the eyes of the Lord."

"You, a clergyman? Sweet Jesus, Lachlan, I never would have guessed. I've seen you in battle. You fight like a warrior."

"A skill I learned as a lad and which I abandoned to become a minister. But when the redcoats came after my congregation, what could I do but revert back to the sword?"

"Bloody hell!" Harry put his elbows on his knees, mug clasped in his hands between them, and stared down into the whiskey. "Then I didn't wrong Margaret. She has been my true wife since the day we stood before you and you declared us as such."

"No, you didn't. But now that you've consummated that union, you must be doubly aware of your responsibilities. There'll be no running away from them."

"I have no intention of leaving, Lachlan." He looked up at his friend. "This is the life I want, the one woman who makes me whole."

"Delighted to hear it, Hamish. Now as soon as you've dried out, head back to your farm. Your wife will be wondering what's become of you."

The rain was abating as Harry Wallace rode back to his home. Truly his home. His wife, his true and forever wife, waited for him there, with their seven children and his best friend. Could life offer more? The only thing troubling him was whether he should tell her he'd believed their marriage false, that he'd slept with her in spite of thinking it was a sham.

He'd eased himself out of their bed that night, the

first night they'd shared it, as soon as she'd slept, as soon as the family slept, to consult Lachlan. He'd whispered something to Brodie, who'd awakened on his mattress by the hearth as he headed out of the house, something about checking on Scotia's hoof. In the light of the dying fire on the hearth, Brodie had looked at him suspiciously for a moment before rolling over to go back to sleep. He'd muttered something about the day with the children "tuckering him out."

Now as Harry put Scotia back into her stall and rubbed her dry, he struggled with the quandary before him. Back at the house, he eased himself inside, got a quizzical but brief glance from Brodie, who once more returned to sleep, and shucked his wet clothes, leaving them to dry over a rocking chair by the hearth. Then, naked, he moved quiet as a shadow back into the bedroom and slid back into bed beside his sleeping wife.

"Good God!" Her muffled exclamation startled him. "Harry, what's wrong? You're cold as ice!"

"Shhhh." He pressed a finger to her lips. "I've been out and about."

Now fully awake, she pulled herself up on one elbow. In the darkness he saw her silhouette looming over him. "Oh, yes?" She spoke in a whisper now. "And where, pray tell, have you been gallivanting off to on our wedding night?"

"Margaret, I had to see Lachlan…the man you know as Edward Morgan. He's an old friend from back in the Highlands." He lay on his back, giving her the advantage of being above him as he confessed. He'd never allowed another living soul such a position, but his wife deserved it. "I thought he was only acting the part of a clergyman. I thought we weren't truly married. And after today, I was desperate to put things right…for you, for us." He paused.

"Go on."

"Well, it seems I was mistaken. It turns out Lachlan is an ordained minister with full powers to unite us both legally and in the eyes of God. So, you see…"

"So I see you rode out into the wind and rain in a desperate attempt to make things right for us." He was astonished at the soft tone of her whispered words. "You couldn't bear to wait for morning and clear skies."

"No, I couldn't. It was too important to us, to you, Margaret. I know how you value being respectable, looking correct in the eyes of the world, and I couldn't…"

She cut off his words by leaning over him to cover his mouth with hers, to press her bed-warm body over his rain-chilled one. The depth of that kiss told him all he needed to know. Margaret Wallace loved him.

She ran her hands down his body as he held her, and she suddenly chuckled.

"Whit?"

"I think we'd best wait until you're warmed up a bit before we resume our wedding night, my love," she said. "The cold and rain hasn't enhanced your prowess as a lover, I think."

"Damn. We'll just see about that, you saucy lass. Give me a minute in your arms and see what happens."

****

"Brodie, box up that fiddle of yours. You're coming to the harvest home supper with us." Harry slapped his friend on the back as he came out of Fox's stall.

"Ah, now, Hamish, you know there's little I wouldn't do for you, but you also know how I feel about church and the like." He met his friend's look dead-on, unblinking.

"Aye, I know, but this isn't a church event. Lachlan won't be preachin'. It's just a supper, and then, as I understand, there used to be a bit of music and dancin'."

"Used to be?"

Harry suppressed a chuckle. Music and dancing. That always caught Brodie's interest.

"Aye, but not this year. Ned, the old lad who used to play the fiddle for the event, passed away last winter, and there's no one in the community who can take his place, unless..." He looked meaningfully at his companion.

"Aw, now, Hamish, lad, you do know how to tempt a man." He turned back into the stall and rubbed his horse's nose.

"Then be tempted and come along. It'll do you good, and the community will be grateful."

"But we can't go leavin' the place unguarded." He came back to face Harry, his hand resting on Fox's shining rump. "We'd be all but invitin' Joe Carmody to attack."

"Carmody and his henchmen, including Michael Kelly, have gone to Richibucto, where he has a store and docks, I've learned. It's a day's ride away, so he and his group will be passing the night there. They won't return until tomorrow. So you see, the place will be safe."

"How would you be knowin' this, laddie?" Brodie narrowed his eyes.

"A man named Gardiner came to the mill yesterday for a few planks, while you were tending the stock. He told me."

"I surely would love playin' for dancin' again." Brodie lowered his head and rubbed his chin. "And if you're thinkin' it would be safe for all of us to leave for a few hours…"

"I do."

"Well, then, Hamish Wallace, you've got yourself a fiddle player."

****

That evening the Wallace family was received with careful politeness at the picnic supper laid out on long plank tables in the churchyard. Even when Edward Morgan and his wife greeted them warmly, the parishioners' attitude had been that of reserved watchfulness, still unready to accept them fully.

The supper was a sumptuous one, with generous servings of salmon, beef, vegetables, bread, biscuits, and a variety of pies. The Fowler children, well instructed in table manners by their parents, ate carefully, quietly. Harry, sitting at the head of their table, felt an intense pride in the clean, neatly dressed, mannerly group. Glancing over at Margaret, he let a smile curl his lips. When she caught his expression, she lowered her head coquettishly and winked slyly. Thoughts of their nights together rushed into his mind as he grinned back. Eppie and Precious had moved upstairs to share the girls' room, he had moved into the bedroom with Maggie, and Brodie had taken up residence in the cubicle he'd formerly occupied.

Her reaction brought an instant response to his nether regions as it brought to mind the passionate lovemaking they'd enjoyed the previous night. *One amazing lady.* He loved her and, most wonderfully, she loved him.

When dusk came, the minister rose, clapped his hands to get attention, and spoke.

"Ladies and gentlemen, children. As you all know, a treasured member of our flock, Ned Landry, has this past winter gone to be with God. For many years Ned played for the dance following this supper, I've been told. He shall be missed." Edward Morgan's voice grew hushed and reverent over the last sentence. He lowered his head, and there was a moment of respectful silence. Then he looked up at the assemblage, and his tone brightened.

"Fortunately, the good Lord has seen fit to send us another musician. Allow me to introduce Mr. Brodie MacMillan, who shares his life with the Wallace family. Mr. MacMillan, if you please."

The clergyman swept out his hand to indicate Brodie, who'd taken his fiddle out of its case and now rose to stand beside him. He bowed to his audience, then drew his bow carefully across the strings. The tune he'd chosen to start the evening was an old Scottish ballad, soft and sentimental. As the first sweet notes slid out into the autumn dusk, a hush fell over the gathering. Transfixed by the music's beauty, not a man, woman, or child stirred. Harry slipped an arm around Maggie, and she rested her head against his shoulder. Brodie was once again working his magic.

For a moment after he'd finished the piece, silence, except for the occasional sniffle or clearing of a throat, held reign over the churchyard. Then Edward Morgan began to clap, at first alone, then slowly joined by the rest.

"Would you be knowin' any jigs or reels, sir?" one of the men stepped forward.

"Oh, aye, of course." Brodie favored the man with a broad grin. "If you and your neighbors will just be movin' back the tables into a circle, we'll be able to have dancin' in the centre."

"Move them away back, lads." Another man came forward. "We'll make a bonfire in the centre. It'll be dark soon, and we'll be needing the light."

Willingly and quickly, laughing and slapping one another on shoulders and backs, even Harry and Brodie, who set about helping, the men moved the tables and benches well back to allow for the upcoming fire and festivities. When Brodie once more took up his fiddle and bow and broke into a rollicking tune, all were ready to dance and swing about in the improvised ballroom.

Harry, grinning, looked over at his friend, his face bright as he played one tune after another.

"He's in his glory." He had to raise his voice to make Maggie hear above the music and laughter.

"So it would seem." She glanced up at her husband. "Yet I feel he carries a great sorrow in his heart. Sometimes when I see him staring off across the fields, I suspect his heart has known severe pain. And I long to help."

"You are." He smiled down at her. "You and the children, Eppie in particular. Brodie needed a place to call home, and you've given it to him. Now, if I'm not mistaken, our friend is breaking into a waltz, and I plan to dance around in the firelight, making a shameless display of how besotted I am with my lovely wife."

He took her into his arms and swirled out into the midst of the dancers, who now greeted them with warm smiles and friendly nods of approval.

"Harry Wallace, you never cease to amaze me." She smiled up at him. "And even though you remain a man of mystery, I give you my heart and my trust."

****

"Aye, well, God only knows what a man'll find in these colonies."

The stubby man, grey sidewhiskers sticking out beneath his cap, paused beside where Maggie sat on a bench, watching Harry dance in the light of the bonfire with Mary Morgan. Eppie was asleep with her head in Maggie's lap.

"I beg your pardon, sir?" She looked up at the man and saw him staring at her husband, a smirk on his weathered face.

"I said, God only knows what you'll find in the colonies," he repeated. "Look there, dancin' with the minister's wife, Highland Harry, the wildest rogue that ever fought the English." He chuckled. "I well remember the night he was driven from mi'lady's bed chamber, pullin' on his coat as he ran. And she was only one of many, legend has it. Seduced 'em, robbed 'em while they slept, then disappeared into the night. Quite the lad."

Something inside Maggie plummeted. Her heart? Her soul? She swallowed hard.

"Surely you're mistaken, sir." She drew Eppie closer, the evening chill and something much colder washing over her.

"Hard to mistake a handsome lad like that,

mistress. I was a groom at Lady Annabelle Spencer's estate. I stabled that beautiful horse o' his—the one with the silver mane and tail—and saw him make his escape on her with that friend of his yonder, the one playin' the fiddle. Highland Harry and Brazen Brodie, they called 'em. Quite the pair. I even helped 'em, hid their horses in the stable until they made their escape." His tone turned to one of bitter remembrance. "I'm a Scotsman, too. The lad was only doin' what the rest o' us would have liked to do but didn't have nerve or skill to attempt. Good luck to ye, Harry boy. And you, too, Brodie MacMillan." He pulled a flask from inside his coat, saluted the unaware Harry and Brodie, and took a long swig. "Glad to see ye're safe and sound."

He turned and walked off into the shadows. Maggie wet her lips and swallowed hard as Harry danced past in front of her and cast her an intimate, suggestive smile.

Good God! She'd suspected he and Brodie might have been something of rogues back in the Old Country, but not this. A seducer who robbed women after he'd made love to them! She closed her eyes and drew in deep breaths. Small wonder he knew how to please her in bed. Nausea roiled in her stomach, the bonfire and dancers blurred, and for a moment she felt a hot weakness threaten to overwhelm her, the same hot weakness she'd experienced twice already that week.

Get a grip. You can't let the children see you upset. You must play out the loving wife until you can be alone with him. Until you can confront him with this infamous charge.

Chapter Twenty-Five

"Margaret, what in God's name is the matter?" Harry followed her down the trail behind the barn in the moonlight as she strode away from him with long, angry strides. The drive home from the evening's festivities had been one of coldly polite silence he couldn't fathom. They'd seemed to be having a wonderful time, and then suddenly Maggie had turned cold as ice. "I cannae make it right if I dunnae know what's troublin' you."

"Very well." She swung to face him, her face pale with anger. "A man at the party this evening told me about some notorious Scottish rebels. He recognized you and Brodie as a couple of them, known as Highland Harry and Brazen Brodie. He said this Highland Harry was not only a highwayman but also a nefarious seducer of wealthy English women, a man who charmed his way into their beds and then robbed them while they slept. Is that you, Harry? Are you the Scottish seducer who has escaped the law in England?"

"Margaret..." *Sweet Jesus!* He tried to take her by the shoulders, but she shrugged away.

"Don't touch me!" She swung away from him. "Don't ever touch me again."

"Margaret, I confess. I was a highwayman and, because of my ability to ape an aristocratic English accent, I also did manage to work my way into manor houses to rob them. I did steal from those houses while the occupants slept, but I never seduced women to rob them." He struggled to control the tremor in his voice. *God damn whoever that man was.* He couldn't lose Margaret…Margaret and the children. They were his whole world. "But in this country I've become someone else. I'm Harry Wallace—farmer, miller, father, faithful husband, and that's all I'll ever wish to be."

"Oh, and who, pray tell, is Lady Annabelle Spencer? And why were you forced to flee her company in a state of partial undress?"

"Lady…? This man told you about her? That means it had to be Parsons, the groom." He rubbed his forehead in agitation. "He must have heard Brodie and me discussing our ultimate plan of escape, our escape to Riverhaven. That's how he ended up here. Of all the rotten luck!"

"Don't wander from the topic, Harry. What about this Lady person—whom I very much suspect wasn't much of a true lady at all."

"Brodie and I were told she'd been given a necklace, a very nearly priceless necklace, believed to have been the property of the late French queen. We decided to make one last big robbery and then head for this place. We didn't realize it was a trap, one very carefully laid by the lady. Apparently her brother, a colonel whose family had bought him a commission in the British army, had been killed in a raid in the Highlands. She believed Highland Harry was the man responsible. And so she set out to trap me.

"She was clever. She'd learned about a man who seemed always to have been a guest in manor houses just before a goodly supply of their valuables went missing. She deduced it was me. She arranged to meet me at a gathering, pretended to become enamored with me, and invited me to her estate for a hunt. I should have been suspicious when I found that famous necklace lying unprotected on her dressing table. I was just about to stuff it into my waistcoat when the bedroom door burst open, and there stood the lady herself, a pistol pointed at my chest.

"Fortunately, she was a dreadful poor shot, and I managed to escape through a window and out to the stable, where Brodie waited with Parsons. We barely escaped with our lives that night. In fact, I believed Brodie had been killed. In fact…"

"You're a disgrace!" She whirled back on him, emerald eyes flashing fire. "You're a disgrace to my home and my children! I thought we were building a respectable life together, something we could all be proud of. Now this! You're nothing more than a sneak thief, Harry Wallace, or whatever your real name is. There cannot be an ounce of respectability in you. A highwayman I might have tolerated, but a professional seducer of women, using his body to…"

"Margaret, you have to understand the bitterness I've felt toward the English, the outrage. Let me tell you about my family and what happened to them during the Highland Clearances. Let me…"

"No, I won't let you. Never again! You're a Lothario, Harry Wallace!"

"Do you know what I think?" Anger was replacing his desire to placate her. How could she believe he was such a man, a man without honor? "I think you're jealous…jealous that there were other women in my past. Good God, woman, I'm guessing I'm more than a dozen years your senior. Did you expect I'd lived the life of a monk?"

"Harry, enough." She became suddenly calm, a calm that sickened him more than her outrage, it was so bitterly cold and unassailable. "For the children's sake, we must go on as if nothing has happened, even though I'm sure that gentleman who recognized you will be spreading the story far and wide, he was so delighted to have discovered you both, as if you were heroes for a great cause. We can only hope that in time the scandal will all blow over. Or perhaps people will find the story too farfetched to give credence to it. In another year or so James will be of age, and you can leave. I thank you for helping us in our time of need, but you will understand I can never again accept you as my true husband. From now on you'll sleep on the trundle bed in our room. We must keep up the appearance of a decent marriage, for the children's sake."

She turned and, head held high, started back up the trail toward the barn. He longed to go after her, to take her into his arms, to kiss her so violently all the sins she'd accused him of would vanish from her mind. Looking at the back of her stern, rigid figure as she marched away, he knew that wasn't possible.

He threw back his head and closed his eyes, a great sigh heaving through his body. Highland Harry had failed for the first time with a woman...and with the woman he loved.

Chapter Twenty-Six

The next morning as he was grooming Scotia he heard what sounded like an animal being tortured. Going out of the barn and rounding a corner to its back, he found Brodie and Geordie seated on a weathered bench, the younger man with Brodie's fiddle tucked under his chin, the bow in his hand creasing across the strings to make the racket that had attracted him.

"That's better, laddie." Harry marveled at his friend's patience as he spoke to Geordie. He knew how much that fiddle meant to Brodie and how it must be paining him to let a novice handle it. "Like so." He took it into his own hands, and a moment later sweet notes floated out into the cool September morning air.

"Uncle Brodie, I don't think I'll ever be able to play half as well as you." Admiration colored Geordie's words when the older man paused.

"But you want to learn, don't you, laddie?" Brodie lowered the instrument and handed it back to him.

"Yes. More than anything."

"Well, then, it's just a matter of practice. Here, let me show you again. Aw, here comes your father." He saw Harry standing a few yards away. "Harry, your son is showing a talent for the fiddle, and I'm inclined to teach him. What do you say?"

"I say well and good." Harry, in spite of the problems roiling around in his mind regarding the ragged state of his marriage, grinned. "It would be grand indeed to have two fiddlers in the family. And"—he winked at Brodie before heading back into the barn—"it would give one of them an opportunity to dance with a certain young lady while the other took over the fiddling at the next gathering."

"Now, there's a thought." Brodie called after him as if the idea had not occurred to him. "Aye, there's a thought. I would enjoy a wee bit of dancin', that I would."

"And Miss Morag Green might just be willin' to partner even the likes of you," Harry called back as he continued on his way.

****

Maggie stood beside the beehive oven. In a few minutes the bread baking inside would be ready, and she didn't want to give it a chance to burn. She gazed across toward the barn where, through the open door, she could see Harry, stripped to the waist, cleaning stalls. The memory of his lean, muscular body pressed against hers in the nights they'd shared rose in her mind, sending a shiver of longing washing over her. In spite of what she'd learned about him, she still loved him, still wanted to be his wife. But how could she be, knowing what she'd been told of his past?

She checked the bread. A few more minutes.

Maybe he had been right in some measure when he'd accused her of being jealous. She looked down at her work-coarsened hands, fingered the shabby grey woolen dress she wore for doing housework, and thought of her hair caught back into a careless queue at the back of her head. How could she compete with the kinds of women who lived in those manor houses where Harry had been a guest? Their hands would be soft, their gowns made of silk and lace, their hair carefully styled. They'd smell of exotic scents such as came from that bottle Harry had given her months ago and which she'd been conscientious in applying behind her ears each evening before they went to bed together.

She grimaced as she watched him straighten up and roll broad shoulders. He was a fine figure of a man. A few drops of perfume couldn't make him forget the beautifully sophisticated women he'd at least romanced if not outright seduced. If she could just erase those images, maybe she and Harry could start again. But life wasn't chalk on a slate. There was no way of rubbing out the past.

The sound of a horse coming up the hill made her turn toward the road. A woman rode into the dooryard and yanked her mount to a halt so roughly the animal threw back its head, jerking its mouth open wide.

"Is this where Harry Wallace lives?" she asked. She wore a low-cut dress that showed ample cleavage. Paint brightened an otherwise plain and surly face.

"Yes." Maggie shielded her eyes to look up at the newcomer in the sun. "He's down at the barn."

She glanced in that direction to see her husband coming out of the door. He paused on seeing the new arrival, then grabbed his shirt from a peg and advanced toward them, a smile of welcome in place as he thrust his arms into its sleeves.

"We have a visitor, Mrs. Wallace?" He shrugged fully into the garment as he came to stand beside her.

"Yes, this lady has come looking for *you*, Mr. Wallace." She stepped away from him as he raised an arm to put it about her shoulders. "You're acquainted, I take it?"

"Harry." The woman, who'd been riding astride, swung her leg over the horse's rear and dropped to the ground, causing the animal to shy. "Harry." This time she moved to stand close in front of him and spoke in a soft, intimate tone. She ran a finger down his chest where his unbuttoned shirt had left it bare, down to the wide belt at the top of his pants. "I've missed you. When are you coming back? That big, cozy bed in my room above the tavern is waiting just for you."

"Whit?" He stumbled back a step. "Who are you, woman? Whit are you talkin' about?"

"How can you pretend you don't know me?" She glared up into his face, suddenly distorted with a semblance of outrage. "How can you deny those lovely nights we shared last spring, when you promised me you'd be free soon, that your marriage was a farce? Damn you, Harry Wallace!" She hit him hard on the chest with the flats of both hands. "You're a bastard through and through. You take advantage of one tavern girl after another, with never a backward glance!" She turned and flounced back to her horse. With an effort she stuck her foot into the stirrup and scrambled aboard the nervous animal. "You'll pay for this, you Highland scum!"

She swung the animal awkwardly about and headed down the hill toward the bridge, her bottom bouncing high on the trotting horse as she fought to keep her seat.

Maggie turned back to the oven and removed the golden brown loaves. She didn't speak. She couldn't. The lump in her throat was too large to allow words. Just when she'd been considering how they might be reconciled, this evidence of his infidelity had to arrive.

"Margaret…" He blocked her way as she started toward the house, the bread on a wooden board.

"Get out of my way, Harry." As speech returned, she barely recognized her own voice, so deep it was a growl of fury. "Get out of my way, or I swear I'll shove this hot bread into your chest."

"Did ye not recognize the horse, Michael Kelly's horse?" He followed her.

"And what difference does a horse make?" She paused at the step to glare up at him. "She might have been riding a unicorn, for all I care!"

"Don't you see?" He managed to get between her and the door. "She was sent by Joe Carmody or, at the very least, Michael Kelly, to make trouble between us. They've heard the story that man you met at the church supper is circulatin' and decided this is the best way to destroy us, our trust. That's why she was ridin' Kelly's horse. Have you never heard of the battle technique of divide and conquer?"

"No, I haven't. Now get out of my way, you great lout!"

"Argh!" Exasperated, he threw up his arms and moved aside.

On the threshold she paused and looked back at him. "We'll not tell anyone of this further disgrace. I'll not have our children shamed by their father's behavior."

She managed to get inside and shove the door shut behind her before the tears came, hot tears that blinded her as she placed the bread on the sideboard and dropped into a chair by the hearth.

I have to get control of myself before the children

come in for supper. I can't let them know what Harry is, what he has done. I have to pretend nothing is wrong, for as long as we need him.

****

Outside, Harry saw James standing in the barn door. *Sweet Jesus, had the lad overheard it all?* He didn't have long to wait for his answer.

"You bastard!" In long, furious strides James crossed the yard to confront him. A moment later Harry dodged as the young man's fist flew past the point where his jaw had been.

He caught him by the arm and swung him about so that his stepson's back was against his chest, the younger's man right arm held bent and immobile between them.

"Now chust you calm yourself, young laddie." Harry held the struggling, panting James in his grasp. "Calm yourself and listen."

"I don't have to listen!" James wrenched against the older man's superior strength and skill. "I know what you did with her when Brodie took us away in the wagon. I thought it was what should happen. I thought you were going to be a respectable man. But no! You must have a strong taste for tavern wenches."

"That kind of slur I won't stand for." Harry gave the younger man's arm a wrench that made him cry out. "And there'll be more where that came from if you don't learn to respect your mother. Now, if you're ready to act like a civilized human being, I'll let you go and explain. Agreed?"

James's only reply was harsh breathing.

"Agreed?" Harry gave him another, this time, less severe wrench.

"All right, all right. Agreed." James, released, stumbled away a bit, nursing his shoulder. "Explain." He glowered over at him, blue eyes hard as winter ice.

"Don't you see?" Harry wiped the back of his hand across his mouth. "This is all a plot by Joseph Carmody. If he can succeed in getting your mother to send me—and probably Brodie—packing, she'll once more be at his mercy." He hurried on, seeing belligerence surge into James's already bellicose expression. "Not that you and your brothers aren't a formidable force, but Carmody sees Brodie and me as professional fighting men, men against whom Michael Kelly and his rabble are useless."

James continued to glower at him.

"Look, you're a smart lad." Harry reached to clap him on a shoulder, but he lurched away. "You must see the logic in what I've said. I swear to you I never had anything to do with that woman. Nor with any woman except your mother since I came to this country. We're married, and I will honor those vows."

"You'd better." Slowly James's stance relaxed, his words cooling. "Or, I swear to God, you'll find yourself shanghaied onto the next timber drogher that leaves Riverhaven."

"A fair punishment…which I'll never be deserving, but still a reasonable punishment for any man who'd be unfaithful to a woman such as your mother. Now can we get to work on the job of trimming that great mare's hooves? I swear I see no reason for your papa to have named her Bonnie."

A corner of Harry's mouth quirked, and slowly—very slowly—James met his grin in like fashion.

Together they turned and headed back to the barn.

Chapter Twenty-Seven

Harry paused to wipe sweat from his face before he directed the next wagonload of wheat toward the chute of the grist mill. The harvest had been good, and now it seemed every farmer in the county wanted his grain ground immediately. He wasn't complaining. Business was booming, keeping him busy from sunrise to sunset and allowing him little time to think of the state of his shattered marriage.

It was a hot day for late September, and no mistake. Looking across the mill yard, he saw James talking to Ezra Gardiner, who waited with a wagonload of wheat. Ezra was leaning down toward the younger man, who stood beside his wagon with one hand resting on the conveyance's board side. Harry couldn't hear what they were speaking about above the throb of the great grinding stone and rush of water, but suddenly he saw James's face blanch, saw him draw back from the wagon, hands clenched at his sides. His eldest stepson stood for a moment as though rooted to the spot, then whirled and headed up the hill toward the house in long, angry-looking strides.

Now whit in heaven's name could that old troublemaker Gardiner have said to set the lad off like that?

****

"Harry!" An hour later, he turned to see Brodie

running down the hill toward him. He'd gone up to the house to fetch a jug of cold water. "Harry, a word…now!"

"Whit?" Harry's Highland accent burst out as his friend ran up the ramp into the mill.

"Shut things down and come outside. It's urgent. We need a word alone."

"Lads." Harry shouted to the three boys. "We'll be shuttin' down for a wee bit."

Glad for the respite, they obeyed.

"What is it, Father?" Robert, covered in chaff, looked like a ghost.

"Yer uncle will be havin' a word with me in private. Take a few minutes to yourselves. Gentlemen," he yelled to the waiting wagons, "we'll be takin' a wee rest period."

There were mutters of annoyance, but since there was nowhere else to take their harvest to be milled, they had no choice but to wait.

"Now, whit is so all-fired important, Brodie?" He followed as his friend led him out of earshot of the others. "We've got more work ahead than I can fathom, and if we don't keep at it…"

"It's James." Brodie turned to him, his expression tense. "He's gotten into that whiskey I stashed down by the river. He's drunk and making all manner of threats. He's got a brace of pistols."

"Whit set the lad off? He was fine just a short time ago."

"Come with me." Brodie took Harry by an arm and pulled him toward Ezra Gardiner's wagon. "Tell Harry what you told James," he ordered, glaring up at the man.

"I just said what the whole community has been whispering behind closed doors for months," Ezra Gardiner muttered, avoiding Harry's narrowing eyes. "I said it was a shame that nothing was being done and that his stepmother had been forced to wed a stranger when everyone knew Joseph Carmody murdered his father."

"Sweet Jesus! Brodie, come on." Harry turned and headed up the hill at a run toward the house. "Gentlemen, you'll have to come back another day," he shouted to the waiting customers.

Before they were halfway, James, riding Midnight, burst out of the yard and bore down on them at full gallop.

"Harry, no!" Brodie jerked his friend out of the path of the charging gelding as he tried to grab its bridle.

"Bugger all, he near run me down!" Harry staggered to regain his footing as he watched his stepson gallop off across the bridge and up the road toward the village.

"He meant nothin' agin you, Harry. The lad's half mad with anger. Remember how you felt when you learned your father had been killed."

"Aye, aye." Harry set off up the road toward the house at a run. "Nevertheless, I have to stop him before he gets himself killed."

"*We* have to stop him." Brodie was running at his side.

"Aye, then, we."

At the house they burst into the kitchen to find Maggie clutching a chair back, her face ashen. "Harry, what in God's name is happening?" she cried. "James rushed in here looking like a thing possessed. He grabbed one of your pistols. I swear he'd been drinking. I tried to question him, to stop him, but he wouldn't listen…"

Harry jerked Brodie's sword in its sheath from the wall inside the door and threw it to his friend, then snatched one of his pistols from its case on the dresser and stuck it into his belt.

"Nothing to concern yourself about, Margaret. A small matter Brodie and I will take care of in the village."

"Don't lie to me, Harry Wallace." She glowered up at him, eyes as hard as emeralds, eyes he remembered had once gazed on him with love and desire and, even in the stress of the moment, brought a shaft of pain to his chest. "You owe me that much."

"We've reason to believe James has decided to take revenge on Joseph Carmody."

"Oh, good God!" Maggie's hand flew to cover her mouth.

"Dunnae be afeard, Margaret." Brodie put a hand on her shoulder. "We're a couple of reliable lads, Harry and me. We've gotten people out of worst pickles than this in a shake of a lamb's tail."

"He's right." Harry met her terrified expression hoping he sounded more confident than he felt. "We'll have our son back here safe and sound in no time. Come along, laddie, times a'wastin'."

****

At the outskirts of Riverhaven, Brodie called a halt.

"We'd best leave our weapons here," he said, holding the snorting, prancing Fox to a pause beside an equally excited Scotia. "If we ride in armed…"

"You're right. We're headin' into a hornet's nest. The small advantage weapons might give us wouldn't be worth the risk."

"Aye. And I've always been right good at talkin' us out of trouble. You're the better fightin' man, Hamish, and a fair treat with the ladies, no debate there. But I've got the gift of the gab, and that just might save us and young Jamie right now."

"You are a silver-tongued devil, and no mistake." Harry rode behind a tree, dismounted, and laid his pistol on the ground. His mouth quirked as he looked up at his companion. "Blessings on your smooth talk, my friend. Our lives probably will depend on it."

He held up his hand for his companion's sword.

****

They drew rein as they entered the village. A group of silent men surrounded the door of Angus Harper's mercantile. A sick sensation roiled in Harry's gut. *Dear God, don't let us have come too late.*

"Come on." He nudged Scotia forward, and Brodie followed. As they trotted their horses down the street, the men turned to look at them.

"Come to get the young fella, have ya?" one of the men leered over blackened teeth. "Better be quick about it, afore he riles Joe any more, or it's his body you'll be takin' home."

Harry dismounted and shot the gathering a cold stare. As Brodie swung to the ground and turned on them, eyes narrowed, hard and cold with threat, they parted like the Red Sea to let the two men pass into the building.

Inside, Harry confronted the scenario he'd feared. James stood holding a pistol leveled at Joseph

Carmody's chest while Michael Kelly and three other men stood behind the businessman.

"Time to come home, James." Harry kept his tone level and calm as he paused a few feet from the young man. "No need to carry this any further."

"Stay away from me!" James's face was sheet white and his hand trembled, but his expression remained deadly determined. "Come any closer, and I swear I'll blow a hole in the old bastard's heart."

"My, my, such language." Brodie stepped forward, wearing an affable grin, his stance as relaxed as if this were nothing more than a mild misunderstanding. "Forgive the lad, Mr. Carmody. He got into my best whiskey and is full of the false courage." He moved closer to James and held out his hand. "Give me the gun, lad. There's work to be done at the mills. We've not time to waste."

"I said, stay away from me!" James was sweating, thin riverlets coursing down his blanched face. "I want him to admit he killed my father...here, in front of everyone. I want—"

"Aye, aye." Brodie was moving ever closer, and Harry held his breath. He knew how disarming his friend could be, but James had point-blank aim at Joseph Carmody's heart. If his friend didn't pull it off, his son would be branded more of a murderer than the entrepreneur himself. "But there's none of us ever gets exactly what we want. Now, Mr. Kelly over there, I imagine he's spoilin' to get another crack at my friend Harry. I've heard Mr. Wallace sent you sprawlin' on your arse more than once, sir."

"You miserable bit of Highland trash!" Kelly's face reddened and his hands clenched at his sides. "We don't need the likes of you two in our village."

"Oh, now, there I have to disagree." Brodie slowly rounded on the man, his gaze focused on the other's bloodshot eyes. "Harry and me...we're hard workers, and myself, I'm clever as a fox." He yelled the last word.

Yelling and whooping erupted outside the mercantile amid the snorts and screaming whinnies of a horse. Fox burst into the room, scattering everything in front of him and knocking the gun from James's hand. It discharged up into the rafters. In the ensuing melee, Harry grabbed his son and dragged him out of the building while Brodie jumped onto his stallion.

"Gentlemen, I bid you good afternoon." He touched his forelock and turned his cavorting horse toward the entrance.

Bending low in the saddle, he rode out the door and into the street, where Harry was flinging James aboard Midnight. Before the crowd could recover from the madness, the three were galloping out of the village, Harry leading Midnight while his son clung to his saddle.

****

As the three rode into the dooryard, Maggie ran out onto the front step. The relief mirrored in her face was worth any risk they'd taken, Harry decided as he watched her shoo back into the house the other children, who'd followed her outside.

They drew rein at the steps, and he saw her swallow hard, fighting, he guessed, to keep her emotions in check as she faced her son.

"James Fowler, that was an insane thing to do!" She batted her eyelashes, not quite keeping tears at bay.

"You could have been killed! And all because of gossip! Ezra Gardiner's gossip, at that."

"He said you knew! He said everyone knew except Papa's children." Blue eyes narrowed in an accusatory stare as he looked down at his stepmother.

"Suspected, James, suspected. Harry and Brodie will tell you no one has any proof. And without proof, there's nothing we can do."

"Your mother's right." Harry held Scotia to a pawing stop. "Until we can prove Joseph Carmody was responsible, we have to bide our time. If we act rashly, we'll only end up in trouble ourselves…maybe even at the end of a noose."

"And you two would know all about ending up there, wouldn't you?" Disgust raged out of the younger man's words. "A couple of highwaymen, aren't you? A pair of murderers, probably rapists, and God only knows what else."

"Get down off that horse!" Maggie advanced down the steps, her face pale, fists at her sides. "Get down off that horse this minute, James Fowler!"

In spite of the seriousness of the situation, Harry couldn't help seeing the humor in the situation as the six-foot-tall, broad-shouldered man obeyed and stood defiantly in front of the five-foot-six-inch woman.

"You'll never, never speak about your father and uncle like that again, do you hear?" She glared up at him, green eyes sparking with the anger of an enraged feline. "They saved your life just now, I've no doubt, by risking their own, and have fought for this family with all their might. If they hadn't come along when they did, I doubt we'd have this place to call home. So take your mount and theirs down to the barn and stable them properly. Then come up to the house. Supper is ready. From the stench of liquor on your breath, a meal and then off to bed are what you need."

To Harry's relief and amusement, James shrank before her angry words. Taking the reins of the horses, he slouched off toward the barn.

"James," Harry called after him. He paused without turning around.

"Make no mistake, lad. When the time is right, we'll see Joseph Carmody pays for his sins."

With a shrug, James kept on toward the barn, but Harry was relieved to see the lad's shoulders straighten a bit at his promise.

"Now, gentlemen, as I've said, supper is ready." Maggie wet her lips and heaved a sigh. *Weary, spent. The lad's adventure has taken a heavy toll. I'm feeling a bit of it myself.* "You'll be needing to wash up around at the back door."

She started back up the steps, and Brodie headed off to the washstand, but Harry caught her by the arm.

"Margaret, it will be all right. The lad just got carried away. It won't happen again."

"I hope not." She looked up at him, sincere gratitude in her expression. "As they'd say in the Old Country, a hundred thousand thank-yous, Harry."

"No need for thanks, lassie. He's our bairn. We both have a duty to look out for him. But if you've a mind to offer thanks of some sort, I'd appreciate your giving me a fair hearing regarding my alleged sins with the ladies." He gazed into her eyes, hoping she saw the sincerity in his heart. "Margaret, you're the only woman I've ever truly loved, the only woman to whom I'll ever give my heart and soul."

"Harry, this isn't a good time." He felt her shrink in his grasp, and he dropped his hand. "Today has left me frazzled. Maybe…maybe in a few days…we can talk."

She walked up the steps, across the veranda, and into the house, leaving Harry with hope in his heart.

He passed Brodie at the washstand and said, "Now I'm off to the barn. I have some talking to do to my son. Then I think you and I should lay a plan for the future."

"Aye." Brodie dashed water over his face. "They'll be comin' after us, and no doubt about it. We'd best be ready." He rubbed the drying linen over his countenance and hands, then started off around the barn.

"Where are you going?" Harry called after him. "Margaret said supper is near ready."

"I'll be back directly." He waved a hand without turning back. "Go and see to your lad."

In the barn, Harry found James rubbing down Midnight with abrupt, angry strokes.

"No need to tear the hide off the poor beast." He leaned on the stall and tried to sound casual, good humored even.

"You made me look the right fool today…you and your outlaw friend." Without turning to acknowledge his presence, James kept on brushing, but with less ferocity.

"Maybe because you acted like one." Harry braced for the reaction. "Ridin' into Joseph Carmody's home territory alone and accusin' him of murder isn't the act of a wise man."

"Oh, and you're far too clever to ever do anything like that." He swung on Harry, blue eyes bright with outrage.

"Now I am. Once, when I was about your age, I wasn't…right after the British had murdered my father and left my mother and wee sister to die in the snow after burning our croft home from over their heads."

James stared. Silence, except for the horses munching hay and moving in their stalls, reigned for the next few seconds. Then the younger man found his voice. "Your father was murdered? Your mother and sister died, too?" The words echoed the shock of Harry's admission. "All at once?"

"Within a week."

"And that didn't drive you mad with anger?"

"Aye, it did. That's why I took to the life of an outlaw…to exact revenge."

"And Brodie…"

"I was wounded several years after I became a fugitive. Pursued by half a regiment, I headed south and ended up at Brodie's mill. He found me hidin' behind sacks of grain, bleedin' like a stuck pig. He took me in, he and his pregnant wife Annie. They hid me until I got well. Not wantin' to put them at any further risk for hidin' a fugitive, I left. I was gone only a couple of days when Brodie rode out on business and soldiers, searching for me, raided his home and mill. They burned both to the ground. Annie, tryin' to save what she could of their possessions, got caught in the flames. When Brodie got back, he found her lyin' dead inside the ruins of what had been their home. She and the wee on' she carried."

As Harry told the tale, he watched James's bellicose expression metamorphose first into disbelief, then shock, and finally the pain of empathy.

"You and Brodie...you lost everything," he said finally, his voice shaking.

"Aye, for a time it seemed that way." Harry went to rub Midnight's neck, avoiding James's emotional countenance. "We turned into the most sought-after highwaymen in Scotland. I even learned to ape British aristocratic speech and infiltrated grand houses to rob them. Our booty we used to help victims of the Clearances...people driven from their small crofts in the Highlands to make way for some lord's blessed sheep. I tell you, laddie, there'll never be a sheep on this farm if I have anything to say about it!"

"But you came here, you and Brodie." James, now full of interest, wanted to hear more.

"Aye, because the shadow of the noose was getting all too real for us. In fact, I thought they'd captured Brodie and hanged him."

"But they didn't." Brodie stepped into the barn carrying one of the bottles he'd pilfered from Joseph Carmody. He pulled the cork from it with his teeth, took a swig, then tossed it to Harry, who caught it. "See that, laddie. You have to be right quick with your hands if you're going to survive." He grinned.

Harry took a drink, then tossed it back to Brodie. He looked at James, who glanced away. "No whiskey for you until you prove you can handle it like a man." *Embarrassed. Guid.* "Now us three men have plannin' to do. After today's incident, they'll be comin' after us, and no mistake. We have to have a strategy in place."

"And there Lachlan would be right helpful." Brodie leaned against the stall. "He was talented in that area."

"Lachlan?" James looked from one man to the

other.

"We may as well tell him, Harry." Brodie shoved the cork back into the bottle with the flat of his hand. "James is going to have to be in on it all, from now on."

"Verrae well. James, our minister Edward Morgan is really Lachlan Cameron, another Highland outlaw we often travelled with. And his wife now known as Mary was actually called Iona, and one of the best warriors you'd ever want by your side in a fight."

James's mouth dropped open.

"But you must swear by all that's holy that you'll never tell a livin' soul." Brodie straightened up and faced the younger man, dead serious. "They're a family now. They're not to be involved in our battles, understood?"

"Understood." Still stunned by the revelation, James had a blank, vacant gaze. "I swear."

"Guid." Brodie slapped him on the shoulder. "Now let's get on up to the house and supper. I'm fair starvin'. Tonight, after the bairns have gone to bed, we'll discuss our defense plans. Bugger all," he said as they started toward the house, "but I wish we had Lachlan and Iona beside us as in the old days."

"By the way, lad, since you're partner in our secrets now, I've another to tell you." Harry walked companionably along beside his son.

"You're never going to tell me you have a wife back in the Old Country?" James came to a dead stop and stared at him.

"No, no, nothing like that." Harry paused and grinned at him. "Nothing so terrible. You know how your uncle has sometimes started to call me Hamish?"

James nodded.

"Well, that is my true Christian name…Hamish Wallace. And do you know what Hamish is Scottish for?"

"No."

"James. You and I share the same name." He threw an arm around the younger man's shoulders and started them both toward the back door of the log house. "Perhaps that's a sign…or something."

Chapter Twenty-Eight

The sound of hooves and wheels bursting into the yard brought Harry out of deep sleep and into a bolt-upright position. Stumbling to his feet from the trundle bed where he slept on the bedroom floor, he stubbed his toe on the door in his rush to get to the kitchen window, and cursed.

In the shadowy light of a near-dead fire, he saw Brodie already up from his bed in the cubicle and staring outside. In the dull dawn graying the sky, he saw a familiar team of Percherons pulling a wagon, skidding to a halt beside the house. Two dark silhouettes were on its seat, the smaller one with a packsack on its back.

"Hamish, Brodie, rouse yourselves!" The larger of the two yelled as he leaped to the ground to tie the horses to the hitching post near the door. His companion followed him. "They're comin'!"

Lachlan. He recognized the voice with its Scottish brogue, undisguised by the English accent the minister had learned to ape. And that had to be Iona by his side. *Sweet Jesus, whit...?*

"Unbar the door, you great Highland louts!" Lachlan Cameron's yell was a command as he came to hammer against it. "We've little time."

Harry, who slept in his breeches, went to obey while Brodie pulled his on. As the new arrivals entered,

Harry started in surprise. In the faint light of the low-burning fire on the hearth, for the first time since they'd ridden the Highlands together he saw Iona in pants, shirt, boots, and leather jerkin, her hair tied back into a queue. A far cry from the demure minister's wife she'd been portraying. The packsack on her back whimpered, and he realized it carried her child.

"Who's comin'?" he asked as Maggie came out of the bedroom and the six oldest children appeared at the head of the stairs.

"Sweet Jesus, man! Joseph Carmody and his gang, who did you think? Get your wits about you! We have to mount a defense, and quickly!" Lachlan snapped back into the role of commander he'd once held among the Highland outlaws. "Brodie, I trust you can still handle a pistol and sword half decently?"

"Aye." Brodie was pulling on his shirt. "I've been spoilin' for a good scrap."

He strode across the room to snatch his sheathed sabre from its peg by the door and help himself to one of the pistols Harry now left on a high shelf beside it.

"Margaret, there's nothing to fear." Harry walked over to her to put his hands on her slim shoulders and look down into her frozen expression. "Joseph Carmody and his bunch may be comin', but this time we're able to mount an excellent defense. Assembled in this room is the mightiest contingent of Highland warriors you'll find anywhere outside the hills of Scotland. We four battled the British authorities for years. Takin' on the likes of Carmody and his unskilled soldiers will be child's play for us."

"Bella," she called, without taking her gaze from his face.

"Yes, Mother?" Bella pushed past the other children, who'd now assembled on the stairs, staring at the fighting force in their kitchen.

"Take Mrs. Morgan's babe. Lizzie, go back upstairs and watch over Eppie and Precious. And all of you, get dressed and ready to leave if needs be. Samuel, harness the team." She turned back into the bedroom. "I'll be ready in a moment, Harry."

"You're coming with us?" Harry hadn't had time to grasp the significance of what she'd been doing before she turned back into the bedroom and grabbed up her work trousers, pulled them on, and stuffed her nightshift inside.

"Of course." She thrust bare feet into her boots and reached for her boy's coat. "With your eyesight, you'll need someone to reload your pistols. The oldest boys will come with us. You've taught James and Geordie to shoot. Robert can reload for them. Equip them, and we'll be off."

Amazed, Harry could only stand aside and watch her organize their family for action and the other warriors headed outside.

"Be very good." Maggie kissed each of the children before she followed Harry to the door. "We'll be back in no time. Samuel, you know the way to Ezra Green's. You're to take the children there in the event we're…detained. Understand? And promise?"

"Yes, Mother." Blanched under his freckles, the thirteen-year-old squared his shoulders and accepted her kiss.

"And Bella, you're to keep the babe in your arms until we return. Lizzie, don't let go of Eppie's hand. And…"

"Come along." Harry had to urge her. "We've no time to waste." He turned to the pale-faced children. "Mind you do exactly as your mother says."

The three eldest nodded, but as Harry and Maggie turned to leave, Eppie appeared at the top of the stairs, Precious by her side. For a moment she stared wide-eyed at her parents. Then, avoiding Lizzie's attempt to stop her, she stumbled down the steps and ran to Harry, throwing her arms about his knees.

"Father!" she screamed, and Harry felt something inside him crack. *Dear God, how I love this family. Don't let any of us get killed...not now. Don't let this wee on' lose another set of parents.*

He picked her up, feeling Maggie's gaze on him, knowing the child somehow sensed the danger of the situation.

"Father will be back soon, lassie." He kissed her cheek and marveled at how it felt as soft as a butterfly's wing. "You do as Lizzie and Bella tell you, and I'll take you ridin' on Goldenbug when I return. Promise?"

She nodded against his shoulder, and he replaced her on the floor. Then he took Maggie's hand, and together they went out into the first light of a grim October morning.

****

"We'll take up positions around the mill." Lachlan, as commander, waved his arm as they stood in the mill yard. "James, you and your brothers secret yourselves under the bridge. Let no one cross it, understood? And don't fire until you can make the shot count."

The three boys, awed by his authority, nodded and headed off, pistols and ammunition in their hands.

"Harry, you and Margaret go down to the far end

of the mill and take shelter behind that pile of deal. You'll be protected and yet can get off a good shot at anyone who rides into the mill yard. Brodie, you and Iona position yourselves in the grist mill. I'll be up on the roof of the saw mill, where you all can see me. I'll give directions when to fire and when to charge…if need be."

Grim-faced, they set off to the assigned positions. This would be a battle for supremacy, a battle to decide who controlled the region, Joseph Carmody or the Fowler-Wallace clan, and they all knew it.

****

At sunrise they came, six of them, led by the big man on the grey stallion. They paused on the brink of the hill. Back at the farm, a rooster crowed. Otherwise, all was silent…as if the entire small world of the valley and pond was holding its breath, frozen before a moment of reckoning.

Finally they started down the incline, walking their horses, spreading out to watch for the least sign of movement. From his vantage point, Harry could see Lachlan crouched, ready, waiting for the moment to give orders.

They were at the bottom of the hill, about to cross the bridge, all six men looking from left to right. Then gunfire rang out from beneath the bridge. Michael Kelly yelled, clutched his chest, and swung his horse away. The animal, screaming its fear of the noise, raced back up the hill, its rider slumped over its neck.

Joseph Carmody, who'd been leading the charge, yelled after his foreman, but a second shot rang out, clipping his stallion's shoulder. It bucked and reared, throwing its rider to the planks of the bridge. Shots from behind the deal pile, the grist mill, and the saw mill flew through the air. To those who didn't know the truth, it appeared a small army had been set up against them. The other four men, yelling and whooping, swung their horses around and galloped back in the direction from which they'd come.

Maggie and Harry stood and embraced.

"We did it, lass. We did it!"

"Aye, that we did, my fine Highland laddie." When Harry looked down into her face glowing with the exuberance of victory, he knew they were once more a team, husband and wife, in this enterprise they called theirs…theirs and their children's.

"Come along." He took her hand and pulled her across the mill yard. "We'd best see what's become of our adversary."

"Fair to middlin' strategy, sir." Harry, grinning from ear to ear, shook Lachlan's hand as the man jumped down from the mill roof to join them.

"Good to be back in harness again…just once."

"Bloody hell, look!" Brodie, who'd emerged from the grist mill with Iona by his side, was staring toward the bridge where Joseph Carmody had fallen. Geordie Fowler was holding a pistol leveled at the man who struggled to get to his feet, grasping the railing. As they watched, Geordie cocked the weapon, ready to fire.

"Geordie, no!" Maggie's cry chorused with the sound of cracking wood as the rotted section of rail gave way beneath the big man's weight. With a cry, he tumbled backward into the water beneath.

"Good God!" Brodie yelled, as they all rushed to stare down at the struggling man in the strong, slow, relentless current drawing him beneath the bridge and toward the dam. "I can't swim. Harry, you?"

"No." Harry was only vaguely aware that James had left the group and had set off running. *Looking for a rope, no doubt.*

A sudden, violent roar of water made him swing toward the mill. The flood gates on the dam had opened, the force sucking Joseph Carmody, screaming, toward its zenith. With a final shriek, the entrepreneur was pulled over its face and sent hurtling down onto the rocks below.

Through the mill's open front, Harry saw James, his hand on the lever that had released the killing flow, his expression as cold and hard as stone.

Chapter Twenty-Nine

"I think it's time to be sharing the truth with these good people." Lachlan hung his sword on a peg by the door of the log house and looked around at the group assembled before the fire. A large pot of oatmeal bubbled over the flames, and the table had been set. Above, the children slept, exhausted from their traumatic early morning awakening. Now Harry, Brodie, James, Geordie, Robert, Maggie, Lachlan, and Iona nursing her baby sat around the table. "Who will begin?"

"I will." Brodie drew a deep breath. "It's high time someone cleared the air between Harry and Margaret. It's high time she knew the truth."

"I'm not sure…" Harry looked from Brodie to his wife and back again. "Sweet Jesus, Brodie…"

"She's been imaginin' the worst." Brodie's determined expression brooked no refusal. "Now let her know the best. Margaret…" He turned to her. "It's true…we four were outlaws in Scotland. I'll let Harry explain to you how I came to the profession later. Right now, you have to know about him." He took a deep breath.

"Harry's entire family was killed during the Clearances. That I'm sure you already know. He took to the highways shortly afterwards, robbin' the wealthy English to help others afflicted by those infamous removals. One day our paths crossed." He paused and looked over at Harry. "We eventually fell in together. For years, with Lachlan as our leader and Iona as a boon companion, we raided and stole. Harry became adept at apin' an aristocratic Englishman and frequently worked his way into positions of trust among 'em. We often talked around the campfire at night of what we'd do when our hell-raisin' days were over. We'd heard of a place called Riverhaven in this province. We'd heard of other Clearance refugees who'd come here. So we decided when we had to flee the Old Country we'd make for this place with the safe-soundin' name.

"Eventually, the redcoats were gettin' too hot on our trail. We decided to split up, Iona and Lachlan goin' one way, Harry and I another. But we weren't content to simply disappear, my brother and I." Brodie looked over at Harry with a weak grin. "We decided we had to make one last big robbery before we left the country. Harry had infiltrated a group in the north of England that was determined to put an end to rebels such as us. At their head was an infamous woman named Lady Annabelle Spencer. Her brother, an officer in a regiment sent into the Highlands to effect the Clearances, had been killed. She was bound and determined to put an end to the outlaws known as Highland Harry and Brazen Brodie.

"We'd heard she'd recently acquired a necklace, a magnificent necklace reputed to have belonged to the late Queen of France, and that she was goin' to sell it to raise a huge force to come against us. The temptation was too great. Harry became Charles Featherstone and managed to penetrate her circle of friends and conspirators.

"On the night we were to take the necklace, Harry was to pretend to be seduced by her in order to get into her bedchamber, where the necklace lay in a jewel box. I was waitin' near the stables, with our horses saddled, to make an escape. Parsons, the groom, the fellow you met at the party, was with me. A staunch Scot, he was ready and willin' to assist.

"All went as planned until Harry suggested Lady Annabelle might like to have her maid assist her out of her gown in the adjoinin' dressing room. She seemed to acquiesce, but the moment he reached for the necklace, she appeared in the doorway, a pistol in her hand. Fortunately she was a rotten shot. Harry managed to get to a window, climb down the vines that coated the manor, and run to the stables, where I was waitin'."

"They gave good chase, that night." Harry took up the tale. "We rode flat out through the rain and sleet with what I fancied was the better part of a regiment on our tails. Then I heard a shot. Glancin' back, I saw Fox go down and figured they'd got Brodie." He looked down at his hands clasped between his knees. "Sweet Jesus, I didn't think I could continue to ride and stay in the saddle." His voice broke over the remembrance.

"Aye, well, over and done with now, eh?" Brodie's lightened tone fought to change the mood of the moment. "We all made it safely here. And…" He turned to look squarely at Maggie. "That was how Harry's robbery by seduction worked. He never made it into a single bed, sad to say." He was all-out grinning. "Now, that's not to say a few other lasses weren't ready and willin'—"

"Brodie, enough said." Harry drew a deep breath.

"Yes, Brodie, you've explained enough." Maggie

stood and rounded the table to put her hands on her husband's shoulders. "We'll manage from here." She bent forward to place a kiss on Harry's temple, and happiness burst over him.

Chapter Thirty

A feeling of contentment consumed him, permeating every inch of body and soul as Harry sat by the crackling fire in the log house and listened to the storm blustering around its corners. Around him his family, engaged in various activities, were safe and warm. He'd never envisioned such peace in his wildest dreams, and now it was his…his and Margaret's.

He remembered other December nights that hadn't been so pleasant. Nights when he and Brodie had hidden, coated with snow and freezing rain, under a bridge while redcoats passed above their heads, when the only warmth had been his mare's warm breath as he held her head to his chest to keep her perfectly still, with Brodie doing the same with the Fox, a few feet from his side, when his heart had pounded at his ribs, the specter of the noose before him.

And he remembered another stormy night, the first night he'd spent in this warm, comfortable house, the first night free from a tossing ship and with the possibility of a new life rising before him if only he had the courage to chance it. Yes, courage. Highland Harry, notorious highwayman and robber, was unnerved by the idea of taking on a family of seven children, of living with a woman the likes of whom he'd never known, of settling down to both and making a success of the situation.

Fear of Joseph Carmody and his bunch hadn't entered into the equation. Hamish Wallace was a fighting man with more skills and tricks than these men could ever dream of. No, it was apprehension of commitment, of staying in one place, of working day in and day out at the same labors, of being respectable.

But then he'd come to know the children, each and every one. Each with his or her strengths and weaknesses. And he'd fallen in love with their remarkable stepmother. Now there was no going back. Nor would he if the chance presented itself. No, Highland Harry was Harry Wallace, husband and father, miller and farmer, businessman and teacher, and that was all he wanted to be. He stretched his sock-covered feet out to the warmth of the fire and languished in the luxury. He'd slept with his boots on for days at a time, ready to run at a moment's notice. Now there was no need. Never would be again.

He looked over at Margaret. His wife. The familiar swelling that always seemed to fill his heart when he thought of her began again as he enjoyed the pleasure of gazing at her. He thought of the letter in his pocket and smiled. Later that night, when they were alone in their room, he'd show it to her and ask her if she'd allow him to accept the position it offered…replacing Joseph Carmody as magistrate in the district the entrepreneur had formerly represented. Asking would be simply his way of including her in the decision. He already knew her answer.

The irony of the appointment made his mouth curl sardonically at one corner. Highland Harry, the rogue of every road in the north of England and a few in Scotland as well—the King's magistrate.

Perhaps he wouldn't have considered taking the job but for one reason. Margaret. She'd see it as the final accomplishment in her quest for respectability for her family. Aye, he'd be respectable…and fair and just. He'd be a good magistrate, and no doubt about it.

The children were gathered around the table examining the things that had arrived that day aboard the *Avon Queen*. The china tea set with its beautifully painted moss roses was the crown jewel of the collection, but there were also books, which Robert was already poring over, and bolts of fine cotton and linen cloth and ribbons for the girls. For Geordie there was a fiddle of his own, for Samuel a saddle for Midnight, and for James a new hunting musket.

He watched as his eldest stepson examined the weapon, then let his mouth tip at the corners as James looked over at him, appreciation in his eyes. The younger man's gaze moved from his stepfather up to William Fowler's old musket that he and Harry had that afternoon mounted in a place of honor above the hearth. Over it, an elegantly carved plaque Harry had labored over in secret declared it to be the property of William George Fowler, born in Scotland, founder of the Fowler Estates in the Province of New Brunswick.

"It's a fine weapon, sir." James held the musket in his hands and looked over at Harry. "Thank you, Father."

A casket of pure gold wouldn't have meant anything to Harry compared to his son's final and complete acceptance of him.

"I'm hopin' you'll bring down a fine, big moose that will tide us over a few months this winter." Harry forced himself to reply over the thickness in his throat.

"And that you'll take me along on the hunt."

"Sure and certain, Father."

Harry returned his attention to his wife. Maggie had at first been apprehensive of this largess, but he'd assured her that inflated prices for forest products in England had made them all perfectly affordable.

Now she sat across from him in the other rocking chair, her head bent over the work in her hands. Although the loose styles of the day hid the fact, his wife was four months pregnant with his child. *His* child. The joy in his heart when she'd first told him had been overwhelming. Although he'd had an idea of how Brodie must have felt when he and Annie had discovered her condition, and Lachlan and Iona, he never would have believed the intensity of the sensations Margaret's announcement had aroused when whispered softly in his ear while they lay in bed two months earlier.

Of course, they both agreed, nothing would lessen their love and commitment to their adopted children, but still…one of their very own. The only bleak thought he experienced after the joy of that moment had been of Brodie and the terrible pain he must have suffered when he'd lost not only his child but his beloved wife as well.

The strains of a lively fiddle jig brought him out of his thoughts and made him turn toward the man seated on a chair at the end of the table. Brodie's expression was bright as Bella and Lizzie began to dance and laugh. His friend had been courting Morag Green these past months, so perhaps he'd once again be granted happiness. Harry fervently hoped such would be the case. Brodie had even been talking of building "a wee house" on the hill opposite the log house, with a bit of a stable behind it for Fox, and maybe a cow and a few chickens…and a bit of land for a kitchen garden…

"Sounds like the plans of a man contemplating marriage." Harry had said with a grin.

"Or a man who just feels this house will be getting too crowded, what with another wee on' on the way and God only knows how many more." But Brodie's expression as he replied told Harry he'd guessed the truth.

It would be good to have Brodie and his family as their closest neighbor.

Margaret paused, the knitting in her hands falling idle as she smiled over at her husband and held up the tiny bonnet that was her work.

"Do you think *he'll* like it?" she asked softly beneath the sound of the children's laughter and the fiddle.

"I think *she'll* like it just fine," he replied, a smile tugging at the corners of his mouth.

"Harry Wallace, I think you'll be quite happy if we have a daughter." She tossed him a saucy sidelong glance as she returned to her task. "I thought most men wanted a son."

"We already have four sons but only three daughters," he teased back. "It's only fair to level the odds."

"Harry, I must tell you." She looked over at him, her eyes bright. "Lillian Green invited me to a quilting bee at her house next week. Iona will be there, and all the…" She paused.

"And all the other respectable ladies of the community." He grinned as he finished the sentence for her. "I'm happy for you, lass, but I must say, I consider you the most honorable of them all."

"Harry." She blushed and pretended to focus her attention on the tiny bonnet in her hands.

"Now, ladies and gentlemen…" Brodie stood to make an announcement. "Tonight I'll be introducin' a new musician, one who I'm hopin' will play a few tunes at the New Year's Ceilidh so that this tired old lad might share a dance or two with a certain neighbor lady. Geordie." He turned to the surprised young lad seated on the bench near him and indicated the new fiddle and bow on the table. "Give us a tune, sir."

"Uncle Brodie, I…" Obviously taken by surprise, Geordie hesitated.

"Come, come, lad. I'd not be urgin' you to anything I didn't think you capable of. And your father has seen fit to buy this fine new instrument. Canny Scots that we are, we mustn't let it go to waste."

Wetting his lips and rubbing his hands on the back of his pants, the boy stood, hesitated another moment, then took up the instrument.

"I'm not very good…not like Uncle Brodie." He looked around at his family, a blush rising up his cheeks.

"Come along, laddie." Harry spoke gently. "Your uncle would not be encouragin' you to do anything you cannot handle. Give us a tune."

Geordie hefted the fiddle, settled it under his chin, paused another moment, then drew it carefully across the strings. Within moments, the strains of the waltz Brodie had played on his first night in the log house once more sounded in the room with gentle mastery.

Harry was astonished. The boy was well on his way to mastering the instrument. He glanced around the room and saw the others were as flabbergasted as he was.

"Music this fine deserves to be acknowledged, Mrs. Wallace." He stood and held out his hand to his wife. She hesitated only a moment before laying aside her knitting and standing to join him. In a moment they were gliding across the plank floor as they had that first night Brodie had played for them. And looking down into his wife's glowing face, Highland Harry knew she shared his happiness as she had then and always would.

A word about the author...

Award winning author of 32 published books, a graduate of Queen's University, resident of New Brunswick, Gail has had articles and short studies published throughout North America and Western Europe.

Visit her at:

macgail@nbnet.nb.ca

**Other titles by Gail MacMillan
available at The Wild Rose Press, Inc.**

Heather for a Highlander
Counterfeit Cowboy
Rogue's Revenge
Shadows of Love
Holding Off for a Hero
Ghost of Winters Past
Caledonian Privateer
Lady and the Beast
How My Heart Finds Christmas

Thank you for purchasing
this publication of The Wild Rose Press, Inc.

If you enjoyed the story, we would appreciate
your letting others know by leaving a review.

For other wonderful stories,
please visit our on-line bookstore at
www.thewildrosepress.com.

For questions or more information
contact us at
info@thewildrosepress.com.

The Wild Rose Press, Inc.
www.thewildrosepress.com

Stay current with The Wild Rose Press, Inc.

Like us on Facebook
https://www.facebook.com/TheWildRosePress

And Follow us on Twitter

https://twitter.com/WildRosePress